illusion&
indemnity

Other titles by S. Usher Evans

The Razia Series
Double Life
Alliances
Conviction
Fusion

Empath

The Madion War Trilogy
The Island
The Chasm
The Union

The Demon Spring Trilogy
Resurgence
Revival
Redemption

illusion&
indemnity

The Lexie Carrigan Chronicles

S. Usher Evans

Sun's Golden Ray
Publishing

Pensacola, FL

Line Editing by Danielle Fine, By Definition Editing

Sun's Golden Ray Publishing
Pensacola, FL
www.sgr-pub.com

For ordering information, please visit
www.sgr-pub.com/orders

The Lexie Carrigan Chronicles

Spells and Sorcery
Magic and Mayhem
Dawn and Devilry
Illusion and Indemnity

Available in eBook, paperback,
hardcover, and audiobook

Contents

Dedication

To that thirteen-year-old girl
who had a weird dream about
evil wizards and peanut butter,
You did this.

One

"I love you *so much*."

"Nicole, I can't breathe."

In response, my oldest sister squeezed harder. Curious onlookers passed by, all laden with boxes and lamps and other dorm necessities, the parents wearing wistful looks of longing as my oldest sister hugged the very life out of me.

"We still have to move her in," came the gruff voice of Nicole's kind-of-serious boyfriend, Guy. He was a mechanic who'd spent the last six months wooing my sister. His latest overture was *insisting* he drive us up to Washington, D.C. from our little apartment in northwest Florida to help me move into my new dorm at Georgetown University.

And since Nicole had neglected to inform him I was a well-trained magical with the ability to transport myself and all my belongings into the dorm, I'd had to sit in the car with them for two days while we made the fifteen-hour drive. And if that weren't bad enough, Nicole slowly devolved from slightly-awkward-girlfriend to super-weepy-sister the closer we got to the capital.

She'd started sniffling again as we drove over the Key Bridge and broke into all-out sobs when we parked. And that was where we were standing, in front of the still-full car, Nicole holding me as if I might evaporate into nothing if she let me go.

"So…I guess I'll go get your key?" Guy asked, catching my eye. Nicole wasn't the most expressive person with him, and she, like me, colored bright red when she cried. This might've been the first time he'd ever seen her so emotional.

Which she was still doing when Guy returned with my key and move-in materials in hand.

"You're going to have to let go sometime," he said gently.

"I g-guess," Nicole said, relinquishing me and wiping her eyes. "P-promise you'll—"

"I will," I said, cutting her off. I'd agreed to return to Florida every Sunday night to watch a movie or have dinner or do something together. Since I could magically transport myself home in the blink of an eye, and Nicole, a Potion-maker, couldn't, it wasn't that big a deal. But I didn't think Guy wanted to find out that magic was real that way.

I felt bad as he hoisted two of my big plastic tubs from the back of his truck and carried them up to the looming dorm building above us. I hurried ahead of him with the key and went the elevator, but he stopped me.

"Nah, I'll just use the stairs. That'll take too long."

"Are you sure?" I said with another twinge of guilt that I could've had all this done in mere seconds. "It's on the fourth floor?"

"Yeah," he said, his smile widening when Nicole walked in the door carrying my bedding. He shifted the boxes in his arms, making the muscles pop. "Let's go."

I resisted the urge to roll my eyes at his overt showing-off, mostly because I was glad Nicole had found a guy who went through so much effort for her.

We reached my room, which was empty, so I chose the bed closest to the window. The room itself was pretty tiny, complete with two wooden desks and two elevated beds pressed against either wall. But it would be home for the next year, and I was excited about the adventure.

"Okay, I'm going to get the rest of it," Guy said as Nicole began sniffling again. "You two…just unpack."

"Are you sure?" I said. "There's a lot left—"

"I got it," he said with a wink before disappearing. I waited a breath then closed the door. And with a wave of my hand, I released magic into the air around me, unpacking the two plastic bins and making up my bed. I sighed happily, finally able to use magic for something.

Nicole didn't flinch at the use of magic, but placed her hand on the newly-made bed and frowned. "You're so far away."

"I'm really not," I said with a sigh. "One phone call and I'm there."

"But you're not *home*—"

"And maybe that's a good thing," I said, opening the door once more. "Guy's obviously in love with you. You two need some time alone together. Without me around."

"I like having you around."

"You don't like being alone with Guy?" I asked. "Why not?"

"I like being alone with Guy, but I don't like Guy being so…" She sighed, slouching onto my desk. "It's all moving a little fast for me."

"Fast? It took you three months to have sex with him."

She glared at me, obviously regretting sharing that bit of information with me. "But moving you in. It just seems so…so much."

"You could've told him no," I said. "It would've made everything easier."

"I know, but he really wanted to do it. And that's sweet. I just…" She stood with an odd expression on her face. "I'm gonna go help him."

"Or, you know, you could tell him about—"

"I'm not going to tell him about *magic*," Nicole snapped with more than a little heat. "We're not *that* serious."

I might've argued that they were, but I'd already had that conversation with Nicole fifteen times this summer.

Guy made another appearance, huffing and puffing as he put down my microwave. "I'm going down for the mini-fridge."

"No," I said quickly. "I mean, I got someone with a trolley to go down. I'm sure they're on the elevator. There can't be that much more."

"Just your suitcase," Guy said, wiping his forehead.

"I'll go get that," Nicole said, resting her hand on his chest gently as she passed by him.

"Good thing you aren't like Marie, or else we'd be here for years," Guy said as she left.

I had to laugh at that. My middle sister Marie was a notorious clothes hound, and when she'd come with us to Guy's family's cabin in Alabama, she'd brought her entire closet in two suitcases for a one-week trip. Considering she had as much magic as I did, and could transport back to her apartment in Las Vegas in the blink of an eye, I knew it was all for show.

"Hey, thanks," I said. "I know you didn't have to drive me up here, and I'm not sure if Nicole will have the words to thank you any time soon. But I really appreciate it."

"You're welcome, kiddo." He glanced behind him and almost tiptoed into the room, a nervous look on his face. "So you think…besides the whole baby-sister-moving away thing… you think she's happy I did this?"

"No, because you moved her baby sister away," I said with a laugh. "But yes, I think once she gets used to the idea of me not being at home," *Or rather, me being able to come home whenever*, "she'll be very appreciative."

"Good, cause my mom's asking when I'm going to marry her," Guy said. Then, he glanced behind him once more and retrieved a small box from his pocket.

"*Whoa*!" I cried, taking three steps back. "That's a little soon, don't you think?"

"I wasn't going to ask her on the trip," Guy said. "But in case it comes up while you're in school, I wanted you to see it. I hope Marie comes home for a visit, so I can show her."

I pressed my hand to my heart, touched that he was so concerned about us. I had no opinions on diamonds, but it sparkled on a pretty silver band. "It's gorgeous. But I think you need to work on her a little more."

"Do you think she loves me?" Guy asked.

"Yes," I said. "But you know…the whole dad thing…"

"I know."

"What whole 'dad' thing?" The man in question, in his mid-fifties, with dark hair and pale skin like me, breezed into my dorm. Guy hid the ring so quickly he could've done it by magic.

"Dad!" I said with a happy smile. "What are you doing here?"

"It's move-in day, why wouldn't I be here?" Gavon said, glancing at Guy. "I wanted to help out, but it appears I'm too late."

"I'm…gonna go help Nicole," Guy said, inching out of the room as if Gavon would strike him down with a glare. To be fair, he could've, but Guy didn't actually know that. My sister's poor boyfriend disappeared through the door, and my damned father had the nerve to laugh about it.

"What?" he said with a shrug. Not for the first time, I noticed the similarities between us—the shape of his nose, the particular peaks and valleys of his hairline. I should've known that he was my father the first time I saw him, and perhaps, deep down, I had.

"I said stay out of it," I said, turning to fluff my pillows on the bed.

"I am staying out if it!" Gavon held up his hands innocently. "I haven't said one word to the man."

I leveled my glare at him, hearing the loophole in his words. "You'd better learn to like him. He's planning on proposing to Nicole sometime in the next few months."

Gavon frowned. "Really? Seems sudden."

"Didn't you propose to mom after knowing her for, like, two days?"

"I was unaware of this society's customs," Gavon said, as if that explained everything. "And besides, it appears Nicole isn't infatuated with him."

"She let him drive me up here," I said. "And when she wasn't bawling her eyes out, she held his hand. I think she likes him plenty. She's just easing her way into it."

"I suppose," Gavon said, turning and seeing more of the dorm. "Sweetheart, this room is really small for two people."

"It's perfect," I said. "I have to live on campus my first three years. It's the rules."

"Yes, but can't I find you—"

"*No.* I want to live in a tiny little dorm with a person I barely know and share a bathroom with twenty people," I insisted. "That's the college experience. I want the college experience."

Finally, a smile appeared on his face. "You look like your mother when you lecture me."

"Dad," I said with a roll of my eyes. "Please don't get misty-eyed. I can only handle one crying family member at a time. Nicole was absolutely—"

A gasp filled the room, and Nicole stood in the doorway, holding my suitcase. Her face had grown pale, and her lips were pressed into a thin line. The suitcase dropped with a thump.

"Hello, Nicole," Gavon said tentatively.

"Lexie, when you're finished, meet us downstairs for lunch." She paused and glared at Gavon. "*Alone.*"

To his credit, Gavon took the hit without as much as a flinch. But he'd gotten the cold shoulder all summer long. As he and I began repairing our relationship after a tumultuous two years, Nicole still wanted nothing to do with him.

I couldn't blame her completely. Gavon was from New Salem, an alternate universe of magicals who'd been banished for trying to enslave humanity in 1692. Gavon was a descendent, and nearly thirty years ago, he'd made a tear between his world and ours. Despite his ancestors beliefs, he'd integrated himself into this world, marrying my mother and starting a family. Things had all changed when New Salem got wind of the tear and pressured him into taking the mantle of Guildmaster away from his rival Cyrus.

Cyrus had retaliated by killing my mother, who died right after giving birth to me.

My sisters and I had been raised by my aunt Jeanie, my mother's younger sister, and up until my fifteenth birthday, I'd no idea that magic even existed. Gavon had met me that first night, and although he'd never intended our relationship to grow any further than a single, forgettable conversation, I'd had other ideas and kept pressuring him to teach me more. But then Cyrus reappeared, and my aunt Jeanie was his next victim. That death I still carried with me—especially as Gavon disappeared again shortly after that.

In mid-March of this year, after I'd been tricked into going to New Salem, Gavon and I finally had a heart-to-heart about his role in everything. Things were still slowly healing between the two of us, especially as we'd been working on a project together all summer.

"So, I might have another lead on closing the tear," Gavon said. "I know you'll be busy with school now, but—"

"Are you kidding? I'd love to go," I replied with a grin. "Where are we going this time?"

"It's a surprise," he replied. "As I'm still finalizing my contacts there. But you'll tell me if you get too busy."

"To help you close the tear?" I shook my head. "Of course not."

"Your schoolwork comes first."

"I don't have any classes on Friday. We could do it then?"

"You might want to hang out with your new friends though."

Yeah, friends. That was something I hadn't really had too much of in my small town, and one of the things I was most nervous about. I'd promised myself I would step out of my comfort zone and try to be more social, even though it made my skin crawl. But I was a Warrior, damn it. I shouldn't have been afraid of meeting new people.

"I'd better let you get to it," Gavon said, using his magic to take the suitcase still in the doorway and transfer my clothes into the small closet. "There, now I can say I helped."

"I feel so bad that Guy had to carry all my crap up the stairs," I said.

"Don't. He should work for it."

"*Dad*," I said with an exasperated sigh. "I like him. Marie likes him, and you know she hates everybody. Why don't you?"

He shook his head, a sadness creeping into his eyes that had nothing to do with Guy and everything to do with Nicole's hatred of him. He crossed the room and kissed me on the forehead. "Have fun at lunch with your sister. I hope she isn't too cross with you."

"She'll survive," I said.

"Good luck. If you don't like it, you know we can always—"

"I *know*." I smiled. "Thanks for everything."

"Thank your ancestors. I did nothing except sign a check," Gavon said.

Except that had the check not been signed, I wouldn't have been able to afford a single credit-hour. "Thanks, Dad."

"Have I told you how much I enjoy hearing you call me that?" he said.

Had you told me you were my father sooner, you would've heard it much more, I thought, but didn't voice it. I was trying to repair our relationship, and bringing up past transgressions wasn't the way to do that. Even if they always remained in the back of my mind.

Two

Nicole had mastered the art of pretending she wasn't angry with me, so our lunch together was actually quite pleasant.

"What do you think you'll miss the most?" Guy asked as we picked at the scraps of our food.

I shrugged. "I don't know what it's going to be like, to be honest. It'll be weird not waking up at home, though."

Nicole smiled. "You're always welcome to come home, you know that."

"Ah, let her live a little, Nic," Guy said, leaning back and throwing his arm around her. "She's got a good head on her shoulders. You did a good job. Now it's time to live *your* life."

I could practically hear the ring glinting in his pocket. Despite the rocky way they'd met, he'd turned out to be a fairly decent human being.

"I am living my life," Nicole said, stiffening under his arm. "It just happens to include worrying about my sisters. Especially my baby sister."

"But you don't have to worry about me," I said. "Guy's right. It's time you started doing your own thing. Find a hobby." *Like Potion-making.*

"I could teach you how to change the oil in your car," Guy said. "You'd look so cute covered in grease down at the shop."

"I think I'll leave that to you, thanks," Nicole said with an affectionate pat and a goofy smile I didn't miss. "I'm not an idiot. I can figure out what I'm going to do with myself."

"Are you going to go back to school?" I asked, hesitantly. Nicole had dropped out of college two years ago to get a job so she could take care of me.

"Maybe," she said.

"Baby, I'd pay for you," Guy said. "If you wanted to go."

Nicole kissed his hand. "I don't know if that's what I want to do. But thank you for the offer."

I pushed the remnants of my pasta across the plate. Just wait until Guy found out how much money Nicole had sitting in a bank across the Atlantic. Not that she acknowledged its existence, other than to pay her apartment rent every month.

"I mean, it can't be as much as this kid's tuition," Guy said with a chuckle. "How you managed to get so much scholarship money, I'll never know."

"And you're sure this is what you want?" Nicole said, eyeing me with an unsaid comment about Gavon. "To be here, in this big, dangerous city? So far away from home?"

"*Yes*," I said emphatically. "It's not like I had a whole bunch of friends back home to stay there for. And we can…talk all the time." I glanced at Guy, hoping Nicole would fill in the blanks. "I'll be fine."

"She'll be fine," Guy repeated, kissing Nicole on the side of the head.

Nicole leaned into him, but didn't look convinced, wearing a frown for the rest of our meal.

Guy suggested we take a walking tour around the city, but I demurred, both because I wanted to get back to campus and start exploring there, and also because I thought he and Nicole could use some alone time before they headed back to Florida the next day.

That just set Nicole off again, and she spent the whole walk back to my dorm clutching me like there was no tomorrow.

"Promise me you'll come home," she whispered into my ear when we were saying our final goodbyes.

"I promise. Nothing could tear me away on Sunday," I said, and I meant it. "Enjoy your time with Guy. He really loves you. I mean, not every guy would take a week off work to drive his girlfriend's sister a thousand miles to college."

She sniffed and glanced behind her to where Guy was cleaning up the truck to prepare for the return drive. "Yeah, I know."

"We'll talk more about it on Sunday, okay?" I said.

"O-okay…"

"Try not to cry the whole way home."

She rubbed her eyes and released me, walking back to the truck. Her shoulders shook and Guy's face softened when he saw her. I heard him murmur, "Come here, baby" as he took her in his arms. He waved at me, and I waved back, But if I didn't go upstairs, Nicole might never let me.

"Drive safe! And thanks again!" I called, before turning on my heel and darting through the still-open door. As I climbed the stairs to my room, the oddest sense of sadness came over me. Before, there had been nothing but excitement thinking about this new adventure and life far away from everything I'd ever known. But here I was…alone.

And although I knew I could pop back to the apartment any time I wanted, or call my sister, it didn't quite feel the same.

Before I realized it, I was staring at my new door, and my name written on a piece of purple cardstock, along with my roommate's. I heard voices inside, so I took a breath and opened the door.

"Lexie?"

"Samantha?"

I waved awkwardly at the black girl I'd only seen in photos and talked to over text. She wore her hair in braids that she'd gathered in a ponytail at the nape of her neck, standing maybe a few inches taller than I did. Her smile put me at ease, but when she jumped up to hug me, I froze. Reluctantly, I returned it, figuring since we'd be living together, we might as well get comfortable.

"So…?" she said, looking at me with an expectant stare.

"So." I smiled, awkwardly.

"Um…I guess I'll get unpacked?" she said, turning to her boxes, still resting on her bed. "My parents already left."

"Yeah, mine too," I said then realized what she was hinting at. "Oh, right! I'll help."

For the next hour, Sam (as she liked to be called) and I unpacked her things and rearranged the room to be more spacious and accommodating. She did most of the talking, telling me about life growing up in a suburb of San Francisco, her school, her friends, and playing lacrosse (a game I'd never heard of, much to her horror).

"You don't know what lacrosse is?" She gaped.

"I mean, we didn't have it in my high school," I said.

"Weird," she said with a shake of her head. "So, what brought you all the way to Georgetown?"

"Just wanted to get away," I said, although that new feeling of homesickness returned. "Do you have any siblings?"

"A younger brother. Mom and Dad want me to take him for a weekend sometime this semester so he'll want to go here. They're both legacies, you know. Mom is a pediatrician and Dad is a lawyer." She paused, for just a breath. "What about your parents?"

Crap, this question already? "Uh…" My face grew warm as I busied myself with folding her shirts and putting them in the dresser. "That's kind of complicated."

"Oh? How?"

I'd rehearsed this, several times, but my heart pounded as I scrambled to come up with the words I'd spent so long memorizing. "My mom died when I was born and my dad… kind of disappeared for a bit after that."

"Oh my God, I'm so sorry." Sam was by my side in an instant, comforting me as if it had just happened.

"It's fine. My aunt…my aunt raised me. But she died a few years ago when I was fifteen."

"Holy crap, Lexie. I'm so sorry I brought it up."

"No, no," I said with a wave of my hand. "My dad…more

recently, he came back around, and we're kind of patching things up."

The look she gave me was all disbelief. "So your dad abandons you to live with your aunt then comes back and expects to have a relationship?"

"I mean, it's…it's more complicated than that," I said, realizing just how horrible all of this sounded. "He's doing his best to make up for it. He paid for my schooling—"

Her brow quirked. "So you forgive him because he's paying you off?"

"No, like I said, there's a lot to it…" My face was burning, and I wanted to get away from this conversation before it got worse. "Anyway, we're not completely cool, but…we're working on it."

"Mm," came the unimpressed voice from my roommate as she arranged her pencils in a cup on her desk. "So what's your major again? History?"

"Yeah," I said, with a small sigh of relief. "Yours?"

"Biology pre-med," she replied. "I'm going to go out for the club lacrosse team. Do you play any sports?"

Does sparring count? "Uh…no. Not any real sports."

"I can teach you how to play lacrosse, if you want. Maybe join the club team with me. They probably aren't that great."

"Um, maybe…"

A lonely feeling crept in through the back recesses of my mind, almost like fog rolling in. Sam was talking about all the things she'd already planned for the two of us to do—after all, we were roommates, it was clear to her that we should be the best of friends—and it was like I was watching a movie. All I could think about was what I *wasn't* telling her. Magic, me being a Warrior. How my father had sacrificed his relationship with my sisters and I to protect us from something even worse. How a madman had killed Jeanie, and how I'd faced my fear and defeated him in the dueling ring.

I miss James.

As soon as the thought crossed my mind, I flinched to get rid of it. I had been fighting that battle for months on end, and I'd been sure I'd slayed that particular dragon. James was Gavon's apprentice, and he'd spent the better part of my senior year getting under my skin and making me fall in love with him. But even more than that, he'd been the first person I'd ever called a *best friend*. There were no secrets between us (I thought), and he'd been the sounding board I needed.

Then he'd kidnapped my sisters to trick me into sparring with Cyrus, so one of us would kill the other, and he would take over Guildmaster after Gavon died.

That whole episode haunted me at night, along with the loving words James had whispered in my ear the night before. It had been a whiplash, from the first taste of love to the hard shock of betrayal, and I still hurt. But some days, especially now, when there was so much I had to keep to myself, it was hard not to think about him.

"Lexie? Are you there?"

I jumped. I'd come to the end of the pile of clothes and was standing against the full dresser.

"What'd you say?" I asked with an apologetic smile.

"I asked if you wanted to go get some dinner? Some of the girls from our dorm are going."

"Um…sure," I said, shaking myself out of my stupor.

"You okay?" Sam asked, taking my arm as we left the room.

"Yeah," I said with a small shake of my head. "Just a lot to take in today, you know?"

"Get ready, because when school starts, it's going to get even worse."

Three

I'd always known college would be an adjustment, but waking up on Monday morning was weird. For one, I only had two classes, the first of which started at ten. After thirteen years of school first thing in the morning, it was strange to languish in my bed while the sun grew brighter outside the window.

Sam was already up, tapping away on her computer and browsing Facebook. Without thinking, I released magic to summon my own laptop to me then stopped myself before it happened.

"Oh, did I wake you?" Sam asked, after I made a noise.

"N-no," I replied, pushing myself off the bed to retrieve my laptop. I sat cross-legged, propped up against the pillows and stared at my laptop without opening it.

"Do you have a Tumblr?" she asked. "Snapchat?"

"Me? Er…not really."

"Your sister wouldn't let you?"

"No, just not…I mean, I guess I never saw the point of it."

"Oh." A pause. "What about your friends back in Florida?"

"Kind of a loner," I replied after a moment. "My sisters and I just text each other a lot."

My stomach growled, reminding me that breakfast wasn't going to be downstairs, but across campus in the dining hall. Luckily for me, I could just as easily transport myself there as—

"Yeah, me too. Do you want to walk over there?"

"W-walk?" That was the last thing I wanted to do. I'd scoped out all the bathrooms in the area over the weekend, looking for places I could transport to and from. It wasn't far, but I was hungry and I hadn't had coffee.

"Unless you'd rather skip," Sam said, hopping out of bed and stretching. "But your stomach's being pretty loud up there."

There really was no way around it. I could lie and say I wasn't hungry (though there was no hiding my stomach's noises), but as soon as I showed up at the dining hall, she'd wonder how I got there quicker than her.

Every step of the way toward breakfast, Gavon's voice was in my ear, asking me if I *still* wanted the normal college experience. I hadn't really thought about what having a roommate was really like, nor considered how much she'd be in my space—and how that would prevent me from using magic. But this was just an adjustment. I'd get used to it.

We piled food onto our plates and ate, our conversation growing more animated as we woke up. My initial grumpiness at not getting to use magic faded as my blood sugar rose, and I ended up rather enjoying the short walk back to the dorm.

"Where's your first class?" Sam asked as we both packed our book bags. Mine was, of course, for show. Whatever I needed, I could summon to me.

"Reiss," I replied, glancing at my phone. "You?"

"Same." She brightened. "What class?"

"Biology."

"Same!" She grinned. "Good news, 'cause I'm horrible at taking notes."

Good news, except that I was already tired of walking and my magic was begging for a transport spell. But it appeared on Mondays, at least, Sam and I would be getting our exercise in.

When I arrived at my biology classroom, my forehead boasted a light sheen of sweat. I wasn't unhealthy by any stretch, but I also hadn't gone on long walks up and down hills while holding a conversation with my roommate.

Our classroom was a large room with a screen at the front and rows and rows padded seats. Some of them were already taken by similarly weary-looking freshmen. A few of them glanced at me, offering a hesitant smile, which I returned. Sam and I took seats in the back.

"Did you get your textbook yet?" Sam asked.

I shook my head. "My sister told me to wait, that sometimes professors don't really use it and it's a waste of money."

"Yeah, me neither," she said.

From the first few moments of class, I knew it would be much different than high school. For one, the professor didn't even ask for our names or take attendance. For another, he handed out the syllabus with the entire semester's classes, homework, and tests on it. If I was smart, I could complete everything within a week.

"Man, if I was smart, I'd do this all this weekend," Sam

muttered, and I snorted. "What?"

"I was just thinking the same thing," I said.

"Lemme guess: you were the valedictorian too?"

I nodded. "You?"

"Same. Smartest kid in school. Smartest kid in my family, too." She shook her head. "Of course, how could I not be with parents like mine? If I didn't get straight As, they'd be on my ass so fast…"

"Mmm." I glanced down at my pen, which had begun writing down notes about the syllabus by magic. I froze and swiped it up, casting a wary glance to Sam. She didn't seem to have noticed, so I relaxed a little. But that was close.

"Open your textbooks to page five, and we'll get started."

I went to summon a book—I'd pay for it later—but then remembered I'd told Sam I didn't have one. She glanced at me with a mirrored nervous expression, but then we giggled at our predicament.

"We'll pick it up after class," Sam whispered.

"Ladies, please keep conversations to a minimum."

I flushed, and Sam bit her lip in a shameful smile.

With Sam right next to me, I had to jot down everything the professor said by hand, but together we managed to get a complete picture. Apparently, Georgetown was serious about which books they recommended, as my homework was to read the first three chapters.

After class, I started to leave for the bookstore, but since Sam had to go as well, we went together. It was already crammed with students, who'd apparently had the same idea I'd had about waiting before purchasing.

Sam didn't leave my side as I threaded through the crowds, assembling the books I'd need for the semester. Each one was a new lesson in expensive, with my massive biology book coming in at nearly six hundred dollars.

"Don't make it cheap, do they?" I said, grateful for Gavon's ancestors.

My ancestors, I corrected silently. Gavon had made it clear that he was simply the current owner of the account, and my sisters and I were free to use our inheritance as we pleased.

Still, I was about to spend a lot of money, and I didn't want him to think I was out buying designer clothes. After adjusting the books in my arm, I pulled my phone out of my back pocket and tapped out a message.

Buying textbooks, in case you were wondering why I just spent two grand.

I wasn't sure how he'd managed it, but Gavon had been able to text from New Salem all summer. Mostly, he preferred to talk face-to-face, but he'd said to send a message if I ever needed him.

A few moments after I'd texted, a response lit up my phone.

Buy me a sweatshirt.

I smiled, spotting one across the store. Hiding my movements as much as I could, I summoned one of the "Proud Dad" sweatshirt, which appeared underneath the stack of books.

"Oh, I didn't see you grab that," Sam said, cutting off my train of thought as I pulled it out from under the stack to look at it.

"Yeah," I said, smiling at the word "dad" embroidered on the front. "Told my dad I was buying books and he asked me to get him one."

"That's so sweet," Sam said, with a bit of longing. "I'm lucky I got a scholarship, but I still had to take out loans. My parents love me, but they don't love me that much."

"Yeah," I said with a small grimace. Had Gavon not interfered, that would've been my fate too. Then, I brightened. "Hey, let me buy your biology book for you."

"Oh my gosh, I can't ask you to do that!" Sam said with a frown.

"Seriously, my dad is…kind of loaded," I said, hating myself a little. "I promise, he won't mind at all. Especially if I tell him I was buying a book for someone."

She hedged for a moment then plopped the book down. "Fine, I'll buy you dinner sometime. With my meal plans."

I grinned. "Deal. No mag—" I swallowed my words. "Deal."

By Wednesday, it was getting difficult to keep magic from Sam. I'd almost used magic in front of her at least ten times, and between driving up with Guy and the weekend with Sam, magic was building and calling for release.

There wasn't any time for it, not between running to and from classes, meeting even more of the girls in the dorm, making friends in my classes who wanted to get coffee afterward. Moments of peace were usually dedicated to doing homework, which was surprisingly heavy for the first week of classes.

Finally, I had a nice three-hour break between classes, so I trudged back to the room and flopped onto my bed. Then, glancing around, I magically turned off the lights, locked the door, and formed an attack spell in my hands.

"My name is Lexie, and I have Warrior magic. I sometimes have visions of the night my mother died, and my dad is the leader of the New Salem Warrior's Guild, but we're cool now and my sister is a Potion-maker and my other sister is a Healer and I just want to tell someone about it."

The words echoed in the empty room, but I did feel better after saying them aloud. The humming beneath my skin quieted as well; perhaps my magic was simply annoyed that it hadn't been acknowledged in a while. I absorbed the purple ball of energy into my body and reached for my phone.

Miss you.

Ready to come home yet? Came the fast response from Nicole. I glanced at the clock; she must've been on her lunch break.

Not on your life, I replied, even as a tear fell down my cheek.

I sat up and wiped away the evidence of my loneliness. Perhaps all the busyness was a good thing, because it meant I wasn't dwelling on how much I missed Nicole and life back home.

Four

Something magical woke me early Friday morning, and I nearly leaped out of bed to the window. In my sleepy haze, I made out a figure standing under the streetlight. A sliver of fear woke me right up before I finally recognized my damned father waving up at me, somehow knowing I was glaring down at him.

"What the actual hell, Dad?" I grumbled to myself, grabbing my room key and flip-flops and marching downstairs as I magicked my clothes into jeans and a t-shirt.

I yawned as I stumbled out of the door. "What are you doing here so early? Is something wrong?"

"And here I thought college kids stayed up all hours of the night," Gavon said with a chuckle. "Don't you remember we'd agreed to do a little work on closing the tear today?"

"Vaguely," I said, yawning. "But I'd assumed it would be at a decent hour."

"It's a very decent hour at our destination," he said with a mischievous smirk.

"Where, in China?"

"Close," he said. "Japan."

"J-Japan?"

"I've been reading up on some texts of Japanese magicals I acquired a few years ago but haven't had the time to investigate fully." He held an old book in his hand—although this one looked much different than the others. "I believe I might've come across a similar spell that was used to create the world, although I'm afraid the details on it are about as light as all the rest we've found. So I thought it might be a good idea to visit the shrine where it was written and talk to some people."

I opened the book and frowned—it was all written in kanji. "Can you read this?"

"With a translation charm, I can."

"Why do I get the feeling I'm about to learn how to do that?" I asked with a small sigh.

Gavon had always been about teaching lessons, even when I was fifteen. If I'd thought that would stop now that I was older, I was sorely mistaken. Although my knowledge of the magical world had grown tenfold since we'd started spending more time together.

"Why don't you give it a shot, hm?" Gavon said in his typical Dad-voice. "Let your magic absorb the script and seek out like-minded magic. Then the words will form for you."

"This is paper," I said nervously. Charms and I had been at odds since I'd started attempting them on my own. Charms required a great deal of precision. Being a Warrior, my magic was more like a wrecking ball.

"If you ignite it, I can reverse it quite easily," Gavon said.

"Can you?"

"Another perk to being your father. As if there weren't so many already."

I flushed, his praise wiping away all remnants of doubt. Closing my eyes, I relaxed my face and released the magic. Almost instantly, foreign magic became apparent, as did the whisper of words I didn't understand. But almost like watching an anime without subtitles, I began to understand the context.

I cracked open an eye and a grin blossomed on my face. There were now English words on the page where the kanji had been.

"Well, there's no fire and you're smiling so I assume things went well," Gavon replied.

"You can't see it?" I asked.

"That requires a bit more complexity, and I think one charm lesson is enough for now," Gavon said. "Besides, I read it cover to cover last night."

Of course he did. "So what does it say?"

"It turns out my original theory was correct. John Chase was neither the first nor the last to create a magical netherworld to trap unsavory creatures. That journal is from the early 1800's, and speaks of a large magical demon terrorizing the countryside. The magicals then couldn't stop it, so they imprisoned it. I'd like to visit the shrine where it says all that took place to find their accounting of the matter."

"So we're going to Japan?" I asked with a little bit of excitement. "I don't need my passport, do I?"

"One of the benefits of traveling by magic." He placed his hand on my arm. "Shall we?"

The farthest I'd ever transported myself was from my house in Florida to Salem, Massachusetts, and that had taken a bit of my magic. Traveling clear around the world left me dizzy and unstable, even though it hadn't been my magic that had brought us here. Gavon, ever the stalwart rock, steadied me as I got my bearings and cleared the spots out of my eyes.

"Are you all right?" he asked, as my gaze focused on his face. "It's a bit disorienting at first, but it does get better with practice."

"How often do you go flying around the world?" I grumbled, shaking my head.

"Oh, your mother and I used to go all the time," he said. "It's been a while since I've had anyone to go with me."

I craned my neck, the magical change subsiding and leaving in its place the wonder and awe of being in a completely new place. Everything was different, from the leaves on the trees to the colors and words on the buildings—even the scent in the air. I was still mostly half-asleep, but the excitement overpowered my drowsiness as I followed Gavon out into the busy streets. As he'd said, it was mid-afternoon in Tokyo, and there were plenty of people out enjoying the early fall sunshine.

"Did you and mom come here? To Tokyo?" I asked, struggling to keep pace with Gavon's purposeful strides.

He scratched his chin. "I don't think we did. Or if we did, it was for a quick sushi dinner."

"What was her favorite place to go?" I asked.

"Rome," he said. "Maybe we'll go there next. C'mon, I don't want you to be out all night."

We walked until we reached the bottom of a tall staircase. I groaned at the idea that I'd have to climb all of them.

"You can't be serious…"

"Unfortunately, there's a bit of magic protecting the shrine," Gavon replied. "No transport spells. We'll have to go in the old-fashioned way." He glanced at me. "Come on, Lexie, you're not even eighteen. Surely you can walk up a few stairs."

Huffing and puffing, I came to the top of the long staircase, yet my nearly fifty-year-old father seemed none the worse for the wear. It occurred to me then that just because he couldn't transport himself into the shrine, it didn't mean he couldn't still use magic to make the climb easier.

"So," I panted, "you gonna teach me that trick, too?"

"If I do, I'll have no hope of keeping up with you during our sparring sessions," Gavon said, conjuring a bottle of water and handing it to me. "Have to retain a little pride, you know."

I smiled and accepted the water, eyeing him for a moment. "As if I could ever beat you."

He turned to me with an amused smile on his face. "You beat Cyrus. He and I are evenly matched. And you were still mostly standing after."

My cheeks grew warm. "But I mean…that was…a special circumstance."

"Adrenaline simply helps you focus, it doesn't increase the amount of magic you have." He smiled as I continued to stutter.

I chewed my lip. I was no longer afraid of Cyrus; knowing I could beat him in a duel gave a girl a lot of confidence—but I was wary of him—and what he might be doing.

"So…what *has* he been up to?"

"The usual," Gavon said. "Undermining my decisions, questioning authority. Wandering the streets of New Salem looking for Warrior children." He grimaced. "Possibly trying to make a few."

"Ew."

"He wouldn't be the first," Gavon said with a chuckle. "I have several half-siblings that came after my father realized he had a gene for Warrior blood. They're all Charmers and Enchanters."

"And your mom didn't think to make any more?"

"She apparently had a Potion-maker," Gavon said. "But the child didn't live past birth. I think my mother might've been afraid to have more. She wasn't the most selfless individual either. Power does that to people, you know."

I cast him a furtive look. "It didn't seem to do that to you."

"No, but I also spent the first eighteen years of my life power-*less*," he replied. "Cyrus was the one who received all the attention, the doting. He was always more powerful—"

"But you beat him," I replied. "In the Guildmaster match. You beat him."

"I still have my doubts that he was fully healed from his match with my mother, and if I'm being honest, I manipulated him a little into agreeing to a match sooner than was advisable for him." He shrugged. "His arrogance was his downfall then, but I doubt he'd make the same mistake again. Age, in this case, works against both of us. Even with the help of magic, the older we get, the less quickly we move. Reaction time goes down."

I frowned. "You're not old."

At that, he laughed. "Come on."

We walked into the shrine, which was sparsely populated with workers helping tourists find their way around. Gavon, however, kept his gaze on me.

"Now, with whom do you think we want to talk?"

"Uh…" I glanced around the shrine. He was asking me to locate the magical person in the room, something I still hadn't figured out. I had a theory that the grounding spell my grandmother had placed on me for the first fifteen years of my life had screwed up my magical radar, but Gavon didn't buy it.

There was no other explanation, because I was drawing a blank. "I don't know."

Gavon sighed, but patted me on the shoulder. "You'll get there, sweetheart. It's the older gentleman over there."

We approached him, Gavon bowed slightly, and I mimicked him. The man bowed then stepped forward to shake Gavon's hand.

"Very nice to meet you. My name is Gavon McKinnon and this is my daughter, Alexis," he said in English.

The man responded in rapid-fire Japanese, and I caught none of it, but Gavon was nodding as if he understood. More magical translation charms at work, I supposed.

"We're here looking for information about the kappa," Gavon said. "Do you have any journals or records of that time?"

Knowing dawned on the man's face. He took Gavon by the arm and led him toward the shrine. They conversed in low voices, and I only got Gavon's half of the conversation, which was mostly agreeing and nodding. The man procured several leather-bound books, similar to the one Gavon had in his possession, then bowed to Gavon as he left us.

"So…?" I asked as we walked down the shrine steps.

"You mean you didn't catch any of that?" Gavon asked with a smile. "The translation charm is the same in text as in words."

I blinked at him.

"Okay, maybe we'll have to practice that concept a little," he said, handing me the journals.

"Spill, Dad. What'd he say?"

"It's as I suspected," Gavon said with a shake of his head. "This spell wasn't recorded very well either, and it appears to be specific to the demon it imprisoned."

"You don't seem surprised," I asked.

"I've been to a thousand dead ends," Gavon said with a heavy sigh. Then, he smiled. "At least now, I have good company."

"I'm not really being much help," I said. "I don't know if I *can* be any help."

"You're going to be helpful," Gavon said, nodding to the journals. "You have homework to do."

"Ugh," I said with a grimace. "As if I don t have enough already."

"Yes, how is school going?" Gavon asked. Before I could answer, his magic enveloped me, and we arrived back in Georgetown. "I'm afraid I've been a little preoccupied with Guild business this week and haven't had a chance to check in on you."

Since he'd prepaid all four years for me to attend, I felt like I owed it to him to be positive about it. "It's good. Different. Really different."

"It's a big adjustment, I'm sure. Do you like your

roommates? Classes okay?"

"Good. Just…it's hard to have magic with a nonmagical roommate."

"Still want that *normal* college experience?" he asked, with a glint in his eye.

"Yeah," I said, yawning now that we were back in the dark campus of Georgetown. "Sam, my roommate, she's really nice. She said she's going to teach me how to play lacrosse. Apparently, it's a sport?"

"Mm."

"I think the biggest adjustment, and I know how strange this sounds, is that I can't just use magic anywhere I want," I said. "I mean, when I was at home, I could use it all the time in my bedroom. But Sam is always around, so I don't get my space." Seeing the look on his face, I qualified, "But I can get used to it. I mean, it's probably a good thing that I mingle with nonmagicals."

"You should seek out some magical friends, too. I'm sure there are a couple at Georgetown," Gavon said.

"Right, and how do I go about doing that? Just walk up to people and fling an attack spell at them?" My shoulders slumped. "Because as you can see, I'm garbage at finding magicals."

"You aren't garbage at anything," Gavon said. "You just need more practice. It's not your fault—you didn't grow up around magicals other than your sisters, so you're not able to tell the difference. I'd start by going to the library or somewhere populated. See if you can find a magical signature. They'll be drawn to yours, too."

"And is there a secret handshake I should know about?"

"Turn around three times and stand on your head."

I stopped then saw his smirk. "Knock off the cad jokes."

"But I get so very few opportunities to use them…"

That reminded me of the sweatshirt I'd bought for him. I summoned it to me from my dorm and handed it to him. He took a moment to stare at it, his smile pure and wholesome leaving a warm feeling in my heart.

"Thanks, sweetheart," he said, folding it and tucking it under his arm.

"Not sure you can wear it around New Salem, but…" I said, awkwardly.

"You'd be surprised what you can hide under a cloak," he said. "I love it. Have I mentioned how proud I am of you?"

"A few hundred times," I said, feeling stupid about it. "Now can I go back to sleep?"

Five

When I woke up, Sam wasn't in the room, so I helped myself to a large cup of coffee, summoned from the mess hall across the campus. I sat in bed, savoring the taste and still amazed that I'd been halfway around the world for about two hours last night. I would've thought it a dream except for the pile of journals sitting on my desk.

Probably should have hidden those, but oh well.

I didn't have any classes, but I did have a mountain of homework, not to mention sifting through the journals. So once I'd finished my coffee (and summoned some breakfast, because why not?), I laid out all my books on my desk, magically expanding it to a dining room-sized table. In one corner, I placed my Latin textbook. Directly across from me, a thick history book on pre-Civil War US history, along with some print-outs. And to my left, the stack of Japanese journals. My laptop and a large cup of coffee rounded out the table.

Sitting back, I took in all the information assembled and let out a little giggle before grabbing the history book and starting to read. Magic and electronics went together about as well as oil and water, but over the summer, with Gavon's help, I'd practiced using a lighter touch. In this case, mimicking the gentle pressure of my fingers on the keyboard, instead of trying to make the circuits do the work for me.

I practiced a few words—listening for the slow *clack-clack-clack* and watching the words appear on the screen. Satisfied I had the hang of it, I read, using magic to document my thoughts as I synthesized. This was the tough part. Sometimes, when I read, my mind would wander, and I'd end up with three pages of internal monologue. Today, I remained blessedly on track, devouring the first three chapters in less than an hour and ginning up some good responses to the discussion questions we'd be going over in class.

As a reward for staying on track, I pulled over the Japanese journals, opening the first to the handwritten kanji and carefully casting the translation charm.

> *In feudal Japan, the kappa monster terrorized the marshlands of Honshu. A magical by the name of Nakamura devised a solution to permanently seal the monsters into their lakes, thus keeping them away from the nonmagicals.*

Well, that was promising.

> *The combination of water from the lake and the kappa's blood, added to a basic containment potion, allowed the magicals to seal the monsters permanently. It has been over fifty years since a kappa has been seen in the nonmagical realm.*

I jotted down a reminder to ask Gavon about that—maybe it was that whole blood thing that made the seal work. And if it meant draining the lifeblood from one of Riley's descendants, I knew where we could get one.

I chuckled darkly.

In the back of my mind, I recognized the sound of the lock turning over, and as quickly as my magic would move, I resized my desk, and readjusted my books just as the door opened. But my coffee cup sat perched precariously on the edge of the desk, and it tipped over in slow motion.

"Oh, crap, Lexie, I'm sorry!" Sam said, walking into the room as my coffee landed on my lap. "Did I scare you?"

"No, it's fine," I said, as the coffee seeped into my jeans.

"Here, let me help clean that up."

Together, we made quick work of the mess, and I very discreetly cleaned the spots off my jeans using magic. "I'm sorry," I said with a shake of my head. "I was in my own world."

"Is that book in Japanese?" Sam asked, standing with a handful of paper towels.

"Uh…yeah," I said with a small laugh. How would I play this one off? "I'm…um, learning."

"That's cool," Sam said. "So other than Japanese, what do you like to read?"

"Uh…" *Magical textbooks.* "I guess a little bit of everything? What about you?"

What followed was a long list of authors I'd never heard of—mostly in the fantasy genre. Sam was apparently a voracious reader and wanted me to read everything she'd read so we could talk about them.

"Ah, fantasy?" My whole life was a damned fantasy novel.

"Oh, come *on*," she said. "You don't love to read about faraway lands and princesses and princes and magic and all that?"

I shrugged. If only she knew. "Sorry?"

"Well, nobody's perfect, I guess," she said. "You know, I think we had the same idea. I went to the library to try to finish up that biology homework, but I kept getting distracted." She smiled. "Want to work on it together?"

"Sure," I said, hunting for the book in the hastily-stacked group nearby and sighing at the empty coffee cup in the trashcan. If I were alone, I could've simply summoned more coffee. Chalk another one up for living with a nonmagical.

The biology homework was more tedious than difficult, having to describe research design and how to develop a testable hypothesis. We knocked out our science homework, and I was able to finish my Latin work while she toiled through her English reading assignment. It was definitely more fun than working in silence, especially when she kept bringing up the naughtier parts of the book she was speed reading.

"Okay, that's enough for today," Sam announced. "It's dark. It's Saturday night. I want to do something fun."

"This isn't fun?" I replied, motioning to the Latin exercises I was finishing up.

"We're in college. We have to get into some trouble," she replied with a grin. "C'mon, I think some of the girls on the floor are going to try to sneak into a club tonight."

"Oh…wow," I said, getting anxiety at the thought of it. "Um, I don't think that's my thing."

"It's not mine either," she said with a shrug. "But my parents told me I needed to branch out and try new things at college."

"Maybe they meant going to new museums," I said.

She puffed out her chest. "It's my first weekend as a free woman. I want to get into some trouble!" She turned to me with large eyes. "Please, Lexie? I don't want to go by myself."

I shook my head. "No, but text me if you get arrested, okay? I'll come bail you out."

In truth, I might've considered going out with them, but I was nursing questions that I wanted to ask Gavon, and I welcomed a little alone time. Once Sam had left with the rest of the girls, I summoned the journal I'd been reading and found the passage about the containment spell. I supposed it made sense to add the DNA of the thing imprisoned. But it didn't quite explain how to unlock the cage.

I pulled out my phone and texted Gavon. *Have you ever tried to recreate Johanna's potion?*

Yes. Wasn't successful.

How so?

"Why so curious?"

I looked up as Gavon appeared in the middle of my dorm. "Good thing my roommate's not here," I said, dryly.

"I checked before I came," he said, looking offended.

I narrowed my eyes at him. "Still, though. So what happened with Johanna's potion?"

"I thought that perhaps recreating Johanna's potion would close the tear. After all, it created New Salem, it's reasonable to assume that there could be some correlation. But when I poured it on the tear, nothing happened. It was a complete bust." He rubbed his face. "But the New Salem potion was designed and probably brewed by a Potion-maker. So perhaps it would take a Potion-maker to brew it properly."

And Nicole wasn't talking to him. "Aren't there Potion-makers in New Salem?"

He shook his head wearily. "As much as I've tried to stop it, there's a barbaric practice of…killing Potion-makers. So our Nicole is the only one who might be able to parse it out."

"Do you think? She hasn't made a potion in…"

"Potion-making is an innate power," he said. "Much like your sparring ability comes from your magic itself. Even as a small child, your sister's ability was incredible. But at the time, she was still a baby, and Potion-making is dangerous."

"So you made it yourself," I said. "And it didn't work?"

"I suppose it was a little deserved," he said sadly. "One of the conditions of my continued presence in Clan Carrigan was that I find a way to close the tear. But it was hard, and as soon as your mom and I got married, and the kids started coming, I sort of let it fall to the wayside."

"But shouldn't that have made you want to close the tear?" I said. "If you knew the danger to us—"

"I didn't, though," he said. "For twelve years, I was the only one who knew the tear existed in New Salem. And I suppose I'd hoped that if I dragged my feet long enough, I could just keep it open forever. Then, I made the stupid, *stupid* decision to tell Alexandra. And the rest, they say, is history."

His eyes took on a faraway, sad look, and I cleared my throat to change the subject. "A-anyway. The potion in this Japanese journal used the blood from a kappa, the demon it imprisoned. I thought maybe Johanna's potion had blood in it."

"No, it didn't," he said. "That much I remember. Unfortunately, I can't tell you for sure because Johanna's original journal remains with your grandmother. But I've been asking my friends for any other journals about the Separation, perhaps one of them might have a copy of the potion."

"I still have that one journal," I replied. It was a blow-by-blow account of the Separation, and had been one of the first books he'd given to me. "But I don't remember there being a potion."

"No, there isn't," he said with a smile. "But speaking of gifts, I found this last week. Thought you might want to have it."

He handed me a photo, and my jaw fell. It was a family photo of Gavon, my mom, and two pint-size sisters. Marie must've been barely two years old, her chubby face peering out from behind Gavon's shoulder. Nicole was hanging off my mom's arm. They looked so happy.

"Incredible, isn't it?" He pointed at my mom in the photo. "You're in there, too. We'd only just found out you were coming. Your mom wanted to avoid telling your grandmother for a few days so we left for London."

Gavon was grinning, but I just couldn't share his amusement. I (obviously) had no memory of this photo. I didn't have any memories of the happy time before I was born, other than what I could glean from magical memories. Sure, I was *technically* in the photo, but as an amoeba.

"I know you don't have a lot of stuff of your mom's, but—"

"Thanks," I said, forcing a smile onto my face. "I appreciate it."

The next morning, I held the picture, staring at it and trying to picture a life where we were a whole family and I was in it. My mom was gorgeous—I could see a lot of Marie in her. Gavon wore the brightest smile I'd ever seen on his face. And my sisters just looked precocious. Unaware of all the tragedy coming toward them like a freight train.

"You're going to burn a hole in that thing," Sam said from her bed. "What is it?"

I sat up. "I saw my dad yesterday, and he gave me this photo. It's him, my mom, and my sisters. Mom's pregnant with me."

"So why the long face?"

"Because…" I looked down at it. "I don't know, I'm being weird about it."

"Yeah, so share."

I carefully considered my words. What I was feeling had little to do with magic. "I guess I've been thinking a lot about what life might've been like if my mom hadn't died. About who I'd be as a person, what kind of friends I might have. How my relationship with my dad might've been different. I've never really missed my mom before. But now…" A lump formed in my throat—surprising me. "I guess just spending time with him is dredging up all these questions."

"Are you okay?" Sam asked.

"Yeah, I guess." I swallowed hard. The lump grew into tears, one of which fell down my face. I wiped it away hastily.

"I mean, it's pretty obvious you aren't," she said. "Your dad seems like he's trying, but it's a lot to process. The guy basically abandoned you and now wants to have a relationship. I know you're a smart person, but I don't want to see you getting hurt. And you're getting emotional over a photo, so it sounds like maybe spending time with him isn't the best thing for you right now."

I wasn't sure what surprised me more—that she'd remembered our first conversation or that she was so worried about me. I had nothing to say that would change her mind about him. So much of what had happened was based in magical loopholes and hard-to-believe politics.

"I know it's hard to understand," I said. "But I'm not letting him off the hook easily. There's a lot of stuff to work through, and we're working through it. I want to have a relationship with him."

"Mmkay…"

She turned to her closet to get dressed, and I sighed as I stared at the ceiling to give her privacy. The gap between what I had said and what I hadn't was weighing on my mind, and it bothered me that I couldn't be completely honest with Sam.

"I obviously have no experience with this sort of thing, but I think everyone's going through some stuff right now," she said, climbing up on the bed next to me. "Maybe it's just 'cause you're in college and on your own, and you're starting to look at your life differently." She gave me a look then brightened. "Hey, look…a bunch of us—some friends of mine from high school that are here—we're going out to have some pizza tonight. Want to join? I think you'd like them. And it might help get your mind off all this other crap."

I almost accepted then stopped myself when I remembered.

"Sorry, I have a…thing."

"No worries," she said with a half-shrug. "But if you change your mind, it's a standing invite. We're all kind of a little different, you know?"

Not as different as I am. "Yeah. Maybe next week?"

Six

"Okay, it's been literally ten days since you've seen me," I said, my words muffled against Nicole's shoulder as she squeezed me.

"It's been so lonely here without you," Nicole replied, holding me tighter. As requested, I'd arrived promptly at six in the evening, appearing in the living room I'd shared with Nicole for almost two years. Things looked exactly the same as they had when I'd left, although I'd only gotten a second to glance around before she'd attacked me.

"Has it?" I replied. "I see beer bottles in your recycling, and I know that's not your brand…"

She released me and had the good grace to blush. "Guy's just been here to make sure—"

"He's your boyfriend, it's okay that he's here," I said with a laugh. "In fact, I'd be mad at him if he wasn't."

"Marie even came over yesterday," Nicole said, wiping her wet eyes. "It's like everyone thought I was going to lose it when you left."

"I mean…" But I was glad. Marie and Nicole's relationship had always been rocky, but ever since she and Nicole had been kidnapped by James, they seemed to have mended whatever had been between them. Or perhaps they'd just come to realize that their arguments weren't all that important since we were all we had left.

"So how are *you*?" I asked Nicole.

"I'm good," she said, although her puffy eyes told me she'd cried more than a few times this week. "Really. Guy's been… well, he's been checking in on me a lot. Bringing me dinner, that sort of thing."

I smiled, remembering the ring he'd shown me. "Sounds like you got a winner."

"He's been sweeter, more attentive—"

"Nicole, he's *always* been sweet and attentive," I said with a laugh. "You've just been too preoccupied to notice it."

"His mom even called me today, checking in on you," Nicole said, breaking off a piece of cheese. "She wants us to go out to lunch soon."

"She wants a daughter," I said with a wink.

"Okay, it's a little soon for that," Nicole said with a frown.

"But…you are thinking about it, right?" I asked, wondering if I should text Guy and tell him to hold off for a while.

"I…" She sighed. "I had to lie to him about why he couldn't come over tonight. I don't…well, I didn't like doing that. It felt wrong."

"So just tell him the truth."

"How the hell am I going to tell him about Gavon? Magic?

I've never had to have that conversation with anyone—"

"Ahem," I said with a glare. "You had to tell me."

"Marie ruined it though," Nicole said, as if that gave her a get-out-of-jail-free card. "But this? This is just like…I don't know. It's scary. And part of me thinks I could just hide it from him forever."

"That's not fair to him, or to me," I said, adding the second part a bit more gently. "Or to you. You *have* magic. It's just a unique brand."

She pursed her lips. "Have you been discussing me with Gavon?"

"No? Why?"

"That's what he used to say."

"Oh." I nibbled on some cheese. "But it's the truth."

"And I don't know how I'd even begin with that train wreck. New Salem? Cyrus? Jeanie? Mom? He'd be halfway out the door before I got past the first sentence."

"I think he's tougher than that." I reached across the table to take her hand. "What is it really? There's something else keeping you from telling him."

She was quiet for a few moments, staring at the summer sausage cut up on the plate in front of us.

"Nicole's a giant chicken, that's why," came Marie's snarky voice as she appeared in the kitchen in a puff of white smoke. My middle sister was blonde and tanned, and her almost too-skinny frame told of wild parties and not a lot else.

"H-hey!" I said, hopping out of my seat to hug her tightly. "What are you doing here?"

"Nicole invited me for dinner," Marie said, plopping down

on the second stool. "So what are we talking about that you didn't want me to know?"

"Guy," I said at the same time Nicole said, "Nothing."

"Guy, huh?" Marie smirked. "How's that big, beefy mechanic doing?"

"He's fine," Nicole said, picking at the counter.

"He's been over every night," I told Marie, earning a scowl from Nicole. "He's trying to soften the blow."

"Or take advantage of her weakened state," Marie said. "Careful, Nicole, you might admit you love him."

"This is unfair, you two ganging up on me," Nicole said, standing to walk to the other counter and grab more wine.

"We just want the best for you," I said, then, with a pointed glare at Marie, added, "Don't we, Marie?"

"Yeah, yeah," Marie said, clearly still annoyed that she'd been given a later time. "So, Lexie, how's that fancy expensive school Dad's paying for?"

The corkscrew cluttered out of Nicole's hand, and she retrieved it from the sink without a word. She wore a tight smile when she came back to sit with us.

"It's…good. Different," I said, ducking my head a little. "I spent like a thousand dollars on books. The food's good, I guess. My roommate's pretty cool too."

"Made any friends yet?" Nicole asked.

I sighed, sitting back. "Not really. It's kind of like with high school. Everyone's nice and friendly, but I don't really click with anyone. I mean, how can I when I can't talk about myself?"

"Get some nonmagical interests," Nicole offered, pouring Marie a glass of wine and topping mine off. "Join a sorority."

Marie and I both choked, and Nicole cackled.

"Can you see nerd-girl over here joining a sorority?" Marie asked.

"No, but I just wanted to see your expressions when I mentioned it," Nicole replied. "Lexie, you're a great kid. Just put yourself out there. You do have a lot of things to talk about that aren't magical-related."

"I don't know. I just feel like I'm holding back all the time." I broke a chip in half before stuffing both into my mouth. "It's like…here, I was always just me. I never had to introduce myself to anyone—and even though I was hiding magic, it was easier to do with people who already knew me. Now people are asking me about myself, and the first thing I want to tell them is that I'm a Warrior."

"Maybe you should find some magical friends, then?" Marie offered. "It's a big city, I'm sure they're around somewhere."

"That's what…" My gaze slid over to Nicole, and I swallowed my comment before turning back to Marie. "Do *you* have magical friends?"

"Of course I do," she said with a haughty sniff. "Well, I wouldn't call them *friends*. They're weird. But they know I exist, and I know they exist, and when we pass each other on the street, I say hi. That's about it."

I sighed, mostly in jest. "Teach me how to be cool like you, Marie."

"It's really not that hard. Just don't be yourself," she said with a wicked grin. "Honestly, Lexie, are you even seventeen?"

"Until October," I said with a half-shrug.

"Which reminds me," Nicole said, finally joining us again,

"what do you want to do for your birthday this year? We should have a party."

I shrugged. "I don't want anything big. Just dinner."

"I could take you out on the strip," Marie said thoughtfully. "Get you a fake ID and we'll go gamble."

"You could do that now," I said.

"I could, couldn't I?"

"*No* fake IDs, and *no* gambling," Nicole said, shaking her head.

"Why? It's not my money anyway," Marie said.

Nicole's lips flattened into a thin line. "You really should get a job."

"Right, like I'm going to get a job when I'm sitting on all that cash," Marie said.

"You're sitting on *one third* of a lot of cash," I reminded her. "And when you look at the math, spending like you do, it'll only last you until forty-five unless you start saving it."

"Says the girl who's going to a sixty *thousand* dollar a year college," Marie said. "Talk about wasting money…"

"Enough," Nicole said, slapping her hands down. "This is going to be a nice family dinner and we aren't going to argue."

"But, I mean, that's what we do?" Marie said.

"So why aren't you getting along with your roommate?" Nicole asked, dragging us back on topic.

"I guess… Maybe it's just me," I said after a moment. Sam had invited me out twice, and I'd declined both offers. "Don't take this as me wanting to come home or anything, but I really feel…a bit adrift right now. Like I'm not sure what or who I am."

To my surprise, Nicole smiled. "Lexie, I'd be more worried if you weren't feeling that way."

"Yeah, I gotta agree," Marie said after a minute. "You have to make your own home away from home."

I smiled, a little relieved to get that off my chest. "And you don't think I've made a mistake by leaving?"

"No!" Nicole and Marie said in unison.

"You're going to one of the best schools out there. It'll open so many doors," Nicole said. "And like you said, you can always pop home whenever you want."

"Do you think you made a mistake?" Marie asked.

"Not really, but…I guess I wasn't expecting to miss home as much as I have. Or to feel like such an outsider."

"You're going to have to step out of your comfort zone, Lexie," Nicole said. "As hard as that is for you. But you can start by trying a little harder to hang out with your roommate. Who knows? She might turn into your best friend."

I could see that, except for all that I wasn't sharing. "She did invite me out with a group of her friends…"

"Did you go?" Nicole asked.

I winced. "It's in like…half an hour."

"*Go*!" Marie said, magically disappearing the food in front of me. Something creamy brushed across my face and something very sticky appeared on my lips. I glanced down at my shirt—no longer the ratty black shirt, but now a skimpy, sleeveless top matched with black jeans and heels.

"But—" I looked at Nicole, who shook her head.

"You need to go."

Seven

I tugged at the shirt, which bared about an inch of skin above the jeans line. I'd magically lowered the heels to flats, so at least I could walk. But the rest of the outfit I kept. After all, I was supposed to be a new person, perhaps this was part of it.

Sam had texted me the information for the restaurant, so I transported myself to an alley nearby. I took a few minutes to ready myself for the social engagement. I forced to my sides and plastered a smile on my face as I marched across the street to the bar.

"Lexie!" Sam grinned and waved me over. There were already five people seated around a large table, but a seat had been left open for me.

"Hi," I said, conscious of every single movement I made.

"I'm so glad you came," Sam said, wrapping me in a one-armed hug. "Guys, this is Lexie. My roommate. Lexie, this is Chris, Dave, Vicki, and Amanda."

I wasn't able to keep up with who was who when she

pointed to them, so I just hoped I could wing it until their names were repeated. "Do you guys go to Georgetown?" I asked, but the question was drowned in the cheering as a giant pizza was brought to the table.

"Help yourself," Sam replied, handing me a slice.

"So, Lexie," came a deep voice beside me, "tell us about yourself."

I turned and my brows rose. The boy next to me was *adorable.* I was thankful for the foundation on my face to hide my blushing and focused on the really difficult task of talking about myself.

"Um…" I started, running through the litany of interesting things about myself. "I'm from Florida, and I'm a history major."

"History, huh?" A guy on the other end of the table snorted. "Good luck getting a job with that."

"My cousin got a job at a think tank with a history degree," Sam replied hotly.

"Yeah, but it's pretty much useless otherwise."

"Er…thanks, I guess." I took a hesitant bite of the pizza and chewed, hoping no one would ask me any more questions.

"So tell us about your family," the Good Luck Guy asked, with an oddly curious expression on his face. "Anything interesting about them?"

I choked on my pizza, and Cute Guy next to me slammed my back to loosen the food. I took a sip of water and shrugged. "Um…my dad and I were kind of not on speaking terms, but we're working it out, I guess? My aunt raised my sisters and me."

Sam shared an unspoken conversation with the guy, but then

looked back at me. "Nothing else?"

Oh yes, I have magic. Thanks for asking. And my dad is the leader of an evil gang, but we're cool now. "Nope. Totally normal over here."

"So you're from Florida, right?" Cute Guy said. "What's that like?"

"Quiet," I said, opting not to eat any more pizza until I was sure no one would ask me any more questions. "Really small town, you know."

"Was the beach nice?" asked Cute Guy.

"Oh, uh…kind of, I guess. I didn't go that much." *Except at night to spar.* "So, tell me about your families?"

Thankfully, Sam pounced on the conversation change, and they all went into details about where they came from. Surprisingly, they all grew up in different parts of the country, but they seemed close. Dave was the name of the cute guy, Chris the mouthy one. Vicki and Amanda seemed related—sisters perhaps—but I still didn't know who was whom.

"So how do you guys know each other?" I asked.

"We went to…camp together," Sam said.

"So, are you liking D.C.?" Amanda or Vicki said. "Have you done anything touristy yet?"

"Not really, I've only been here a week or so," I said.

"We should go to the museums next weekend," her sister said.

"Can't," Chris replied. "I have dinner at my grandmother's."

"Again?" Sam replied with a groan.

"Every weekend. It's my curse."

I opened my mouth to chime in that my grandmother had

excommunicated me, but stopped myself. How would I explain *that* to anyone?

The loneliness of having to hide myself and my feelings crowded in on me again, but I pushed it away. Marie and Nicole were right; what good was it for me to move away and reinvent myself if I didn't give anyone a chance?

"Your family thing didn't work out?" Sam asked, after the conversation died down again.

"I mean, it did, but they told me I should've ditched them and made some friends," I said, toying with my napkin.

"Family's the best, aren't they?" Sam laughed. "I'm glad you listened to them. I think you fit in nicely with this group."

"Really?" I said, glancing around.

"Yeah, once you relax a little," she said before lowering her voice. "I think Dave's extra glad you came."

My face warmed again, but I snuck a look at him. He was having an argument with Chris over whether the Washington football team was better than the Dallas Cowboys.

"And they have that billion dollar stadium, but what they shoulda done was invest in some damn wide receivers."

"And you think Dan Snyder's any better?" came Dave's retort. "Tell me, when was the last time they won a Super Bowl?"

I smiled, even though they'd forgotten me. There was something so *normal* about sitting in that restaurant with this group. Something that made my soul feel happy.

How often do we play ballfoot?

Cold water washed over my burgeoning excitement, and I hated my thoughts for bringing James back to the forefront. It had been a source of pride to know that James would ask me pop culture questions, because, as he said, I was the only person he could make a mistake around. One more falsehood that he'd planted early to make me feel wanted.

"What's your favorite class?" Dave asked, once the firestorm died down.

I cleared my throat. "I'm taking a class on colonial America at the moment, and it's interesting to dive into detail on all the intricacies that led up to the war."

"She was reading Japanese the other day, too," Sam said.

"Uh." *Crap.* I'd forgotten Sam had caught me. "Kind of. Self-taught. I…er…watch a lot of anime." It was the only thing I could come up with that sounded reasonable.

"That's cool," Dave said. "What were you reading?"

You got this, Lexie. "I'm interested in folklore, so it was an old book I found in the library. Talking about demons and monsters and all that." I tore off a piece of pizza. "Totally weird."

"Hey, whatever rocks your world," Sam said. "So what shows do you like?"

We compared notes on our favorite TV shows, and there wasn't much difference between the five of us, except for Chris, whose likes were firmly in the sports arena.

"You don't play any?" Dave asked. "Even in high school?"

I shook my head. "I kept busy, though. Other stuff."

"What kind of other stuff?"

"Um…" *Think, Lexie, think.* "Fencing."

Sam's eyebrows shot up. "Fencing?"

"Yeah," I said, very proud of myself for thinking on the fly.

"My dad taught me. I'm pretty good at it. Undefeated, basically."

"So why'd you stop?" Dave asked.

"Just too busy with college," I said. "Hard to find time to do anything fun when I'm running to and from classes."

"You'll have to show me sometime," she said with a meaningful look at Chris. "I'd love to learn how to use a sword and poke people when they're being assholes."

I worried I might have to actually *learn* how to fence in order to keep up the lie, but soon the conversation was lost in another rapid-fire argument over football. I exhaled, pleased I'd managed to have a conversation without lying *too* much. It actually wasn't that hard to skirt the truth, once I'd had some practice. Although I was pretty sure I never wanted to get *too* good at lying.

Unlike some asshole magicals who would remain nameless.

We ate our fill and had talked for another few hours after that. As much as I wanted to keep in the conversation, I still struggled to add anything valuable. I felt like an idiot hanging around until the group dispersed, but whenever I started acting like I was about to leave, Sam would stop me and pull me back in.

But it was getting late, and we all had classes and homework to deal with, so we split the tab and went our separate ways. Sam told me she and Chris were going to grab coffee before returning to the dorm, and since I didn't want to be *that person*, I turned and began walking toward the alley to transport myself back to the dorm.

"Hey, Lexie, wait up!"

I cursed, checking all around me for remnants of magic. Then I spun around and smiled as Dave jogged up to me.

"H-Hi," I said, taking a step back.

"Do you want some company?" He grinned, and my pulse skipped. "It's getting kind of dark."

"Uh…" I wasn't looking forward to walking all the way back to my dorm. But I supposed I didn't *hate* the idea of walking back with Dave. "Sure."

"I still can't believe you chose to come up here from Florida," he said, stuffing his hands in his pockets. "I mean, there's the *beach*."

"It's not that exciting," I said. "I mean, it's gorgeous in the summer, but I…I don't know. It's kind of lost its luster for me recently."

"The best Waco could do for me was a pond." He grinned at me, and I had to smile back. It was a little infectious. Or perhaps it was the slow realization that a really cute, nice boy from Texas was concerned enough about me to walk me back to my dorm.

At once, my old fears crept into the back of my mind. Questions about who he was, or why he was so interested in walking me back. Could he be working for Cyrus? Could it be something else?

"You got quiet. Is everything okay?" he asked.

I turned to him and wished I was one-tenth less spastic. "Just…got a lot on my mind, I guess."

"I get that," he said. "I'd never want to leave Florida either."

I laughed, but there wasn't much humor in it. I wished the only thing bothering me was missing home. "I'd take you there one day, but I don't want to burst your bubble. It's really quite boring."

He laughed, and it echoed on the nearly empty streets, releasing some of the nerves bunched between my shoulders. I was worrying for nothing, and I knew it. Dave was just a normal nonmagical guy with very pretty brown eyes and a casual kind of stance with a southern twang that screamed cowboy.

"Well, this is me," I said, stuffing my hands into my pockets again. "Thanks for walking me. Where's your dorm?"

"It's not that far," he said. "It was really nice to meet you, Lexie."

"You too," I said, wondering what the protocol was. Did I kiss him? Hug him?

"Let's do the museum thing some time," he said. "I haven't been in a while. Which is your favorite?"

"American history," I said, and he laughed.

"Yeah, history major, right?"

"Yeah," I shifted to my other foot. "I've always liked history."

"Me too." He took a step back and waited for a moment. "Well, I'll see you around."

I waved weakly as he departed, and once he was gone, I quickly swiped my card on the door and bounded up the stairs, worried that he'd come back and we'd have to continue our awkward encounter. Halfway up the stairs, it dawned on me that I might've just agreed to a date with Dave.

Or he'd proposed it, and I'd just left it hanging.

But…that wasn't right. He probably meant with Sam and the group, right?

I reached my floor and was surprised to see Sam already back in the room.

"How'd you get back so soon?" I asked.

"You and Dave were talking for a long time," she said with a curling smile. "He likes you."

My face probably turned into a tomato. "Uh…"

"No, it's cute! Dave's a nice guy. Real gentleman, you know? Texas boys. They raise them right there…" She turned to me and laughed, presumably at my stricken expression. "Oh Lexie. Did you date in high school?"

"Yes—No. I mean… Museum," I blurted before gathering my words. "I mean, he asked me to go the museum sometime. Is that a date or…?"

"I don't know, when is 'sometime'?"

I swallowed. "I don't know. I kind of froze."

"You are the cutest thing in the world," she said, crinkling her nose. "Why don't I connect you guys on Facebook and you can talk more?"

"Yeah, yeah," I said, walking to my closet to find my pajamas. But while I was walking by the window, I froze as a puff of green disappeared from the sidewalk below. I blinked once, twice, waiting for something *or someone* to walk out of the darkness. But nothing did.

Perhaps I'd just been seeing things. That my mind was so confused about Dave that it had conjured anything to sabotage my excitement, to remind me of the last time I'd become *twitterpated*. But this wasn't the same. Dave was obviously nonmagical. He was a nice, normal guy Sam had vouched for. There was absolutely no reason for the nervous churning in the bottom of my stomach.

Eight

The second week of college was even more insane than the first. Between walking across campus with Sam for breakfast and having lunch with her as well, I wasn't lacking for companionship. Dave and I had connected on Facebook, but that was as far as it had gotten. I wasn't about to make the first move, although somewhere in the back of my mind, I knew he was waiting for *me* to do it. So until one of us decided to be forward, we'd be in this odd version of a cold war.

I just couldn't bring myself to do it, not when I was aching for some alone time. Sam was great, but after two weeks of seeing the same person, and not being able to use magic *at all*, I was growing cranky. Finally, after a particularly long day, one where my magic was sparking at my fingertips, I bit the bullet and texted Gavon.

Up for a sparring match?

Not at the moment. Any particular reason?

I pressed my phone against my chest. How could I put it

into words?

Don't take this as me wanting you to get me an apartment but…it would be nice to have some alone time to use magic.

Meet me downstairs in five.

I sat up, grinning at the prospect of getting to use magic again. Taking the steps two-by-two, I rushed down to the ground floor. Would we go to the sparring beach? Another adventure? I was just excited to be able to talk magic with another human again.

"Hey, Dad," I said, jogging up to where he sat on the park bench. "Are we going on another adventure?"

"Not today," he said, shaking his head. "I was actually in the middle of an experiment, thought you might be able to help. Would you be willing to come back to New Salem with me?"

I hesitated for a moment. "What for?"

"Don't worry, your pact remains solid, no matter where you are," Gavon said, as if reading my mind. "The potions I've been brewing are back in my library, and I didn't want to move them. If you've got the time…"

"A-all right," I said with a nod. "Let's go."

I clamped onto Gavon's arm and felt the familiar hook on my navel as we transported through the tear. Only this time, we landed in his library, the warmth of the fire doing its best to beat back the persistent chill. Magic hummed along my skin, reminding me that this place wasn't supposed to exist. Having spent the past few months deep-diving into all things New-Salem's-creation, being in the world again gave me a new appreciation for just how complex the magic used to create it had been.

Gavon walked over to a set of black iron cauldrons, each bubbling with a different colored liquid. Potions and I had never really gotten along, so I was content to keep my distance.

"What are you doing in here?" I asked.

"I don't have Johanna's potion, but I can remember some of it," he said. "It was a combination of a magical pocket, limb regrowth potion, and a barrier spell." He pointed to the cauldrons. "So I brewed all three to see what might happen. Perhaps if I used the same *type* of potion, it doesn't matter."

I nodded. "What did you need me for?"

"Well…" He cleared his throat and smiled a bit bashfully. "I'm not sure what this will do. If it explodes, I'll need you to help throw up a barrier spell to protect the books. And you sounded a bit lonely, so I thought you and I could talk about what's bothering you, too."

I rose and cast a spell, my purple magic shimmering around the cauldrons and Gavon. "I don't know if anything's really bothering me. I guess I just…am looking for a little reprieve."

Gavon put on a pair of large goggles and slid on thick gloves, although he used magic to ladle potion into three separate cups.

"And you still don't want me to get you an apartment?"

"I think it would be the same anyway," I said with a sigh. "It's not that I mind Sam. She's pretty funny, actually. And we do get along but…" I held my breath as he combined the first two potions. They popped and fizzled, but didn t explode.

"But?" Gavon said, looking up at me.

"But…I was trying to talk to Sam about…" I chewed my lip, finding myself *yet again* sanitizing the truth. "About James. But there's big chunks of my life I can't talk about. So I feel like an idiot because… well, I can't tell her the whole truth." I stuck my hands in my pockets as he readied the third potion. "And I thought if I had a magical friend, I could be honest with them."

"You know…you can tell your nonmagical friends about magic," he said, holding both vials in his hand. "Your roommate, even. You aren't bound by Danvers, so you're not forbidden to talk to your friends about it."

"I know, but how am I supposed to make friends in the first place when I can't tell anyone anything about my life?"

"You're a brilliant, funny, awesome kid. You'll make friends just being yourself. Magic isn't everything about you, you know." He glanced up at me, his eyes three sizes too big under the goggles. "By the way, can you write this down?"

"That's such a dad answer," I said, rolling my eyes as I went to his desk. There, in a journal, I found a long list of experimentations already done, the last three very similar to what we were doing currently.

"One part regrowth spell added into container of one part magical pocket," Gavon said. "Adding barrier spell to container." He paused. "Make sure you note all of that. It matters which goes into which container."

I nodded, making sure I'd gotten all of it.

"Okay…" He took a breath then combined the two.

I waited for an explosion or even a pop, but all that came out was a low hiss.

"Was that it?" I asked.

Gavon pulled off his goggles and stepped outside my barrier. "Let's see, shall we?"

He stood in the center of his library and poured the potion

in an infinity symbol. It glowed bright white and then blossomed into something like a bubble, pushing the air away as it rose up.

"Ah! We did it." He beamed at me, as if I'd been the one to make the thing.

"Did what?" I said, turning my head to stare at the floating thing in the center of the room. "Is that like…a second New Salem?"

"Oh no, no," Gavon said, sliding his finger in the center of the bubble and creating a hole in the center. "It's a magical pocket, although it might be a bit more persistent than the one you've got to store your books."

A few months before, he'd helped me put together a pocket to store my growing library of books, but it wasn't anything like this. More something I could keep things in.

"What do you mean by persistent?" I asked.

He opened the bubble wider, making it big enough for us to walk inside. The bubble room, if I could call it that, had almost transparent walls, but Gavon's library on the other side was fuzzy, like looking through a waterfall.

"Fascinating," Gavon said, tilting his head upward. "But exactly what I thought might happen. If you'll step back a little, sweetheart."

I moved to the center of the bubble, and before my eyes, bookshelves appeared, lining the room from corner to corner. And then, like a reverse vacuum, the books appeared, filing into place one by one. I went to one of the filled bookcases, surprised to see my own books in the mix, along with others I'd never seen before.

"I thought this might be a good compromise," Gavon said with a fatherly sort of smile. "If you won't let me buy you an apartment, you can take this magical pocket with you. When you need a break from your roommate, or just want to be in magic, you can have this."

I quirked a brow. "Did you know this was going to be successful?"

"I had a feeling it might be," he said, plucking a book from the stack and flipping through it. "I knew I was close, and this was the last combination of potions I hadn't tried. But you know, one can never be too careful when you're experimenting with combustibles."

"But don't you need this room to experiment on the tear?"

"I can just make another," he said, closing the book and putting it back. "After all, this may not be New Salem, but it's certainly a place that could sustain life."

At that, I couldn't disagree. What I had wasn't so much a pocket as a giant purse where I stashed all my magical books. This was much…homier. Especially with the leather-bound chair that appeared, along with a lamp.

"This is perfect," I said, sinking down into the chair. "Thanks, Dad."

He beamed.

Gavon helped me transport back from New Salem, which was the easiest way I'd ever escaped from that place. I decided not to share that with him, though. To him, New Salem was merely home.

"I wish I could take you around to meet the people here one

day," he said. "Mary, in particular, would love to meet you."

"Oh, who's she?" I asked. "A girlfriend?"

He laughed, shaking his head. "Perhaps if I hadn't made the tear. But your mother is the only one for me."

I didn't really want to dwell on Gavon dating anyone, so I changed the subject. "How do I get into the pocket?"

"You'll need to summon it first," Gavon said. "It's a magical entity, so it won't take much. Once you feel it, use your magic to find the door then just walk through. Go on," he said, stepping away from me. "Give it a shot."

I closed my eyes and summoned the bubble, and as Gavon said, it came without much effort. In the grips of my spell, it felt like any other bubble, almost like if I pushed too hard it would burst. But I found the small entryway, no bigger than a piece of paper. So gently, I pushed open the sides.

"Well done!"

I opened an eye to the strange-looking opening, hanging in mid-air. "That was pretty easy." With another concentrated movement, I closed the opening and it disappeared. But I could still feel it hanging nearby, ready to call at any moment.

"If you do it a few times, it'll get even easier."

I nodded and sought out the bubble, but my hands moved through air. "So like, if I bring it to my dorm, would anyone see it?"

"Nope, it'll be invisible," he said.

"Great, so I can hide in there," I said with a cackle.

"Lexie…" He sighed. "Are you okay? You sound like you want to be anywhere except your dorm."

"I like Sam," I said. "Honestly, I do. But, I just…I don't

know if I'm ready to talk to her about magic."

"I think she might be a bit more open-minded than you think," he said. "And if she does react poorly, we can perform a simple memory charm on her and she'll forget the whole thing."

"I guess…" I forced myself to smile. "I just need to get to know her better, that's all."

He nodded and brightened. "Whatever makes you happy, sweetheart."

I left him there and walked up the stairs to my dorm, thankful Sam wasn't there. I closed my eyes and summoned the bubble once more, pushing open the sides to reveal the opening. I stepped through, closing the door behind me and standing in the center of the room. My dorm was still visible on the outer edges and between the book stacks, and the air conditioner rumbled in the distance, but it was dulled significantly.

I plopped down on the cushy leather-bound chair, inhaling the scent and turning on the light overhead. Opening my hands, I summoned a book—any book—from the stacks, ending up with a biography of Abraham Lincoln. Then, procuring a cup of hot tea and a secondary table to set it on, I released a sigh of contentment.

My own little hovel.

Somewhere far away, the door to the dorm opened. I could just make out Sam's outline, walking into the room and throwing down her stuff. She stood near to the bubble, as if she were searching for something. I worried for a moment she might see it. But she shrugged and went to her desktop, plugging in her headphones.

And although I felt a little guilty, I stayed in my bubble until she went to bed and turned off the lights. Then I transported myself out.

81

Nine

My new little secret reading room was just what I needed. When Sam stepped out of the room, I dove inside, curling up on that exquisitely comfortable chair with a book and spending a few hours doing homework or reading through the new books Gavon had given me. His library was expansive, and there seemed to be no end to the books in my little haven. Unfortunately, when Sam came back into the room, I had to transport myself to the bathroom then walk in the door, as if I hadn't been there all along.

"Where've you been?" Sam asked. "Hot date?"

I shook my head, cringing that Dave and I still hadn't gone beyond friends and the occasional errant like on a post. "Just been doing homework."

She nodded. "Where at? You've barely been in the dorm?"

"Um…I concentrate better at the library." Well, it wasn't a complete lie. My bubble did have a library in it.

"So hey," she said. "My first intramural game is tonight. My folks might be there, and I know they're dying to meet you. Do you want to come?"

I blinked. Sam's parents lived in California. "Really? That's a long trip for just a game."

"Oh." She laughed. "No, they're on a business trip for my dad."

"Right, that makes sense," I said. I was already on the fence to go, but meeting her parents made me less interested. "Maybe. I've got a lot of homework to catch up on tonight."

Sam's face fell. "Oh, okay. Well, if you change your mind, let me know."

After she'd gone to class, I transported myself into my magical bubble and shook off the guilt of being a bad roommate. I did, after all, have work to do.

One of my pet projects over the summer had been to digitize Gavon's boyhood journals, the ones where he'd painstakingly documented every combination of potions ingredients. He'd told me the tear had happened when he'd thrown out the scientific process and tossed whatever he could get his magic on into a pot, but there was probably still some value in reading through the journals. In any case, since the ingredients were so similar, I had begun adding them to a spreadsheet on my laptop, if only so I could keep track of what was used—and practice a little magical data entry. I was now advanced enough for my magic to read the journal for me and type the ingredients, something I'd only recently mastered.

So with that spell working, I summoned another journal— the one Gavon had given me that explained the Separation in explicit detail. I wasn't sure who'd written it, but I hoped it might hold some secrets I hadn't understood the first time I read it.

For a story written in one- and two-sentence blurbs, it was actually fairly riveting. I was glad I wasn't alive during the bloody war where the magicals warred over the right to use magic wherever they wanted. I could understand why the magicals back then would want to enact such a nuclear solution as the Danvers Accord, especially as I got through the last few, bloody months. The war culminated in the creation of New Salem and the execution of James Riley (the old one, not my stupid ex).

Johanna, John's daughter, had been the brains behind the idea of New Salem. It had taken them several tries to complete the effort, using a coven squared—a hundred and sixty-nine magicals, killing twelve of them in the process.

And all that good work had been undone by some eighteen-year-old Warrior.

I summoned my laptop, which had completed entering the information for this journal. I scrolled through the list, which was pretty long, but also pretty repetitive. There were maybe twenty ingredients he'd used in different combinations. Then again, there probably wasn't much in New Salem to choose from. It was fairly barren.

What we needed was Johanna's potion. My grandmother hated me almost as much as she hated my father, but perhaps she might be willing to give us the journal if we told her what we were up to. She seemed like the kind of woman who focused on the greater good and all that. The trouble would be getting hold of her. She'd all but excommunicated us, and I could barely set foot in Salem, let alone walk up to her front door.

I turned back to my laptop, pleased I could still get wi-fi in my little magical pocket. I searched for 'Irene Carrigan Salem Massachusetts' on the internet and, surprisingly, a Salem address came up.

I just had to laugh. For all her magic and effort to try to keep me out of her life, I could just as easily send her a letter. Way to go, nonmagicals.

With her address in hand, I opened a blank document to start writing, then changed my mind and summoned a blank sheet of paper from my notebook. She might be more willing to read if I hand-wrote it. Old school and all that.

Dear

Dear Gram? Irene? I decided on the latter. After all, she'd excommunicated me from my family. She didn't get to be called "gram" anymore.

Dear Irene,

I'm trying to close the tear. I understand from Gavon there was a great deal of research that exists somewhere in Salem. Obviously, neither of us are able to access it now. Could we arrange a meeting so you could pass the information on to us?

I chewed on the pen tip, thinking. It wasn't too passive-aggressive, although I wanted to add some choice phrases about how horrible she was.

We hope to resolve this matter soon.
All the best,
Alexis

I read and re-read my note a few times, but became distracted by the sound of a phone ringing and Sam's voice.

"Hey, Mom. Yeah. No, she's not here."

Was that disappointment in her voice? I strained my ears to listen.

"Yeah, I don't know if she's coming. I know. I don't know why she doesn't really like me." She paused and sighed. "No, Mom, I can tell she doesn't like me. She's been avoiding me these past few days. No, I don't think I did anything but…I don't know. It's fine."

I sat back in my chair, frowning. Sam thought I didn't like her? I supposed that made sense, considering I had been avoiding her and hiding in my little magical hole. And also avoiding her. And also I was the world's worst roommate.

"Okay, see you in a bit. Love you."

She hung up and put the phone down on her desk then headed to her closet to pull out workout pants and a t-shirt.

Hating myself, I sealed up the envelope and transported to the bathroom, where I checked my face in the mirror to make sure I didn't look too guilty.

Then I walked into the room, my backpack slung on my arm as if I'd been out all day. "Hey, is it too late to come tonight?"

Sam blinked, wearing nothing but her sports bra and shorts. "You want to come watch?"

"I mean…I have no idea what lacrosse is," I said with a smile. "So you'll have to explain it to me. But you're my roommate so…that's what you do, right?"

Although Sam tried to explain the game on the way to the field, I still had no idea what it was about. It didn't matter though—her thousand-watt smile was all I needed to know.

The field was well-lit, and a small crowd had gathered, mostly wearing uniforms. An older black couple waved emphatically from the sidelines, and Sam's smile grew three sizes.

"I can't believe they came," she said under her breath. "Mom! Dad!"

After giving Sam a bear hug, Sam's mom turned to me and pulled me in for the same. Her dad shook my hand firmly.

"Lexie, these are my folks, Rose and John Hoyle," she said. "Mom, Dad, this is Lexie, my roommate."

"We've heard so much about you," Mrs. Hoyle said with a beaming smile. "Valedictorian of your school, full scholarship? History major?"

I coughed uncomfortably. "Um, yeah…"

"I gotta run, but Lexie, you can sit with my parents, okay?" Sam said, patting me on the shoulder before jetting off.

A jolt of nervousness slid down my spine at being seated next to her parents, who I knew very little about and who seemed to know an awful lot about me. But I swallowed my apprehension and told myself to be brave.

"How are you liking school?" Mr. Hoyle asked as we settled into the bleachers.

"Good. Different than I thought," I said, watching the players gather on the field.

"You're very far from home, aren't you?" Mrs. Hoyle asked.

"Uh, yeah. Florida."

"And your parents aren't worried?" Mr. Hoyle asked.

I shifted uncomfortably. Sam must not have told them. "Um…my parents are… Well, my mom died when I was a baby and my dad…um…" I hadn't really thought about a better way to phrase this. "He's been away for a while. But he's back now. My aunt raised me."

"Your poor father. Is your aunt pitching a fit to have you so far away?"

My face warmed. Why hadn't this gotten easier? "She passed away, too."

Mrs. Hoyle hissed at her husband and threw her arm around my shoulder. "John, quit making the girl uncomfortable. I'm so sorry for your loss."

"Thanks, I guess," I said. "But it's all right, really."

Mrs. Hoyle didn't remove her arm. "You'll have to come over for dinner this weekend. Sam'll bring you."

"Are you guys staying the weekend?" I said.

"Oh my gosh," Rose said, pressing a hand to her forehead. "I forgot we aren't in California. It's just so much like home. Samantha on the field like this."

I half-smiled. "I mean, I'd love to come out to California sometime. I've never been."

"So tell us, what's your favorite class?" Mr. Hoyle said with a smile that told me he wouldn't ask any more questions about my family.

The game passed fairly quickly, and the small talk mostly focused on history and their jobs as an attorney and pediatrician. And despite my protestations, Mr. and Mrs. Hoyle took Sam and me out to dinner to a nice restaurant in Georgetown. I had to admit, it was strange to be with an intact family. One that hadn't been ripped apart by magic and death, secrets and lies. It made me nostalgic for the time when my own little family was normal, even though we weren't. When it was just Jeanie, my sisters, and me.

"So, Lexie, what do you plan to do when you graduate?" Mrs. Hoyle asked me, pulling me from my memories.

"I don't exactly know," I said. "I just really like history, so I thought it would be something nice to study."

"You could go into politics or law," Mr. Hoyle said. "I'd be happy to get you an internship at my firm, if that interests you."

"Maybe…"

"John, don't encourage the girl. Lexie doesn't seem like the politician type—and she's too sweet to be a lawyer."

"Are you saying I'm not?"

I grinned as they got into a little good-natured spat, until Sam cleared her throat to quiet them down. "We *just* started school, Mom. No need to worry about graduation for a little while."

Mrs. Hoyle gasped as if Sam had just said the sky was purple. "You *absolutely* need to worry about it. You've got to get internships and job references before you graduate or else you'll be behind everyone else."

"Okay, but give us maybe a month," Sam said with a heavy eye-roll.

I laughed with her, but inside, I was curious. What *did* magicals do when they grew up? My life had been in such turmoil since the day I'd found out I had magic that "what I wanted to do when I grew up" hadn't really gotten a lot of thought. I'd wanted to come to Georgetown, but that was merely an excuse to get out of the small town I'd grown up in. And now I was here, faced with adulthood and having to have a purpose.

Unlike Marie, I didn't see myself breezing through life in a fancy apartment and sunning myself all day. I thought about the things I enjoyed—reading, researching magical stuff with Gavon, sparring. A lawyer? A history professor? Or was I going to sit in an office somewhere and push paper?

"Now look what you've done, Mom," Sam said, patting my head to get my attention. "You've broken my roommate."

After dinner, Sam's parents drove us back to the dorm, and took a long time saying goodbye to their daughter while I stood awkwardly in the common room. She grinned bashfully as she joined me walking up the stairs to our room.

"So…those are my parents."

"They're great," I said. "Really. They care a lot about you."

"You should see the rest of my family. They're all interested in my business. Want to know my grades, if I've met someone yet. What I'm doing after I graduate."

I paused. "Do you know what you're doing?"

"Not at all," she said with a worried look. "Do you?"

"Nope."

She laughed then stopped. "Hey, I'm really glad you came

out tonight. I feel like you've been a little distant lately, and I hope I didn't do anything to make you mad."

I flinched. "No, it's just me being weird. I'm sorry."

"Cause if I'm coming on too strong or—"

"Sam, you're golden," I said with a grin. "If anything, it's me. You're great."

"Cool," she said.

My phone buzzed, revealing a text from Gavon. *Up for a trip to Rome tomorrow?*

I grinned, shaking my head and replying, *Sure, can't wait.*

"What is it?" Sam asked.

"Um…" Some things were just too unbelievable to share. "Funny text from my sister."

Ten

A little after lunch the next day, I found Gavon sitting on the bench outside my dorm, proudly sporting his Georgetown Dad shirt.

"Well, thanks for not waking me up at two in the morning again," I said, grinning as he looked up.

"I figured you needed your rest, being a college kid and all," he said with a smile. "Ready to go?"

"What are we going to Rome for?"

"Remember when I said I was working with a friend who might be able to get us some journals from the Separation?" I nodded. "He found a few things. I thought you might want to go with me to retrieve them."

I frowned. "Is that it?"

"That and I thought you might want to see the city?"

Half an hour later, there I was, in a city I'd only read about, craning my neck to absorb everything I possibly could. It was as fascinating as Japan, although this time, the round-the-world transport spell didn't bother me as much.

"It's not as far, and you're getting used to it," Gavon said by way of explanation. "But we do need to get you out more. There's a whole world out there at your fingertips and you've barely scratched the surface."

"Well, we're out here," I said, fighting a blush and the latent annoyance. "So what are we going to do here?"

"First, I want to show you something."

We walked along the city, Gavon pointing out various tourist traps and other statues. Every corner I turned, I'd see something else recognizable. But the most incredible was the Trevi fountain. Larger than life, the figurines looked alive, and it was incredible to think they were carved out of marble.

"Wow," I said.

"That's what I said when I first saw it," Gavon said, his eyes taking on that wistful look once more. "It was my second or third time in this world. I told your mother I'd always wanted to see Rome, because it was all I'd read about as a boy. So she took me here. To this." He sighed with a smile growing on his face. "This was where I first kissed her. And where I proposed the first time."

"The first time?"

He smirked. "Took her a few times to agree to it. This looks a little different now, though. It's been almost twenty years since I've been back."

I watched him as he reminisced. His face had lost some of the sadness it always held, and he looked younger. I wished Nicole could see him like this, could get past some of her anger to see how much he really loved Mom, really loved her. But perhaps that didn't matter to Nicole.

"What was it like growing up in New Salem?" I asked, as we stopped to get an espresso Gavon promised would be the best I'd ever tasted.

"Well, for me, it was very normal," he said, handing the cashier a Euro note. "I lived with an older magical for most of my childhood. Woke up at dawn to help him to the privy, then did chores like mopping the floor, dusting, that sort of thing. Practiced magic with him when he was feeling up to it. When he wasn't, he'd send me over to Alexandra's to spar with Cyrus." He shivered. "I hated that."

"Why?"

"I always lost," he said. "I've only beaten him a handful of times—including, of course, to become Guildmaster."

I scowled, thinking about him living on after all the pain and misery he caused. "And there's no way you can kill him, right?"

"There is one," he said. "I could renounce my position as Guildmaster and sever connections to the clan."

I stopped mid-stride. "So why haven't you done that yet?"

"Because it affords me *some* power. Without it, I'm blind to what the Council is planning, and that includes Cyrus. He's unable to hide all his activity from me. If I gave that up, I'd lose the insight."

"But you'd be able to kill him?"

"Theoretically."

"So…what's the hold up?" I asked, stopping. "Give up the Guildmastership, challenge Cyrus, and kill him."

He turned to me. "Because if I fail, I'll be dead and there'll be nobody to stop Cyrus. I'd much rather wait until I have a solution to the tear before I cross that bridge." He smiled, but there was something fake about it. "Come on, we're nearly there."

I wanted to discuss more, but Gavon kept changing the subject. Finally, we arrived at an old bookshop, and Gavon held the door open as I walked inside. It smelled of spices, coffee, and old books. The front wall was lined with tins, each with a hand-written description on it—everything from Darjeeling to green teas to flavored teas of hibiscus and lavender. And on the other walls, tables, and everywhere there was a level spot: books.

"Always smells so good in here," Gavon said, inhaling deeply. "You don't know the types of teas I had to drink as a boy. Liquid dirt."

"Ah, is that Gavon?" A middle-aged Indian man with thick glasses and graying black hair emerged from the shadows.

"Sahil," Gavon said, grasping the other man's hands like they were old friends. "It's so good to see you again."

"Likewise, my friend," he said in a thick British accent. He peered over Gavon's shoulder to look at me. "My, my. Your little girl has grown up, hasn't she?"

I blinked and looked at Gavon. "Have I met him before?"

"No," he said with a shake of his head. "Sahil, this is my other daughter, Alexis. The baby you met was Marie, her older sister. Lexie, this is Sahil. He trades in magical items, like potions ingredients and, more importantly, books."

"Nice to meet you," I said, shaking his hand.

"Did you have any luck retrieving those books I asked for?" Gavon asked.

"As a matter of fact, I did," he said, handing Gavon a stack.

"What are these?" I asked.

"Sahil used to live in London and has a lot of insight into some of the oldest magical families," Gavon said. "Most of the magical clans don't like to part with their old books, but occasionally, you'll get lucky. In particular, I asked him to find any books owned by members of John Chase's family."

"Why?" I asked.

"Magicals love their books," Sahil said, plucking one of the old books out of the stack. He flipped open to the end, where hand-scrawled paragraphs filled the last few blank pages. "And they sometimes used them as diaries."

"I'm hoping we might find another version of Johanna's potion in them. It's the best we can do, since Irene's banned me from her library," Gavon said. "I promise I'll return them within the week. I appreciate the assist."

"I had a tough time getting these," he said. "There seems to be an uptick in interest in the old ways—the Danvers Accord, the specifics behind it." He leaned on the counter, his brown eyes sparkling. "Know anything about that?"

I swiveled to Gavon, and there was something unreadable on his face. "Not a thing. But next time someone comes in, would you tell me about it?" He slid a piece of paper with his phone number across the table. "I have a pair of teenagers, so I text now."

"Of course," he said. "You know, the people who are interested usually come bearing this symbol."

He summoned a sheet of paper with a symbol of a flame inside a circle. If Gavon recognized it, he didn't show it.

"Wait, what's going on?" I said, turning to Gavon. "Why are

people interested in the Danvers Accord?"

"There have always been magicals who didn't agree with the pact," Sahil said. "It's so bothersome—the inability to perform magic around the nonmagicals, no specialties, that sort of thing. But the pact is iron-clad—has been for over three hundred years. If there was a loophole, someone would've found it by now." He smiled. "But sadly, you two are the only strange magicals who've come into my shop of late."

"Okay, so what was that about?" I said, as we walked out of the shop. "People looking up loopholes in the Danvers Accord?"

He shrugged. "No idea."

I stopped him. "Seriously? No idea? 'Cause it kind of looked like you had an idea."

"It's always been something of a concern for me," Gavon said. "As long as the Danvers Accord remains in place, there's no problem. As Sahil said, people have been trying to get around it for centuries and no one's been able to beat it yet."

"But…" I slowed my gait. "We're not bound by it. You, me, Nicole, Marie…everyone in New Salem…"

"Mm-hm." He winked at me. "And that's why we're working to close the tear."

"Okay, great, but *we* aren't going to live in New Salem," I said. "And so aren't we one giant loophole?"

"Theoretically."

"*Dad*," I said, grabbing his arm. "You're not telling me something."

"That's because I haven't yet come up with an answer I find appealing," he said. "You're right—you, your sisters, and any children you might have would have specialties. Your children and grandchildren would have magic at birth, instead of fifteen." He sighed. "I don't know how I would resolve that issue. With our bloodline, there would certainly be another Warrior eventually. And I can't guarantee that child wouldn't have funny ideas about things."

As much as I wanted to tell him not to worry, I couldn't. It was a legitimate concern.

"Couldn't we just add an addendum to the Danvers Accord or something?" I asked. "Like, not take away specialties or anything. But like a pact we could add the Guild onto. If they wanted to, of course."

"I've thought about it," Gavon said. "It would require the presence of every clan in the world—or at least a representative descendent of the original signatories. All the Clanmasters."

"I bet Sahil knows a bunch of them."

"He does, and I'm sure they'd be amenable. Clan Carrigan, on the other hand, might not."

I shrugged. "I wrote a letter to Irene asking if she wanted to meet with us. Maybe we could ask her then?"

"Did you cast a fire-retardant charm on it?" he asked, glaring at a speck on the sidewalk.

I laughed and shook my head. "No, but she wouldn't just burn it because I sent it, right?"

He made a noise.

"I mean, she'd at least read it…"

"I'm sure she will," he said, but he didn't sound convinced. "I don't think it would be a wise use of our time anyway. In my younger days, I'd wanted to bring the inhabitants of New Salem here," he said. "Ashley, your great-great uncle, said if I could close the tear, he'd consider it. I even had a signed letter from Alexandra stating she'd be willing to adhere to the accord. But sadly, all that went down the tubes the night Cyrus killed your mother."

"Maybe she'll answer my letter and we can readdress it."

"And maybe pigs will fly."

"If they're enchanted, they will."

Eleven

When Sunday rolled around again, I transported myself down to Florida. Once I landed in Nicole's living room, I exhaled loudly. There really was nothing like coming home.

"Is that you, Lexie?" came Nicole's voice from the kitchen.

"Yeah," I said, following the sound.

Nicole stood over the stove, stirring a large pot of something that smelled delicious with a frown on her face. "Come taste this and let me know what it needs."

She ladled me a small sip. "Nothing. It's great," I said.

"No, it's not," she said. "It's Guy's mom's recipe, but I don't think I did it right. It called for rosemary, but I thought thyme might work better and now I think I screwed it up."

"You didn't screw it up," I said, taking a seat on the kitchen table. "You're overthinking it."

She shrugged and returned to the pot, a scowl on her face. "It's good to see you. I haven't heard from you in a few days, so I thought you might not come."

"Seriously?" I rolled my eyes. "I wouldn't miss this."

She turned from the stove to plant a kiss on my forehead. "I'm glad you still want to come down here. So, how's school?"

"It's good," I said. "Busy. I went to my rooommate's lacrosse game and Rome on Friday."

"R…Rome? As in, Rome?" Nicole blinked at me. "As in… the city in Italy?"

"Yeah," I said, gauging her reaction. "Um, we're still doing that project. So we had to find some books there. '

"Ah." She rose from the counter and went back to the pot. "Were you…successful?"

I considered my response. Was Nicole asking about our project because she was interested or because she didn't want me to be uncomfortable? "I've got half the books to look through, and Gavon's looking through the other half. So we'll see."

"Mm-hm. And how close are you to completing this goal?"

I heard the undertone of annoyance and hedged my response. "Pretty close. Gavon's looking for a potion that could seal the tear so…"

"And he was looking for that potion twenty years ago, too," Nicole said. "So forgive me if I don't believe this is anything more than him trying to look like he's solving the problem."

I might've argued, except for our brief conversation about Cyrus, and how Gavon could've killed him. It was almost like… he was afraid of challenging Cyrus. Like he thought he might lose.

"You know my opinions on the matter. I just don't want to see you get your hopes up—and get hurt when he doesn't follow through."

"You could always help us," I said. "He mentioned he might need a Potion-maker's eye. You've got some kind of power that we don't—"

At that, she barked a humorless laugh. "He used to tell me that, too. That I was special and unique. That's just what you say to a kid when you don't want them to be disappointed." She returned to the stove. "Trust me, I'm very happy driving myself around and going to the store for my food. I don't need magic."

"Speaking of not needing magic, how are things going with Guy?"

Her eyes darkened. "Fine."

"That doesn't sound fine," I said. "What's wrong?"

"Nothing's wrong."

"Nicole—"

"When there's something to tell you, I will tell you. Until then, *drop it*."

"Well, that certainly sounds like something that needs telling," Marie said, appearing in a cloud of white magic. "Are you gonna dump him?"

"Is it any of your business?" Nicole said, angrily grabbing two bowls from the cupboard. "I don't ask about your boys of the month."

"My boys of the month aren't trying to become your brother-in-law, either," Marie said. "Spill, I'm very curious."

I leaned forward. "Me too."

She sighed, rubbing her forehead. "There's nothing. Just having to think about whether I'm still serious about him. He's obviously very serious about me. I just…I can't be serious right now."

"Fair enough," I said, albeit a little sadly.

"I don't buy it," Marie said. "You're crazy about him but you're just scared to admit it to yourself."

"When I want your opinion, I'll ask for it," Nicole said, placing the stew in front of both of us. "Now eat before I throw you both out."

Chastened, Marie and I ate, with nothing but the sound of spoons against porcelain as conversation.

Finally, Nicole cleared her throat. "Lexie, how did that thing go with your new friends?"

"Oh, um…." Had it really only been last week? "Good, I think. It was just a pizza thing. One of the guys…he was kind of cute. He friended me, but nothing's happened since then."

Marie put down her spoon. "Have you texted him or anything? You're so weird, maybe he thought you weren't interested."

"What would we even have to talk about, though?" I said, shrugging off her insult. "I feel that way with everyone I've met. Like, I went out to dinner with Sam's folks, but it was like I had to censor myself. Every other question was about family or my childhood. And I can't just be like 'oh, hey, well, my aunt died when a madman cast an attack spell at her cause he's pissed at my dad.'" I paused, casting a look to the side. "Sorry, Jeanie."

"She would appreciate the phrasing," Nicole said, patting my hand. "But we've gone over this. You have more to offer than just magic. What about history? TV shows?"

"And I mean, yeah, we talk about that. But I guess…I guess I still want someone who not only watches Buffy and is studying the same classes as me, but also happens to have magic. I guess I just don't know where to look for that."

Nicole looked to Marie. "Didn't you say you had some magical friends in Vegas?"

"Friends is a strong word."

"Magical people," Nicole said with a roll of her eyes. "Why don't you take Lexie to meet some of them?"

"*Fine*," Marie said with a loud exasperated sigh. "Just don't get your hopes up, all right? If you're looking for some perfect solution to your problems, you're barking up the wrong tree. But I guess I can show you around tomorrow."

The next morning, I ducked away from Sam after class to avoid our usual lunch. Hiding in a bathroom, I transported across the country to meet Marie in her apartment—a swanky, upscale penthouse with white furniture and void of any personality. It made me afraid to eat anything, even though I knew I could magically clean it up. Marie was still asleep, having completely forgotten she'd promised to take me around. But after some prodding and summoning a large americano, we set off in the mid-morning heat.

"Where are you taking me?" I asked.

"There's a couple of restaurants and bars that cater to magicals here," Marie said. "Mostly backrooms where high schoolers with newfound powers can use them. I rarely see anyone over eighteen because, let's face it, who wants to hang out with a bunch of immature high schoolers?"

"Did Jeanie know about these sorts of things? Was there one back home in Florida?"

"No," Marie said. "And Gram wouldn't let us go to any of

her little clan meetings either until you were of age."

I paused. "Wait, so you remember Gram and the clan and Salem?"

"Of course," she said. "Gram knew I didn't give a crap about her, so she didn't bother blocking my memory. Or maybe her magic is just weaker than mine and it didn't stick. I mean…" She sighed. "My magic centers on human emotion and the mind, so Dad thinks that any kind of memory charm won't work on me anyway. A lot of stuff doesn't work on me. He's always testing different spells and getting all dorky over my reaction."

Dorky was an apt description of Gavon. "What else do you guys talk about?"

"Random stuff," she said. "Sometimes I ask him questions about magic. Sometimes we talk about Mom. Sometimes he's yelling at me cause I'm hungover and he wants me to do more with my life than waste his money." She grinned cattily. "But it's his fault he gave it to me without restrictions."

At that, I had to agree with her. "What does he want you to do?"

"Doctor or something like that," she said, making a face. "But what he doesn't get is if I start healing everything that moves, then maybe someone's going to notice something, right?"

"Sam's parents asked me what I wanted to do with myself," I said. "And I guess I have no idea what adult magicals do, either."

"Lexie, you're not even eighteen. Hell, I'm twenty. Neither of us should have to make any decisions about anything for at least another ten years."

I choked on my spit. "Um. You are an adult."

"A very *rich* adult," she said. "Ergo, I don't have to do anything I don't want to."

"But you're taking me to this magical meet-up place?"

"Because I want to. And I'm sick of feeling like I'm on an ocean liner in a storm whenever you're around."

"What's that supposed to mean?"

"You're unsettled, Lexie," she said. "And until you figure out who you are or whatever existential crisis you're having, you're gonna be unsettled, and I'll have to pop antacids."

I stopped mid-stride. "You can feel that deeply into my emotions?"

"Not…" She sighed. "Dad thinks we've got a stronger connection than most because we're blood opposites. You know —a Healer and a Warrior. Yin and yang. A long time ago, it was pretty common for there to be pairs like us." She rolled her shoulders. "Anyway, I can always get a sense of people's emotions, like a knowing in my gut. But with you, it's more prominent, like I can see your aura." She shivered. "It's become stronger since we've reconnected, especially after all that crap with your James guy."

I had nothing to say to that except, "Wow. That has to be the most you've ever talked to me about your magic."

"I mean, what am I gonna say? I'm the only Healer out there." She put her hands on her hips. "And I've managed to find friends. You've got at least three other Warriors to talk with, and you're moping. Suck it up, buttercup, and figure it out."

"To be fair, two of those magicals have tried to kill me…"

The restaurant we arrived at looked like every other Italian restaurant ever created, with checkered tablecloths and the lingering aroma of baking garlic bread. The hostess seemed to know Marie, because she offered a small wave when we walked in the door, and nothing more.

Marie pushed open the backdoor marked *Staff only* to reveal a space larger than the restaurant out front suggested. The ceiling extended nearly fifty feet into the air and almost a football field in front of me. And everywhere I looked—couches, chairs, televisions and kids my own age glued to their phones or to the television, playing some shooting war game and screaming at each other.

"Um…are you sure this is the right place?" I whispered to Nicole. "I don't see anyone magical—"

Before I finished my thought, one of the kids nearest to me summoned a red plastic cup and took a long sip before returning to his video game.

"Ah," I said. "So this is… it?"

"This is your big place where all the magicals hang out," Marie said with a knowing smirk. "Your millennial magicals right here. Impressed?"

I was sure my face told my disappointment. I couldn't put my finger on what I was expecting. Maybe people sparring? Potions bubbling in the corner? But a bunch of teens playing video games? If I wanted that, I could go to the student union.

"I tried to tell you," Marie said gently. "Magicals aren't like the ones you and I know. Not like Gavon and James and the New Salem folks. These guys can't use magic to heal or create attack spells. The most magic they use is for convenience—

summoning, transporting, and maybe a little potion-making for a hangover cure. They aren't going to be getting into a sparring ring with you."

"So why did you bring me here?"

"Because I'm trying to prove a point," Marie said. "You spend all this time waiting around for the so-called 'right' people to get you. Instead of just putting yourself out there, as you are, to everyone. Maybe it's time you tried hanging out with *them* on *their* terms and finding a new interest. And instead of focusing on all the stuff that's different about you, talk about what you guys have in common. For crying out loud, ask them about *themselves.*"

More surprising insight from my selfish big sister.

"Oh hey, that's Eileen," Marie said, nodding to the woman in her mid-twenties walking over to us. "She kind of runs the place."

"Hi, Marie, glad you could come back," she said then looked at me. "I can only assume this is your sister?"

"Chill, Lexie," Marie said when I opened my mouth to respond. "Yeah, this is my little sister. She wanted to make some magical friends, so I brought her here."

"Well, welcome," Eileen said, although she didn't look like she meant it.

"So you're magical?" I asked.

"Oh my God, Lexie," Marie said as Eileen made a confused face. "Do you not know how to tell if someone's magical or not?"

My face warmed. "Not really…"

"Everyone here is magical," Eileen said, her gaze still

watching me warily. "Otherwise, we wouldn't be able to perform magic in here."

"Oh, right." I kept forgetting about that.

"So can I assume we'll be seeing a lot more of you?" Eileen asked. "We've got some magical tutors who come in every Saturday morning to give lessons."

My already warm face grew even hotter. "Um, I've got a tutor, thanks."

"And besides that, she lives in D.C.," Marie said. "Got any connections for magical friends she could make there?"

"Not like either of you," Eileen said. "There's the school in Arlington, but it's pretty restrictive about who they let in the door. Usually like to start magicals before they age into it, you know?" She tilted her head in my direction. "I'd really recommend finding a tutor though. You could use some rudimentary lessons."

My face burned as Marie laughed. "I'll keep that in mind…"

Twelve

I wasn't sure what was more embarrassing—that I'd made a fool of myself in front of the only non-family and non-evil magicals I'd ever met, or that they thought I needed remedial magical lessons. I wasn't that stupid…at least I didn't think I was that stupid.

I lay in bed, forming an attack spell in my hand. I'd spent so much time focusing on what made me unique, like this magic, my quirky interests, my weird family history, that I was out of practice finding commonality with people. James and I had fit like puzzle pieces, two identical Warriors with similar backgrounds. I didn't have to try with him—I was just me and that was the girl he… Well, he hadn't fallen in love with me, just made me think that.

Maybe Marie was right—maybe I needed to stop looking for a replacement for James and start making new friendships. It would require some effort, but—

The door opened, and I sucked the magic back inside as Sam

came in. "Hey, roomie!"

"Hey," I replied, staring at my hand where the magic had been.

"What are you looking at?" she said, tilting her head in my direction.

"Just thinking," I said, sitting up. "What's up?"

"Oh, my afternoon class was cancelled," she said. "So I am open to suggestions on how to spend my life today. I was thinking about going out into the city, if you wanted to join me."

"No" was on the tip of my tongue, but I kept my mouth shut. If I was really going to start trying, it needed to start right now.

"Sure, let's go."

It really was a gorgeous day, with a crystal blue sky and a cool breeze that kept the sun's warmth at bay. It was my first taste of a northern fall, and considering it was September, I wasn't looking forward to the frigid winter.

"Me neither," Sam said with a shiver. "I don't even own a winter coat. I'm so underprepared for this place."

"Why did you decide on Georgetown, then?" I asked.

"Getting as far away from my parents as I could," she said with wide eyes. "I mean, don't get me wrong. I love them. But they're so…overbearing. My mom calls every day to ask how my grades are going." She paused, giving me a look. "But I guess I shouldn't complain."

"You can complain," I said, shrugging. After all, it was nice to hear someone else do it for once. "My sister Nicole used to be like that. I think she's backed off a little now, though.

Thankfully."

"It must be hard not to see them all the time," she said. "Your other sister is in Vegas, you said?"

I nodded, wanting to tell Sam that I'd seen Marie mere hours before, but clamming up. I still wasn't ready to tell her yet. Baby steps.

Given the lead to navigate, Sam took me deep into the heart of the city. The neighborhoods of Georgetown were architecturally interesting, but the people in them were definitely the richest I'd ever seen. I went into one store, saw the $80 price tag on a white t-shirt and promptly decided there was nothing I needed to buy in there. Sam oohed and aahed over the sweaters and dresses, wincing when she looked at the price tag and buying nothing.

While she did that, I scanned the people in the shop and outside. Tourists, joggers running along the canal, and young professionals eating and enjoying brunch. We found a reasonably priced coffee shop and sat in the corner, sipping americanos and people watching.

"You've been quiet today," Sam said. "Something on your mind?"

I sighed, looking into the black coffee at the bottom of my cup. "I guess…I had all these ideas about how life would be, and I'm finding it's nothing like I thought it would be."

"I completely understand," she said softly. "It's like…I just woke up one morning and here I am, on my own. Totally independent. I could skip class if I wanted to."

"You'd lose a letter grade."

"Well, yeah, but you get my point," she said with a laugh.

"My parents used to control every moment of my schedule, and now…well, it's up to me." She leaned back in her chair. "And yet, I'm still nervous to do anything they might disapprove of."

I nodded. "For me, I guess, it's more that I thought when I got to college, I'd find my place immediately. Not to sound… whatever, but I've always felt different, you know? I never had any friends—real friends—in high school. Nobody I was able to just call whenever and talk with for hours." I grimaced. "I mean, maybe I did. But he turned out to be an ass."

"He?" Sam asked.

"My…ex. We were friends first. Best friends last year. Until he turned on me."

"Yeah? What happened?"

He kidnapped my sisters so I'd duel this evil guy and get him out of the way. "He changed after we slept together."

"Ah, yeah. The whole Buffy-Angel thing?"

I smiled. "You like Buffy?"

"Girl, I *love* Buffy. We should do a marathon." She grinned then it softened a little bit. "If you ask me, and you are, since we're talking about it, maybe you're self-selecting yourself out of friendships? I mean, you won't go out with me and my friends. Dave says you haven't texted him *at all*."

My face warmed. Dave and I…hadn't done a thing. I'd almost forgotten he existed. Was that a bad sign? "Well, I mean…"

"I get it now," she said. "You've got some hangups after your last boyfriend. But that doesn't mean you shouldn't go out to trivia with us on Thursdays. And we all really like you so I don't really know what the problem is."

"It's me," I said with a heavy sigh. I couldn't believe her friends even *noticed* me, let alone liked me.

We grew quiet for a while, people watching and pointing out interesting things on the street. Mostly expensive cars that people had no business driving down the crowded streets.

"This place is crazy," she said, playing with the lip on her coffee cup top. "So much money. What do people do with it all?"

"Waste it?" I said. My sister certainly did.

"If you had a million dollars, what would you do with it?" Sam asked.

"I'd still get a job," I said, trying not to look guilty. "A million doesn't actually last as long as you think."

"A billion then."

I chewed my lip. "Hm…" I took the question and re-worded it in my mind. I had money, but if I could do anything, really, truly anything. What would it be?

"I think I might start a library," I said quietly, thinking about the large stacks of books in my magical pocket. "But I don't know if anyone would be interested in that."

"A library?" She frowned. "What kind of a library?"

A magical one. "Just a library, I guess. I've got…a lot of books. Been accumulating them over a long period of time. My dad has a pretty sizable collection, too. Maybe he'd donate some."

"A library full of books," she said. "Can't you just go to your local one?"

"Uh…these are special books," I said, realizing I must've sounded strange to her, talking about old books. "You can't really find these in regular libraries."

She nodded. "You should show me your collection sometime."

"It's back in Florida," I said, wondering what she'd say if she saw my pocket. "But if you come to visit, maybe."

"Oh!" Her eyes lit up. "I forgot, there's a really good bookstore around here. It's a bit of a walk, but would you want to check it out?"

"A bookstore?" I laughed. "That I'm always down for."

The walk was long, but not unmanageable, and Sam and I talked about our love of books the whole time. She was still trying to convince me to read the latest young adult fantasy novels, although I was sure I had enough magic in my own life to last me a thousand books. The look of horror on her face when I told her I was interested in political nonfiction and biographies was classic.

Finally, we arrived at the bookstore. I noted the iron bars on the windows, which seemed a little weird for the neighborhood. We walked inside, and Sam made a beeline for the contemporary romance section, squealing about some author's new book that she hadn't known was out.

I left her there, wandering to the back of the store, then up a back staircase to the second floor. This place reminded me of a bookstore in New Orleans I used to visit, until I found out that Gavon had been stocking it with books for me to "discover."

Alone on the floor, I closed my eyes and searched the room for any magical books. A book appeared in my mind's eye, and my eyelids snapped open. It was close; not in this room, perhaps on a third floor.

Before I got too excited, I pulled out my phone and tapped out a message.

You didn't stash any books in Georgetown for me to find, did you?

A moment, then: *I did not. Why?*

Just making sure.

Slipping my phone back into my pocket, I circled the room, running my hand along the shelves, searching for that thread of magic that I was holding onto. I couldn't find a door or stairway to the third floor, but maybe it was hidden for a reason…

"Can I help you?"

I spun on my heel, coming face to face with a middle-aged woman with a kind smile. "I…uh…"

"Are you looking for our collection of magical books?" she asked.

It took me a moment to realize what she'd said. "Oh…um… yes?" I squinted at her, trying to figure out how I would tell if she was magic. But there was nothing special about her.

"We don't usually get young magicals in here," she said, giving me a strange look as she walked to one of the shelves. "Mostly it's older retirees who come looking for books. Come on, I'll show you the stash."

She moved a shelf of books on a roller, revealing a hidden doorway and another staircase. As she led me up a back stairway, I released magic toward her, hoping it was sensitive enough to find the spark of magic within her. Or *something*. I thought this method was rather intrusive, but it was all I had.

"Most of what we have is from the eighteenth century. After the Civil War, with the advent of modern technologies, magic's become somewhat obsolete. After all, they can't use it in front of magicals, so what's the point, hm?"

"Yeah," I said. If only I had that luxury. "So no more books?"

"You might find a small one here or there, but mostly, it's kept within families."

I sighed, picking up the book my magic had led me to. It was a post-Separation book, but only barely and it was pretty clearly a niche book.

Thirteen Ways To Improve Your Magical Herb Garden.

"Thanks," I said, putting down the book. "Not quite what I was looking for."

She shrugged and turned to go, and yet again, I struggled to find something magical about her that would've clued me into her magical abilities.

"I'm sorry," I blurted, unable to stop myself. "Are you magical, or…?"

"Oh, no," she said, giving me a curious look over her shoulder. "My husband and kids are."

I frowned. So much for all that effort.

"You look like you might need some help," she said with a sad smile. "What are you, fifteen?"

"Almost eighteen," I said. Was I really that idiotic-looking?

"Here," she said, scribbling on a sheet of paper. "These guys might be able to help you. My kids attend their weekend sessions. Really helped them get acquainted with having magic and understanding what they can and can't do."

I looked down at the address, suddenly relieved. "What is it?"

"Just a school for magicals like you," she said.

A school I didn't need, but I would absolutely take the chance to see more magicals. "How old are your kids?"

"Fifteen and thirteen," she said. "My daughter attends the pre-magic program. Learning history and all that. It's a nice way to make friends before you come into your magic so you're all in it together."

"Yeah, I guess that would've been nice." I slipped the paper into my pocket. "Thank you for this. And for all your help."

I found Sam downstairs, nose-deep in some brightly colored book. "Ready to go?" she asked. "Find what you were looking for?"

"Yeah, I guess," I said then shook my head. "Not really."

"Bummer," she said. "What were you looking for?"

"Just…something."

Thirteen

I had classes in the morning, but as soon as they were over, I was marching over the Key Bridge, phone in hand, letting the GPS navigate me toward the address the lady had given me the day before. After huffing and puffing up another ridiculous hill (what was with this city and hills?), I finally found the restaurant.

Taking a deep breath, I pushed open the door, a small bell tinkling above my head. The hostess caught my eye immediately and her face brightened.

"Hi, you must be looking for the back room," she said. "Come with me."

I squinted at her back as she led me through the restaurant, searching for something that would tip me off to her magical state. But yet again, I came up with nothing. She opened the door marked *Employees Only* and I walked through.

Inside, I found a much different venue than Las Vegas. There, it was big screen TVs, squishy couches, and video games.

Here there were conference rooms with older magicals standing in front of dry erase boards with two to three students at rapt attention. In one room, there was a cauldron bubbling and an assortment of ingredients as two kids peered into it.

"Hello, can I help you?" A twenty-something man wearing a polo shirt appeared in the center of the room in a puff of brown smoke. I got the distinct impression he wasn't enthusiastic to see me.

"Um, hi…" I said awkwardly. "I'm Lexie. I got this address from a bookshop over in Georgetown?"

He summoned a clipboard and read it quickly. "Are you looking to enroll or…?"

"Enroll?"

"This is a magical training school," he said, narrowing his eyes at me. "And you have very weird magic."

"Yeah, so I've been told," I said, averting my gaze awkwardly, then looking back up to him, confused. "What do you mean, magical training school?"

He sighed and shoved a pamphlet into my hand. "Read this. I'll see if I can't find someone else for you to talk to."

He disappeared in a puff of brown smoke, leaving me to read. *Arlington School for Magicals*, it read, and inside gave a fairly fluffy overview of their curriculum and expectations. It was the oddest thing I'd ever read, having been basically self-taught in magic. But here was a school that not only went over the basics of summoning, transporting, and potion-making, but held competitions and gave out certificates.

Well, what the hell?

I looked around the room, seeing the conference rooms for

what they were—classrooms. This was a place I probably could've used at fifteen to understand who and what I was. Or, like the bookseller had said, even a preliminary class of some kind; something so I didn't just wake up at midnight on October sixteenth and start shooting fireballs out of my hands.

Then again, most of these kids couldn't even manage a *single* fireball. They woke up on their fifteenth birthdays and were able to summon and transport, and that was it.

"You look lost," said a girl who'd been sitting on a couch across from me. I pegged her at maybe fifteen, with long dark hair that hung to her mid-back.

"I am very lost," I said, looking down at the pamphlet. "I was just told to come here because I needed help with magic. I didn't even know something like this existed."

"Oh, well…yeah." She shrugged. "It's a pretty old school. Do you have a clan or no? I've seen that with a few kids around here."

"That's complicated," I replied. "So, okay. This is a magical school. How does one enroll? What do you learn?"

"All kinds of stuff," she said. "And enrolling, that's the tricky part. There's a waitlist, usually, as this school attracts some of the best from around the country. The cost is pretty high—twenty grand a year."

I choked on my spit. "Are you serious? For magical training?"

"It's not just magical training," she said. "It's also about networking. My cousin Shaylene got a six-figure job out of college cause she went to class with the son of an investment banker in New York." She gestured to the room. "If you ask me, it's less about magical training here and more about setting your kids up for a bright, nonmagical future."

"Huh." I had no room to talk based on my tuition at Georgetown. If I asked him, I was sure Gavon would spring for a semester here. But it hardly seemed worth it. "So why even train in magic if that's not the point? I mean, you can't use magic outside these walls, right?"

"It's still important within the walls though," she said. "Rich magicals send their kids here to get a shiny certificate that they can show off to all their rich magical friends. They'll even charm it so it looks like some prestigious school for their nonmagical friends."

I half-smiled. "Sounds like a waste of time to me. Unless you're learning something you can't learn on your own?"

"I mean, who has time to teach anyone magic anymore?" she said, summoning a textbook then sending it back where it had come from. "My parents certainly don't. He does real estate and my mom's a civilian with the government. The day I turned fifteen, they sent me here."

"And how long ago was that?"

"Six months?" She shrugged. "Magic's kind of overrated, but they said if I kept up my studies, they'd buy me an Audi."

I nodded, not sure what to say to that.

"So…what do you think about all this can't use magic in front of the nonmagical crap?"

"Uh…" Should I be honest? "It's all right, I guess?"

She blew air out between her lips. "It's bullcrap. We have all this power and we can't use it. I couldn't believe it when my parents told me."

"You didn't know about magic?"

"Of course I knew about magic," she said. "But I didn't realize how strict they are on magical use. I tried to use magic in front of my best friend. Couldn't even get the words out. It was like I was choking to death on my own breath."

I nodded; having never been on the other end of that experience, I couldn't relate.

"What makes it worse is my great-aunt Irene—"

"Hang on," I said, holding up my hands. "You're in Clan Carrigan?"

She nodded. "How did you know?"

"Irene is my…" Again, the question of being honest held me back, but I pushed through. Irene could deal with it. "She's my grandmother."

"Irene's daughters died in a fire, I thought," she said, eyeing me. "Like twenty years ago."

"That…" I scowled. *Thanks a lot, Gram.* "No, we didn't. She just doesn't want anything to do with us."

"She's kind of a pain. Really strict about a lot of stuff. My parents are considering leaving the clan," she said. "Irene's like our fifth cousin twice removed, so we aren't really that connected. And now that we found this place, we can get our magical training here. Irene likes to train all the kids at her compound in Salem."

I glowered. "She does, does she?"

"I went once. Told my mom it was horrible, and then I got to go here instead."

"Oh, you're still here." Brown-smoke Polo Shirt was back. "Can I answer any questions for you? What clan are you with?

Do you want to set up an appointment?"

"I'm not technically with any clan," I said. "But since I'm a legal adult, I'd like a tour. Right now."

Technically, I wasn't an adult for another month, but he was pretty much a jerk, and I didn't want to tell him that. I left my new, young friend sitting on the couch, summoning books to herself, and followed the older man around the space.

"Our curriculum has been refined over hundreds of years," he said, sounding about as bored as I felt. "We have a board of directors from some of the most prominent families in the United States and around the world. Getting accepted here is a privilege that many seek but few actually get. We're *super* selective."

"I go to Georgetown," I shot back. "And my dad's loaded." Then, for effect, "And my grandmother is Irene Carrigan."

His eyes widened, but his tone softened considerably. He showed me each of the rooms and introduced me to a few teachers who were without students. I tried to keep the annoyance off my face as they spoke to me about all the things that would've been really useful at fifteen.

"Any classes on knowing a magical from a nonmagical?" I asked, in the middle of discussing the potions curriculum with the old professor.

"Er? I don't believe that's something we teach here," he said, adjusting his glasses. "It's just something you know."

"Apparently, I didn't get the memo."

"Forgive me, but your magic is very strange. I've never met a magical like you before."

I nodded. "It's a long story. Maybe if I enroll, I'll teach a class."

We ended the tour, and the only thing of value I learned were the names of the board of directors, which might help Gavon and me if we could ever get Irene to agree to adjust the Danvers Accord. I also got a glimpse of their magical book library, but found it wanting. Gavon's was much more impressive, which I would be sure to tell him the next time I saw him.

I thanked the tour guide with a promise to return if I thought they could help me then headed for the exit. But before I got there, I was stopped by the girl I'd chatted with when I'd first gotten there.

"How was it? Ready to plunk down some cash?"

I shrugged. "Hardly. I don't think there's anything here these guys can teach me that I can't teach myself."

"I kind of figured as much." She gave me a once-over. "Look, there's a group of students here that have this little club." She handed me a flyer. "It's kind of a not-official group of magicals. It's less about getting better at magic and more about being able to *be* magical, you know? Without all the restrictions."

I took the flyer, immediately recognizing the symbol as the one I'd seen in Rome. The one Sahil said had been used by magicals interested in undoing the Danvers Accord.

"Thanks. I'll check it out."

This symbol—it couldn't be a coincidence. It could also be nothing. But it could be something.

The Danvers Accord was iron-clad. Nobody'd been able to

break it.

Except those who weren't under it in the first place. A whole group of people. One, in fact, who'd made no bones about wanting to redo what the Separatists had started. If I'd learned anything about magicals, it was that they were good at finding loopholes. There was definitely a queasy feeling in my gut about this flyer—this symbol I'd now seen twice, with people who wanted the same thing.

I snapped a photo and sent it to Gavon.

Found this flyer when I was meeting with some D.C. magicals. What do you think it's about?

Probably nothing. Wouldn't worry about it.

I frowned. *But we saw the same symbol in Rome? And that guy said it was a group. Maybe it's something to look into?*

Leave it alone, Lexie. Not worth you getting involved in.

"Oh really?" I said, looking at the flyer once more. *So why are you involved?*

Because it's my problem to deal with. I'm not discussing it with you further.

"That isn't an answer," I snapped to no one in particular.

"Yes, it is."

Gavon was behind me, looking more annoyed than I'd seen him in months. His appearance said more than his stormy gaze did.

"No, it isn't," I said, crossing my arms. "What aren't you telling me? And why aren't you telling me?"

He sighed, shaking his head. "Focus on school, Lexie. This isn't your problem to solve."

"I can help—"

"No, you can't," he said. "I thought I said I'm not discussing it with you?"

"And yet, here you are, discussing it," I said.

"Because I need you to promise me you won't go looking into this," he said. "Promise me."

"No," I said. "Because I'm an adult—"

"Not technically for another—"

"—and I'm tired of you lying to me about everything."

Gavon stared at me, the fatherly indignation disappearing as my words echoed around us. "I'm not lying to you, Lexie."

"Selectively informing, whatever," I said, although much less harshly. "What's the big deal? Am I in danger?"

"No," he said with a swift shake of his head. "If you or your sisters were, I'd let you know so you could be prepared. This has absolutely nothing to do with you. And because it has nothing to do with you, I don't want to involve you in it so it continues to have nothing to do with you."

"But—?"

"Please, Lexie, as a favor to your old man, just let it go."

I sighed, shrugging half-heartedly. When he begged like that, it was hard to keep pushing. "Fine, I won't go to this meeting or whatever."

"Good." He smiled. "Where did you get this thing anyway?"

"I went to a magical prep school," I said, pulling the other pamphlet from my pocket and handing it to him. "Heard of it?"

"Oh yes," he said with a derisive snort. "Jeanie was briefly sent here."

"She was?"

He nodded with a sad smile. "Briefly. They knew what I

tried to tell Irene. You can't train what doesn't exist."

"Dad, come on." I pursed my lips. My aunt hadn't had a lot of magic. "Be nice."

"I am being nice," he said with a look. "Your aunt was a giving, kind woman, but a magical powerhouse she wasn't. I always thought she could've done with some potion-making lessons, but she never seemed interested."

I stared at the pamphlet again, embarrassment rising to my cheeks from that lady who'd suggested I needed lessons. "Think I should enroll?"

"Hardly," he said with a hearty chuckle. "You'd probably run circles around everyone there. But if you need a training session, you could always ask me."

"I think you train me plenty on our little jaunts, thanks," I said.

"And speaking of…" His eyes sparkled. "Ready for another trip?"

Fourteen

For the third time in as many weeks, Gavon and I transported across the Atlantic. This time, our destination was the south of Spain, close to Seville. Instead of a back alley, we landed in the middle of a desert-like field with low, thorny bushes.

"Really?" I said, looking around for any sign of civilization.

"We can't get any closer magically," he explained, guiding me out of the field and onto a main road. "We're going to meet with a Clanmaster, and she's got many of the same magical protections around her village as your Gram. So we transport most of the way, walk the rest."

My track record with Clanmasters was pretty abysmal to date. "Does she like you?"

"The Clanmaster?" He smiled. "Of course. Josefa and I are old friends. Clan Vargas used to be the preeminent experts on potion-making, before the Accord, of course. I've been trying to rip a magical hole in the other magical pocket I'd made, to no avail, so I thought she might have some insights."

"Nicole's busy?"

"Ah-hah," Gavon said with a cough. "Well, as your sister isn't really speaking to me right now, I had to ask someone else. And I also thought you'd benefit from meeting some more magicals your own age. Ones without funny ideas."

"And you don't want to spring for a semester at the Arlington School?" I asked, half-jokingly.

He smiled. "I would, if you really wanted to. But I think you'd be bored. Remember, all the kids there are limited to simple things like summoning, transporting, and charms. Easy things you've already mastered. So this way, you get exposure to young magicals and I don't have to pay another expensive tuition."

"True…"

"And probably more importantly," he said with a grimace. "Celeste Davis, the school's director, is close friends with your grandmother. She'd appreciate a nice endowment, I'm sure, but it might not erase all the ill will your grandmother has toward us."

"I guess," I said, stuffing my hands in my pocket. "I still haven't gotten a response to my letter, by the way."

"Are you expecting to?" he asked, raising a brow.

"No…yes?" I said. "Maybe. I just can't understand why she hates me so much."

Gavon clasped his hands behind his back. "Because she's threatened by you."

"Why?"

"Our magic is much more powerful than theirs. They've had

years under the Danvers Accord to limit and reduce their magic to what it is today. Even if Cyrus had been half as powerful…" He licked his lips. "The only reason your mother stood a chance against him was because—"

"Because she was using my magic," I finished for him. "So that's why Irene is so afraid of me?"

He nodded. "It's silly. It's not enough to have power, you have to want to use it. And you've never wanted to take over Clan Carrigan, have you?"

I frowned. "I just wanted to be included."

"I know, sweetheart," he said with a sympathetic look. "If I could change your Gram's mind, I would. But I'm afraid I'm the least likely person to do that at this point"

"You think?" I said, dripping sarcasm.

He shook his head, staring out into the open road with sad eyes. "I think her hatred of me has blinded her to the fact that you guys are Mora's children, too. You're all that's left of her. One day, Irene is going to realize that and regret that she didn't get a chance to see you guys more."

I stared at the dusty road, trying to come up with a response somewhere in-between blasé and the torrent of feelings that came from talking about the mother I never knew. Instead, I just remained silent, promising myself I'd figure a way to articulate it better some day in the future.

We arrived at a small village of white houses and tile roofs and almost immediately, I felt an undercurrent of magic. It was faint, not at all like the zip-zip of New Salem. But enough to let me know there were more than a few magicals in the houses around us.

"Okay, I can feel this magic," I said. "So maybe my magical radar can only detect the presence of a lot of magicals, not just one?"

He smiled as the door opened in front of us. "We'll keep working on it. Ah, Josefa, you look as lovely as ever."

The woman who walked out was heavy-set, with graying black hair and a bright smile that put me at ease. She gathered Gavon into a bear hug—the first such hug I'd seen anyone give the man. The woman spoke Spanish quickly, but Gavon nodded as if he could understand her perfectly.

"Josefa, this is my daughter, Alexis," he said, then smiled wider. "Sorry, Lexie."

"*Díos mío.*" The woman took my hands gazing at me as if she'd met me before, then shook her head and spoke rapidly. I caught nothing of what she said.

"Ah, Josefa," Gavon said, obviously recognizing my deer-in-headlights look. "Give us a moment. Lexie, you still don't know how to do a translation charm on words, hm?"

I shook my head. "Still trying to get the hang of the written one."

"It's basically the same process." He put his hands near my ears, but not touching them. "Do you feel that space between your ear and my hand?" I concentrated, imagining a small dome around either of my ears, like a pair of headphones. "Create a magical barrier in that space then use your magic to translate the sound waves."

Instead of arguing with him, as I usually did, I closed my eyes and listened. Josefa began talking again, slowly, as if she were helping me through the process. I imagined the sound coming from her mouth, hitting the barrier, and transforming into words I could understand.

"*Que paso a...* Potion-maker?" Like tuning a radio, Josefa's words suddenly made sense in my mind.

"Got it? Good job," Gavon said, patting me on the shoulder. "Josefa, this is my youngest daughter. Nicole, the Potion-maker, is my eldest."

Josefa shook her head. "You cannot be serious. This is your *youngest?* She's got to be sixteen? Seventeen?"

"Eighteen almost," I said, blushing. I wasn't sure I'd ever get used to people knowing about me before I showed up at their front door.

"And a freshman at Georgetown," Gavon said with a proud smile and hand on my shoulder. "My other two are doing quite well, too."

"I would expect nothing less from your children, Gavon," Josefa said. "Come in, come in. Let's have a look at you."

She grabbed my face, turning me around two or three times as if she'd known me forever. She commented on how much I looked like Gavon, how smart I must be to be attending Georgetown, was I dating anyone, asking so quickly I barely had a chance to answer her before she was on to the next.

"Josefa," Gavon said, interrupting with a smile, "we were hoping you could help us with a potion. As you know, we're trying to close the tear I made between this world and New Salem. We've been experimenting with magical pockets." He held out his hand, palm-down, and a magical pocket appeared beneath it. "I've been trying to recreate the potion I used to create the tear, using this pocket as a guinea pig. But I still haven't been able to crack the code."

Josefa nodded, running her hand along the edge of the pocket. "Have you tried recreating your potion in reverse? Sometimes that can help undo what's been done."

"We haven't," Gavon said slowly, his brow knitting together. "I'm not quite sure what I did or how I did it."

"I have a list of ingredients," I said, hoping I was offering something helpful. "I mean, I took all your potions and put them into a spreadsheet, then took out all the duplicates." They both stared at me like I was speaking in tongues, and my cheeks warmed.

"Well," Gavon said. "Let's see what you've got."

I summoned my laptop from my dorm and showed it to them. "See here, on this sheet, I've got all the ingredients themselves. On this other one, I've got all the combinations. I thought it might be useful to tick off how much of each you used, and in what combination."

Gavon squinted at the screen, looking as confused as I'd expect a man who'd grown up in New Salem to look. But even Josefa scratched her head as I slowly explained the spreadsheet, but eventually, she nodded.

"And are these all the ingredients you used?" Josefa asked. "That you can remember?"

"Maybe," Gavon said with a shrug. "Obviously, most of what's available in New Salem is created by magic from a small kernel of the original. But the options are limited."

Josefa furrowed her brow, thinking for a moment. "It's going to be difficult to recreate the potion exactly then. The ingredients you used would've had their own magical properties, different from what we could procure. Even if you brought something from New Salem, it would have a different ratio of magic."

"That's a good point," Gavon said. "Can you think of any other potions that might be similar to these ingredients that could cause a tear to be made?"

"We can certainly look through my library," Josefa said, catching my eye. "But I wouldn't want to bore Lexie."

"Not boring at all," I said, perking up.

My traitorous father decided otherwise. "Lexie would be an apt research assistant, but I was hoping she could spend some time with some of your younger clansmen."

"Dad…" I frowned. He was trying to get me to be social instead of spending all day in a library? Did he even know me?

"Oh, Martin would love to take her around," Josefa said, clapping her hands. "Martin!"

A puff of orange smoke appeared in the center of the room, and out of it stepped a young man, probably a good foot taller than me.

"Lexie, this is my great-nephew, Martin," Josefa said with a knowing look. "Martin, show Lexie around. Take her to your grandmother's house. I'm sure she's got some food cooking. She *always* has some food cooking. Maybe some croquettes today. Make sure you show her everything."

I gave Gavon a 'help me' look, but he shrugged. "We shouldn't be long, sweetheart."

Trying my best to keep the frown off my face, I followed the tall Spaniard out of the house and into the warm afternoon air. He was all right, I guess, if not for the disinterested look on his face.

"So, I'm Lexie," I said, after a long string of silence.

"American?" Martin asked.

"Yep," I said, taking in the village once again. Every building was white, perhaps to reflect the hot sun, which was pretty sweltering even in September. Nobody was out and about except for Martin and me, so it felt a little like a ghost town.

"So did you grow up here, or…?"

"Yep."

"Great." I supposed I'd have to make the conversation here. "So, what do you do for fun?"

"Play Halo."

I couldn't help but laugh. So much for Gavon's plan to introduce me to interesting magicals.

"What?"

"It's just…I've been around nonmagicals my whole life. Thought I was missing something, but it turns out you guys are the same as them. Everyone plays video games and lives on their phones."

"I mean, there's not much to do around here. Not with my great aunt looking over my shoulder all the time." He shrugged. "If you're looking for something more fun, magic-wise, there's a group of people who meet up and act like they can do more than zap each other in the ass."

I blinked. "Seriously?"

"Yeah, but don't get your hopes up. They keep promising a lot of stuff, but they never deliver." He crossed his arms over his chest. "Two years I've been hearing this guy talk about it. Oh, it's coming, he says. Just need to figure out the kinks."

"What?" I asked.

"The end to the Danvers Accord," he said, glancing at the house behind us. "But don't tell the old people. Even Josefa told me to steer clear of it, and she's been trying to get potion-making back in the mainstream for years."

"I've heard a little about it. Group with a flame in a circle?" I asked and he nodded. "Gavon told me to steer clear of it, too."

"You call your dad by his first name?"

"Um. It's complicated," I said. "But you really think they're *actually* trying to bring back specialties? Or are they just blowing smoke?"

He chewed on his cheek. "Who knows? You've got Warrior magic, Josefa says. Why would you keep that from other people?"

"Because it's dangerous. And in the hands of one idiot like Cyrus, you could cause a lot of damage."

"Who's Cyrus?" he asked.

"The asshole who killed my mother and aunt," I snapped. "And if giving up my Warrior magic means that nobody gets orphaned at a few hours old, then so be it."

He shrugged. "Sorry to get you so mad."

We walked the rest of the way to Martin's grandmother's house (I assumed), where there was, indeed, a large spread of food being cooked by Josefa's sister. She drew us inside, making us sit and placing a plate of shrimp and fried eggplant in front of us. Martin took a plate and disappeared.

"Kids these days," Ana said. "So you're Gavon's little one, hm? Josefa said you were a Potion-maker."

"No, that's my sister," I said. "I'm a Warrior, like Gavon."

"Is your sister married?"

I actually laughed. "Soon to be engaged, I think."

"Pity," she tutted. "Josefa would set her up with one of the young men here, just to keep her around. In the old days, your father might've sent her here to learn. The Vargas Clan used to be the most well-known in the world for our potions. Once upon a time."

"But you don't…" I thought about what Martin had said. "You don't want to do away with the Danvers Accord, do you?"

"Of course not," she said with a shake of her head. "It would be nice if it were a bit looser, but sometimes we've got to sacrifice for the greater good."

Just then, Gavon and Josefa breezed through the door. "I wish I could tell you more. Maybe you should get that daughter of yours to take a look at it?"

He thanked her, not mentioning that Nicole wasn't speaking to him. "Ready to go, Lexie?"

"You can come back and visit any time, Alexis," Josefa said. "And bring your sister! I'd love to see how her powers have matured."

"I'll certainly try." I wouldn't go out of my way to tear Martin from his video game, but Josefa seemed nice enough. And if I could get Nicole here, even better.

We left the way we'd come, hiking out of the village into the desert hills. Sweat dripped down the back of my neck, but I was more curious about what I'd missed.

"Why didn't you want me around?" I asked, after a moment.

Gavon smiled, almost too nicely. "I thought you wanted to meet more magicals?"

"I do, but come on," I said, wiping my brow. "Why did you want to get rid of me?"

"I wasn't getting rid of you," Gavon said, although the tops of his cheeks turned red. It could've been from exertion, but he didn't look bothered by the heat. Probably another charm. "She gave me a stack of books on potions for barriers, but we didn't find anything concrete."

"And you didn't want me there because…?"

"I told you, I wanted you to get to know more magicals. How was Martin?"

"He plays video games and he doesn't talk to me, so a typical guy," I said, stopping. "And he also told me about that group of magicals that you don't want me to know about."

He sighed. "Lexie…"

"Hey," I shrugged. "You asked."

Fifteen

I couldn't shake the feeling that Gavon wasn't telling me something—and that it had something to do with those magicals I'd heard about from the Magical Academy. Something strange was afoot with the Danvers Accord, and while I didn't think Gavon was doing anything *evil*, I also didn't like his reasons for not including me.

Sure, I got that he wanted me to stay out of it. I got that he wanted me to focus on college and fun and not get pulled into another death match. But at the end of the day, I *always* got sucked in. If I knew what was going on, I could avoid it.

At least, that was what I told myself as I walked into the Arlington School for Magic the next afternoon after classes.

It was busy, with small, three-person classes led by an older magical. In one room, three girls were practicing levitation. In another, a couple boys were appearing and disappearing. I shook my head—this place would've been really great at fifteen. Or thirteen. It would've been nice to know magic existed.

Whatever.

Knowing that the polo-shirt-wearing magical might try to kick me out again, I quickly scanned each of the rooms, looking for the girl I'd spoken with a few days ago. Kailey was her name, I thought. I asked a passing girl who looked maybe fourteen, and she pointed to a room in the back. There, I found a group of kids very mundanely writing their homework in a room with snacks and a vending machine. Only instead of math and science books, they were reading old magical books.

"Oh hey!" Kailey said, looking up as I opened the door. "Lexie, right?"

"Yeah," I said smiling. "Hey, listen, I was wondering if you could show me to that meeting thing you were telling me about?"

She made a face and looked around, as if I'd just screamed obscenities. "Ssh! You can't talk about that here."

"O-okay," I said.

"Let's go outside," she said, grabbing my elbow and leading me toward the door. She didn't speak until we were in the alley, and far, far away from the door. "The director is really pissy about this kind of stuff. She says anyone caught doing this group stuff will be expelled from the school."

"Yikes," I said. "So…what is it, exactly?"

"I can't say outside of the meetings," she said. "It's a pact. You know what that is?"

"What kind of a pact prevents you from speaking?" I said with a frown.

"Oh, it's this whole complex thing," she said. "I think they call it a chain barrier? You can't just show up. You've got to be approved by Trent." She laughed, almost a little surprised. "Huh, I guess you're approved. I normally can't even say his name."

I shrugged. I wasn't an expert in pacts, but the more I found out about this thing, the more curious I became. "There's nobody named Cyrus involved, right?"

She thought. "Not that I know of. I've never heard the name."

Well, Cyrus couldn't be the only bad person in the world. "So when's your next meeting?"

"Tonight, at a school over in northern Virginia," she said, blinking. "Wow. I guess you really are approved."

"I guess so."

"Which is good," she grinned devilishly, "because I'm kind of grounded and wouldn't be able to get there otherwise. Can you meet me at my house at like seven? We can transport there together."

"Oh…um…" Sure, I was all for *me* breaking the rules. But I wasn't sure I felt comfortable abetting Kailey in rule-breaking. Did that make me a bad influence?

Then again, she was my only lead into this weird group, and since Gavon wasn't spilling the beans…

"Fine. Seven, it is."

I transported to a very nice house in the suburbs at the address Kailey had given, keeping to the darkness. The houses were bigger than I'd ever seen before, mansion-like with perfectly manicured lawns and big, bushy trees. Each driveway held a luxury SUV or car. Pretentious was an understatement.

"Psst!" Kailey appeared in her window, waving at me. "I'll be right down."

She kicked her feet out of the window, in an attempt to shimmy down. Without thinking, I used my magic to surround her and gently waft her to the ground.

"Holy shit," she said, eyes wide. "How did you do that?"

"Um…magic?" I said, blinking.

"No, but like…this is in the open. I can't even say the word m…m…" She shrugged. "See? Can't even say it. And you just friggin' levitated me."

"Well, I have weird magic," I said, glad the darkness was covering my flushed face. "So can we get on with it?"

She showed me a piece of paper with a location at George Mason University, and I used my magic to find it then transported us both there. It was an empty classroom, though.

"Oh, this isn't where we're meeting," Kailey said, by way of explanation. "Just the landing spot. We've got to walk the rest of the way."

So we ventured through the campus, which was verdant and lush, and filled with kids and activity. We stopped briefly to watch a pair of kids break dance in the middle of the quad before going on.

"Why couldn't we just transport into the meeting space?" I asked.

"Oh, there's a ton of barrier spells around it. It's for the nonmagicals," she said, twirling a lock of hair. "But it also means we can't get inside through magic. And he likes for us to walk in so he knows who's coming, too."

"Do I need to know some kind of code?"

"Nah, if I vouch for you, it'll be cool. And besides that, if you weren't approved, I couldn't even be talking to you about it." She giggled. "This is so weird. I've tried to tell other people about it and it's never been this easy."

When we got to the conference room, I felt the presence of magic. It reminded me of the magical barrier I'd put up around my apartment once upon a time, a sizzling perimeter that promised pain if anyone unauthorized came through the door. Luckily, with Kailey leading the way, I was able to pass through it. Perhaps in hindsight, such a barrier wasn't the smartest idea for whomever was trying to protect this meeting space.

But from the looks of things, this seemed like an amateur operation anyway. There were certainly magicals here, but I pegged most of them at fifteen and sixteen. They sat in groups on the floor, playing on their phones and taking selfies with each other.

"C'mon, let me introduce you to my friends."

Kailey's friends were like her—rich, magical, and very, very bored. They oohed and aahed at my strange magic, but I wisely declined to show them the real power. Something told me it was better to keep things under wraps until I knew what I was dealing with. My gut was churning uncomfortably, and not just from the group of young magicals who were decidedly much cooler than I was.

A middle-aged man walked into the room, and the chatter quieted.

"Get into your pairs," he said, and like clockwork, everyone rose, myself included, and walked to opposite sides of the room. As a new person, I didn't have a pair, so I followed Kailey, who whispered explanations in my ear.

"That's Trent," she said. "He's the guy in charge. Every day we start with sparring—"

I held up my hand. "You guys can't spar."

"Hah!" She lifted her chin. "Watch us."

"Ready," Trent said. "And begin!"

I held my breath and waited for the fireworks as both sides of the room formed multicolored balls. But even with my limited sense of magic, I could tell they were…not real attack spells. They might've stung, but I doubted they'd even leave a bruise.

One by one, the would-be Warriors released their attack spells into the room, where they limped along until disappearing into nothingness in the middle of the room,

"Way to go!" cheered one boy on one side of the room. "You only got three feet last time."

Each of the kids congratulated themselves on their performance, as if they'd accomplished something fantastic.

"Wow," I said.

"Impressive, huh?" Kailey said with a grin. "Trent says with practice, we might even get to the other side of the room."

"Kailey. Who is this?"

Trent had zeroed in on me, and it was all I could do not to wither under his gaze. I had to remind myself that he wasn't from New Salem, that he was a regular magical like the rest of them. Because he sure gave me a Cyrus-like vibe.

"This is Lexie," Kailey said. "I found her wandering around the Arlington School. Thought she might be interested in what we do here."

"And why is that?" he said, boring a hole into my skull with his fierce gaze. I already didn't like this guy with his pencil mustache that seemed too hipster for the crowd. I also didn't like the way he looked me up and down, as if I were some kind of abomination.

"Um… 'cause she thinks we should be able to use magic whenever we want?" Kailey wilted slightly, and my Warrior instincts kicked in. "And she can—"

"What *exactly* are you trying to accomplish here?" I said, my voice carrying across the room. "You know these kids can't use attack spells."

He shrugged. "We've been able to find ways to create something similar. It's not as effective as a true Warrior would be, but it's close enough."

"Whoever's been telling you that has been lying to you," I said, more to myself than to him. I was pretty sure I could knock out every single kid in here without blinking an eye. "And for what purpose are you training these kids to use attack spells? Gonna be hard to take this show on the road when you can't use magic in front of nonmagicals."

"We have our ways."

"Care to share?" I pressed. "I'm exceedingly curious."

His angry glare broke, and he averted his eyes. "Can I have a word in private?"

"Sure," I said, glancing at the rest of the class, who'd been watching intently.

I followed him outside the room, ready for a fight, but his face grew weary.

"There's no plan," he said quietly. "But these kids are restless. It's unfair that they've been given this great gift and can't use it freely. So I have to keep telling them something great is on the horizon or else…" He met my gaze. "Do you understand?"

"Yeah, but…" I looked back into the room. "Isn't that just false hope?"

"It's mostly young kids, just turning fifteen. Once they get out of the house, they integrate more with the nonmagicals. But until then, it's just something to do." He smiled, and it felt slimy, even as his voice sounded sincere. "You seem like you're pretty well on the right path. Got a good head on your shoulders. Not sure we can help you here."

His gaze melted into one of worry, and then he disappeared in a puff of light blue magic. For a moment, I didn't understand, but then puffs of magic started appearing all over the room.

"Sean Scythes! Get your ass over here right now!"

"You are in big trouble, Quinn Malcer!"

"Eric Stroinski, you are *grounded*!"

Parents had appeared in the middle of the supposedly impenetrable space. How, I had no idea, but I guessed there might've been a snitch in the room. Hence my initial suspicions that the spell they'd used had been ill-thought out.

"You can forget about the car, Kailey Ann!" A middle-aged man wearing a suit had Kailey by the arm and was wagging his finger in her face.

"*Dad*, it's not that big a deal," she said, looking to me for help.

I shrugged, having no dog in this fight. I'd never been more grateful to be in college.

"You must be Alexis."

A strong, authoritative voice rang out behind me, and I turned to see a formidable black woman with short hair and eyes that pierced my very soul like Irene's had.

"Must I?" I squeaked.

"Irene mentioned you were attending school nearby," she said. "I suppose I'm unsurprised to see you here in the midst of this nonsense."

I scowled. "I wasn't aware she knew anything about me. Considering she excommunicated me."

The woman quirked a smile. "She was right. You do lack some basic respect."

"Care to explain what the hell this was about?" I gestured around the room. "Or what the hell this is?"

"Only if you would care to explain your presence here."

My neck burned. "I was invited by Kailey."

"Do us all a favor and stay away from our magicals," she said. "They don't need to be exposed to any more crackpot ideas."

"Hey, I wasn't the one exposing them," I said. "You should talk to that Trent guy."

Her eyes flashed. "Who?"

"The one who was orchestrating this whole thing," I said. "Like I said, I'm just an innocent bystander. He said his name is Trent, and that this whole thing is just a way to pass the time with the kids. It doesn't sound like anything too nefarious."

She opened her mouth to respond, but I felt a presence appear right behind me, and a familiar hand on my shoulder.

"Ah, Celeste," Gavon said. "I see you've met my daughter."

"And the ringleader arrives," she said, narrowing her eyes. "Causing trouble as usual."

"Merely coming to retrieve my child like the rest of the parents here," he said, squeezing my shoulder with a promise of a lecture sure to include a collection of disappointed looks. "I know it's difficult to believe after what Irene's told you all these years, but it's not my intent to corrupt your children." He smiled. "In fact, we'd love to have a chat about ways we can prevent this sort of thing—"

"I don't believe a chat with you would be very helpful," she said. "And I'll be warning my charges to stay away from your daughter."

He sighed heavily. "As you wish. Good evening."

With his firm grip still on my shoulder, he led me from the small conference room. Once we were safely out of the area and in the open, he finally spoke.

"What are you looking for, Alexis?" he asked, shortly. "Trouble? To give me a heart attack?"

"I'm sorry," I said, looking at the ground. "I swear I wasn't trying to get in trouble this time. I just met this girl Kailey and she invited me—"

"After I expressly told you not to get involved?"

"Well, yeah, I mean…she's like fifteen. How much trouble could it be?"

"Obviously, a lot," Gavon said, gesturing to the building. "You don't get Celeste Davis to show up with a boatload of the world's most powerful parents for nothing."

"Who is she?" I said, shivering a bit.

"She's the director of the Arlington School for Magicals, and a Clanmaster," Gavon said. "And now, she thinks you and I are ringleading this ridiculous group of people who want to practice attack magic. So you can probably forget about asking her if she'd be interested in updating the Danvers Accord."

I chewed my lip. "I still don't understand why everyone was getting up in arms. They can't even form attack spells."

"I don't care about them. I care about you not listening to me," Gavon said. "As I still haven't gotten a straight answer as why you keep wanting to include yourself into something that blessedly doesn't concern you."

I didn't have an answer I was comfortable voicing yet, so I just kept quiet.

"Celeste could've been an ally," Gavon said after a long pause. "She's Irene's friend, but might've been willing to listen. Especially if we still wanted to update the Danvers Accord. You still want to be a part of that, right?"

I nodded.

"Then I suggest you quit getting involved in this," he said. "And get back to school before you make anyone else angry."

Sixteen

Aware that I'd potentially screwed something significant up for Gavon, I kept my nose in books and school for the next few days. I didn't even open my magical bubble, only using magic to transport to Florida for Sunday dinner with Nicole. In this case, I was glad that she and Gavon weren't on speaking terms because she would have lectured me as badly as he had. Instead we shared a nice, quiet dinner and watched a movie.

I hadn't heard from Gavon in a few days either, which suited me fine because the course workload had taken a decidedly upward turn. Sam and I were stuck in the library most of the week, and too tired do much else but talk about how tired we were at night.

"My brain is mush," she said, pressing the heel of her hand against her head. "How can one class be so mind-numbingly exhausting?"

I put down my Latin book and nodded. "Thanksgiving can't come soon enough."

"How am I supposed to compete at trivia tonight if I can't even remember my name?" she said. "Last week was bad. We missed a question on Jefferson. If only there was a history buff hanging around that would come to our games and help us win."

I rolled my eyes with a laugh. She'd been not-so-subtly hinting that I should give her and her friends another shot by joining them at their weekly trivia nights for days now. I still wasn't convinced that they liked me as much as Sam was making out, and the idea of going out with a group that I had nothing to say to didn't really interest me that much.

"Dave was just asking me, do I *know* anyone who reads historical biographies? Who'd know the difference between Jefferson and Jackson."

"Well, obviously, *big* difference there," I said to the ceiling.

"See? We need you, Lexie." She wiggled her eyebrows. "Dave needs you."

I groaned. "I think I've outlasted the statute of limitations on that one."

"No, you haven't. I've been telling him *all* about you," she said, rolling onto her stomach. "He gets that you're weird. But he still thinks you're cute."

"Oh, gee, thanks," I said with a laugh. "Why are you so interested in seeing me date him?"

"Because I *really* think you'd get along great with the group," she said. "And I don't see you with any other friends. We want to adopt you."

I hesitated, face burning. "Did he really say I was cute?"

"Yes, he did," she said. "So no excuses, you're coming

tonight!"

About an hour later, Sam and I were walking into the same restaurant where I'd first met her friends, and I was determined to do better this time. I would have a conversation with Dave, and if he asked me out again, I wouldn't leave it hanging. I would be social and engaging, and not let my magic hold me back.

At least, I hoped I would.

"You guys remember Lexie, right?" Sam said, as we walked up to the table. Thankfully, she re-introduced me to the group. Vicki and Amanda, twins with pale skin and dark hair, waved emphatically. Chris, the sneering, pretentious boy from Maine, gave me a slight nod of disinterest. And, of course, Dave rose and held out chairs for the two of us.

"Such a gentleman," Sam said, settling in one of the open seats. "Don't you think, Lexie?"

"Um, yeah," I said, sharing a smile with him. "Nice to see you guys again."

"'Bout time you came to join us," Vicki said. "We've been telling Sam that she should invite you."

"She's been busy," Sam said, pulling a slice over to herself. "I didn't think it was possible to have more coursework than high school."

"You're telling me," Chris said. "I was barely able to get out here today. Have a ten-page analysis due tomorrow. Currently on page zero."

"I told you that you should've started that ages ago," Sam said, shaking her head.

"Yes, Mother."

I caught a look between them and wondered if they were seeing each other. Sam hadn't mentioned a boyfriend…then again, I also hadn't asked. I was officially the worst at friendships.

"So, Lexie," Dave said. "How are your classes going?"

"They're good," I said, scrambling for something interesting to talk about. "Busy." But all I could think about was the Danvers Accord, the magicals I'd met, and all the other things I couldn't talk to this group about. I couldn't even name a nonmagical book I'd read lately.

"Lexie's learning all about lacrosse," Sam said, saving me from making a bigger fool out of myself than I already had. "She came to my game last week and met my folks."

"Aw, how are John and Rose?" Vicki asked. "I need to come visit soon. Your mom makes the best pound cake."

"She so does." Sam sighed wistfully. "Lexie, when you come visit, you'll have to pack your sweatpants, 'cause my mom will feed you until you explode."

I grinned, but lost myself to thoughts about how I'd come visit her in California. Magic, obviously, but how could I play off visiting for a day? I'd have to stay for a week. And I'd have to tell them about what plane I was on, presumably. Her parents would want to pick me up from the airport.

This whole nonmagical friend thing was making my head hurt.

Luckily, the trivia announcer tapped on the mike, getting the room's attention. I sat back in my chair, annoyed at myself for all this overthinking, and glad we'd have guided conversation from here on. Trivia, at least, I could handle.

"First question: Wellington is the capital of which country?"

"New Zealand," I said, without missing a beat.

"Yeah, New Zealand," Sam said, elbowing me. "I'm already glad to have you on our side."

"I do have a lot of useless knowledge," I said with a laugh. "And it's not often my sisters appreciate it."

Chris took the paper up to the front of the room and we waited for the results. We'd gotten it right, but so had several others in the room.

"That one was pretty easy," Dave said, looking up at the screen. "What about this one?"

"Next question: What does the Olympic motto '*Citius, Altius, Fortius*' mean?"

"Faster, higher, stronger," I said to Chris as he scribbled down the answer. Dave quirked a brow in my direction, and I blushed. "Uh…I take a Latin class."

My stroke of luck continued, with questions related to flags, wars, and even a random question about limericks and the author of Peter Rabbit. Even Chris voiced his appreciation for my knowledge, which judging from Sam's look of shock, was high praise coming from him. Dave saved the day with the answer to a random 80's song, which only our table got right. In the end, we won a $20 gift certificate to the bar, which Dave handed to me.

"Oh, I couldn't," I said, handing it back to him. "I mean, you got that last one."

"Yeah, but you got all the other ones," Dave said, pushing it across the table. "You can use it to buy us dinner next week when you come back."

I laughed. "You got it."

The game over, Vicki and Amanda left, making me promise I would come back and spend more time with them. Chris left shortly after, whining about the paper that he hadn't started and Sam giving him an earful about better time management. And then it was just Sam, Dave, and me, sitting around the table, picking at the leftover pizza and talking about theories about a popular zombie TV show that we all watched. After a while, I forgot that I was magical and all my strange quirks. I was just a college kid nibbling at pizza with some friends. I'd been incredibly stupid for avoiding Sam's invite for so long. And maybe Gavon and everyone else had been right; there was a lot about me that I could share.

"You're coming next week, right?" Sam said. "I mean, it would be pretty crappy of you to take our shared twenty-dollar gift card and not buy us all dinner next week."

"I'm coming back," I said with a short glance at Dave. He'd been talking to me most of the night, when we weren't in the throes of trivia madness. I kind of liked his thick accent, too.

"Well, Lexie, I've gotta head out," Sam said with a smirk. "Dave, would you be a gent and walk her home?"

All the pizza turned sour in my stomach. "W-what?"

"Relax," she said. "I forgot I have to do some work at the library tonight. Dave's good. He'll get you back to the dorm in one piece."

You damned liar. The words died on my tongue as she walked away cackling. She was setting me up.

And just like that, I was alone with Dave again.

"So, you ready?" he asked, having the good grace not to look like he'd had any part in this.

The walk was silent at first, as I had nothing in my repertoire to handle Dave alone. Instead, I pointed to his wrist where there was a small black dot.

"What's that tattoo mean?" I asked, pointing to the small symbol on his wrist.

"Oh, that," he said, turning over his wrist to show me the symbol better. "It's this group I belong to."

Red flags waved in my head. "You got a tattoo because you belong to a group?"

"Yeah, I mean…it's small, so it's not really noticeable. Kind of like a fraternity, you know?" He shrugged and rolled up his other sleeve. "I've also got this one here, and a couple on my back. I don't know, I like tattoos. But don't tell my mom. When I have to go home, I wear a watch so she won't see it."

At that, I had to smile. "Yeah, I think my sister would murder me if I got a tattoo."

We walked in silence for a few more minutes, and I kept wondering if I should bring up us going to the museum, or if he would bring it up, or if we'd just continue to walk in silence until we reached my dorm, and he'd think—

"So…I hear there's twenty museums around here we could amuse ourselves with."

Exhale. "Oh yeah," I said, trying to play it cool. "I've been so busy I haven't gone to see any yet. And it was the one thing on my list when I moved here."

"Want to go together?"

My heart pounded and a thread of anxiety had snaked its

way from the top of my head down to my toes. "Uh, sure," I managed. "When?"

"This weekend?" He stopped and grinned at me, and I just knew he could see right through me.

"This weekend could work," I said. Gavon hadn't been asked me to come out with him in a while, but I could easily tell him no if he did. "Yeah, that sounds good. But I mean…we don't have to go to the museums. I'm sure it's kind of boring."

"You said you're a history major, so I just assumed…" He chuckled. "I'm an engineering major, so I doubt you'd want to take any field trips to what I like. Maybe the Hoover Dam, so we could look at the hydroelectric generators."

I smiled. "My sister lives in Vegas. Maybe I'll make her take me there."

"You visit often?"

About once a week. "We talk a lot. Same with my other sister in Florida."

"Family's important," he said with a nod. "I've got one sister, she just turned fifteen, so it's a bit of a mess back home. Glad I'm not there."

"Fifteen's a rough age," I said with a snort.

"Why? What happened to you?"

I paused, considering my response. It wasn't even the magic part that stopped me, rather, sharing something so personal with a complete stranger. My relationship with Gavon began and ended then, and everything had gone so wrong so quickly after that. Not to mention Jeanie's death.

"Sorry I asked," Dave said after a long pause.

"No, it's just…" I swallowed, being careful to pick my

words. "My aunt…the one who raised us, she died when I was fifteen, and it's kind of hard to talk about."

"Oh man," Dave said, looking genuinely sorry. "I didn't mean to—"

"No, it's fine." It was actually getting easier to speak about the more I did it. "Anyway, fifteen was weird for me. And the last few years have been even weirder. But my dad and I started reconnecting. We hang out a lot," I chewed my lip, "I mean, he lives near here. He paid for Georgetown, so…yeah…"

Dave raised an eyebrow at me, and I knew exactly how it sounded. But there was so much more to our relationship than that, but I couldn't go into it. Not without coming clean with the big secret in the room.

"Anyway," I said. "What's your family like?"

"Pretty normal. Mom and Dad in Waco. Just Penny and me. I've got a few aunts and uncles, grandparents back in Texas, so we're all pretty close."

"And they let you move to D.C.?" I asked. I was only able to convince Nicole to let me go after promising to come home for dinner every Sunday night.

"Ah…yeah," he said with a shrug. "Well, this is you, right?"

I glanced at the dorm in front of me. "Yeah, this is me." I bunched my hands in my jeans pockets, yet again faced with the embarrassment of what happened after the end of a date. "So… this was fun."

"Yeah," he said with a smile. "I don't think I got an answer on this weekend's museum trip."

Hadn't he? I guess not. "Sure. Let's do it. Museums are okay, if you want. Or we could do something else."

"American History museum it is," he said. "This weekend?"

"Cool," I said. "See ya!"

I closed the door behind me and made sure he was far enough away before sighing and leaning against it. I'd survived several major steps today, but they left me feeling sick. And even though I'd shared a lot with Dave (probably too much about my crazy life), I thought about what would happen if I told him everything, and a shot of fear slid down my spine. It wasn't just the fear of telling him, making it real. It was also knowing that I'd lied to him about almost everything up until that point. Would he understand?

It would be so much easier to date a magical. There was never anything to explain, never anything to feel bad about. If only I could find someone my age with magic—

"Still wearing those emotions on your face, aren't you, Lexie?"

James Riley, my former fling, ex-boyfriend, and evil magical extraordinaire, sat ten feet from me on the common room couch.

Seventeen

An attack spell was in my hand before I could even think.

"You have one minute to tell me why I shouldn't blow you into next year," I snarled.

"Put that thing away," James said, sounding infuriatingly familiar as he stood. "The nonmagicals might see."

"As if you care," I said, keeping the attack spell above my head. "And you have thirty seconds now—"

"I'm not here to hurt you," he said. "If I was, I couldn't be within five miles of you. Your pact, remember?"

My hand twitched. Magicals made habits of creating loopholes around pacts, and I didn't trust James for one second. Still, it made sense to suss out what he was here for, just so we could be one step ahead of him.

Finally, I slowly lowered my hand, and reabsorbed the magic. "What are you doing here?"

"I need your help."

I burst into laughter. I wasn't even sure what was funnier—

that he wanted my help, or that he thought I would give it.

He clicked his tongue against the roof of his mouth as I wiped away tears. "When you're finished."

"Oh, go to *hell*," I said. "Why would I ever consider helping you after what you did?"

"Because you don't know the whole story." He actually sounded serious.

"I am *so* sure," I said, standing upright. "Please, James. Enlighten me what I missed while I was fighting for my life in a sparring ring."

"You weren't ever supposed to go into that ring," he said in a clipped tone. "You were supposed to go to your father. Tell him what Cyrus had done, and then they would've found your sisters. Most of the Guild hates Cyrus already, so it would've been easy to frame him for it. Gavon could've kicked Cyrus out, and then I would be free from…" His voice cut off abruptly as if something were choking him from the inside.

I was only a little concerned. If he choked to death on his spit, I wouldn't mind.

"I…" Another cough and a frustrated shake of his head. "I didn't have a lot of time to put together a plan, so that was the best I had."

I stared at him. "So instead of, I don't know, sending a text, leaving a note for me, you decided it was better to just take my sisters and let me think they were in danger? Just to frame Cyrus and kick him out so you could be Guildmaster?"

"This isn't about the Guildmastership," James said. "I just said it was because I…couldn't speak the full truth. I wish I could tell you more, but I just…can't."

"You can't." I couldn't believe my ears. "You show up here, asking for my help, and you also just happen to be unable to tell me why you need help or why you tricked me in the first place?"

His gaze bored into me, and for a brief moment, I allowed the hopeful thought that what I thought to be the truth wasn't, and he was coming to provide some explanation, as Gavon had. But I squashed that idea quickly. James was *not* Gavon. He'd never done anything to prove that he gave two craps about me or anyone else but himself.

He broke his gaze and stared at the ground. "I'm sorry for what happened. I had a plan—you just didn't follow it. And by the time I found you, you were already agreeing to the match. There was nothing I could do at that point."

"You *kidnapped* them, James."

"Lexie…"

"It's *Alexis* to you," I snapped. "I don't believe one bit of this story. Not after you spent an entire year worming your way into my good graces. Not after you told me you loved me and then… well, then…" I couldn't finish. The hurt was still too fresh to think about. "And so far, you haven't given me one good reason I shouldn't blow you into next year."

"Cyrus is going to kill me," James said. "I need the protection of your clan's pact with the New Salem Guild."

Well, okay, *that* got my attention. But only momentarily. Gavon had spent many, *many* hours lamenting to me how he wished he could wipe the floor with that guy, but the rules of the Guild prevented it. "Cyrus can't kill you. You're in the Guild."

"He's figured a way around that, trust me," James said,

glancing to the side. "But he can't come within five miles of you."

"So go 4.9 miles away from me," I snapped.

He sighed. "It doesn't work like that. Cyrus can come within five miles of you, as long as he has no intention of hurting you. So he could literally be next door, and as long as his goals don't include you, your pact wouldn't apply."

My heart skipped a beat. "What?"

"Hence why I need to be actually *in* your clan to get your protections." His face broke into a hopeful smile.

"You want to join my…clan?" I asked, raising my eyebrow. "Fat chance. Gram won't even let me in the clan."

"Not that clan," he said. "The one you started when you and Gavon signed the agreement. The clan that includes you and your sisters."

I furrowed my brow. "That's not…an official clan."

"Official enough to have a binding pact with the Warrior's Guild." He shrugged. "You didn't know you were a Clanmaster, did you?"

I didn't, and I was pretty sure if I told my sisters, they'd laugh me off the planet. "Whatever. Even if I did have one, why the hell would I let *you* join it?"

"Lexie, please," he said, taking a step forward. "We were friends once—"

"Friends?" I couldn't believe my ears. "Friends. You want to even *go* there with me? You're lucky I'm letting you breathe in my presence."

He exhaled, as if he wanted to say something in response, but couldn't. I almost wanted him to; it would've been delicious to throw it back in his face.

"Lexie, I am begging you to help," he murmured quietly. "And you're the only person who can help me. Otherwise…I'm a dead man."

"Then start talking about all these things you can't tell me about and maybe I'll start believing you," I said. "In the meantime, there's a lovely alley down the street that would be perfect for garbage like you. I suggest you make yourself at home."

I smirked as I turned to walk up the stairs then screamed as James appeared in front of me. "That's not really going to work, remember? We have magic?"

"Get *out*," I barked, forming an attack spell.

"Come on, Lexie, please help me," he said, turning on that damned smile of his. Pleading wasn't going to work, so he was going to try charm? Lucky for me, I'd developed a thick skin when it came to his nonsense. Perhaps it was the six months of wallowing in my own misery that had done it.

"Go away, James. I don't want you here. I don't want to help you. I was really happy pretending that *you* didn't exist, and I'd like to go back to that."

"Why? So you go on a date with *Day-ve*?" he said, mimicking Dave's Texan accent. "Sounds like a real winner."

"Probably won't lure me into a trap and try to kill me," I said.

"You sure about that?"

I inhaled and exhaled. "Get out of my life, James. I don't want you here."

He sighed, and for the briefest moment, I felt bad for being so mean. But then I remembered the last six months of humiliation, thinking about how much I'd fallen in love with him, and how much it had hurt to know it had been a lie. This was just James—manipulation, sweet-talking until he got what he wanted.

I answered his green, puppy-dog eyes with a middle finger and a slamming door.

I paced angrily in my dorm, grateful Sam was still at the library. There was a really good chance James was lying about everything. He didn't need my help at all, and he was there to destroy something. My college career, maybe. Or maybe even me.

But if that were true, he wouldn't be in the area. Gavon and I had made that pact iron-clad. Just in case…

You awake?

A few moments later: *Everything okay?*

I chewed my lip. Should I tell him James had shown up? If I did, he might show up himself and they might have it out. Besides that, I could handle James on my own. I didn't need him swooping in to rescue me. But I did need something else.

Just wanted to make sure that pact is still working.

I held my breath.

I got a photo of the pact, sitting on Gavon's desk in New Salem, along with the text, *Just read through it again. Nobody from New Salem Warrior's Guild can come within five miles of you or your sisters if they have any intent to harm you.*

I almost put my phone away, but then a nasty voice that sounded like Nicole reminded me what had happened the last time I hadn't told anyone about James. Gavon and I were on the same side, and he was already mad at me. Might as well be honest.

James showed up at my dorm, asking me for help. Thought you should know.

I smirked, staring out the window and waiting for Gavon to get back to me. Oh, if James thought I was going to make the same mistake twice.

Don't worry about him. He's working on something for me and shouldn't have come to you.

I stared at my phone, incredulous.

Did you forget what he did? Why are you working with him at all? Why isn't he in wizard jail?

There were extenuating circumstances that we've discussed in detail. Best just to send him on his way. Also, there is no such thing as wizard jail.

"Best. *Best?*" I sputtered at my phone, not believing what I was seeing. How could Gavon be so nonchalant? James had taken my sisters—*taken them.* All in the pursuit of getting me and Cyrus in the ring. How could he lie about that?

Furious, I marched back downstairs. "Where are you?"

"Did you reconsider?" James asked, appearing in a puff of smoke. "I was already getting comfy in that alley."

I swallowed, leveling a glare at him. "What do you want from me? The truth, please."

"I have told you all the truth I'm physically able to," he said. "Cyrus wants me dead, and I need your pact's protection."

"Then what, you'll kill my sisters? Me?" I narrowed my eyes. "What are you working on with Gavon?"

"You told him I was here?" James said with eyebrows raised. "Good job, Lexie. You're learning."

"I told him you were back," I snapped, glaring at him. "He said I should send you on your way."

"And yet…here you are," he said with a smile. "Are you sending me on my way or…?"

"What are you working on with him?" I asked.

"I can't tell you."

"Can't or won't?"

"Both," he said. "But I want to, very badly." He smiled, as if he'd gotten an idea. "You know the thing we made at the beginning of school last year?"

"The pact?"

He nodded. "That is something…" The words died on his tongue, and he rubbed his neck. "That is something."

"Something what? Still in effect?"

"Something re…" He released a loud breath. "Something r…rel… Dammit."

"You're not making any sense. Are you having a stroke?"

"Possibly." He ran a hand over his face. "Look, I wish I could tell you more, but I can't."

"Then maybe I'll ask Gavon," I said, crossing my arms across my chest. "He told me you shouldn't have gone to me. And that I should send you on your way."

"To my death? Okay then." He shook his head. "There are things I can't tell him either."

"Like what?"

"Same things I can't tell you." He made a noise of frustration and gave me a stare-down. "Look, let me in or don't, but I was getting comfortable in the alley, so I'd like to get some sleep before I die."

"Were you…really in an alley?" I asked. "There are hotels around here. Less than a mile down the street."

He shrugged. "I wanted to be here in case Cyrus pops out of the woodwork and tries to murder me. So you could hear my screams for help."

I chewed on the side of my lip. "Can he really be nearby?"

"I didn't mean to scare you," James said. "But the point is… your pact gives you protection. I need that protection, maybe just…" He sighed. "Temporarily. A week will do."

"What do you need to do in a week?"

"Figure out better provisions. Or, if I prove that I'm not here to hurt you, you might consider extending it."

"Doubtful." I could give him a week, though. "We should make a pact though. That you won't bother me or my sisters."

He conjured a paper and handed it to me. "We already did, dummy."

I took the paper, surprised to see my own words reflected back at me. The pact James and I had signed at the beginning of my senior year. There, in plain words, had been the starting point to our friendship. An agreement I'd thought to be iron-clad, keeping our interactions to just the sparring ring.

"Well, this thing is useless, obviously," I said, pointing to the words on the page. "Because you did harass my sisters."

He laughed. "If anything, I think it would prove that they were in no danger. I merely moved them from one place to another. My intentions were pure, as always. Not one hair was harmed on their heads."

I glared at him. "They were just kidnapped, James."

"One week," he said. "That's all I ask. Please."

The soft plea in his voice did me in. Gavon had said they were working together, and perhaps his excuse was plausible, even if I didn't forgive him. And our original pact remained in effect, I supposed, because we hadn't mutually agreed to break it.

"If you hurt my sisters, my roommate, or anyone else I care about, I will rip out your insides," I said, raising my gaze to him with all the fury I could muster. "And if you are tricking me—"

"I'm not, I swear."

"I will make you regret it for the rest of your life," I finished. "Now, what do I have to do?"

"Say the words, Clanmaster Carrigan," he said with a smile.

I chewed my lip for a moment, calling on the magical hum underneath my skin. James could very well be talking out his ass, but...I was able to sign a pact. I suppose that did make me Clanmaster of my little family.

"James Riley, I allow you temporary membership to my clan on the understanding that you are speaking the truth and nothing but the truth." The magic burned my tongue, more proof that what I was saying was binding. "This agreement will end in one week or if I find out that you're lying to me."

He closed his eyes, inhaling and sighing, as if a weight had been taken off his chest. "Thank you, Lexie. I appreciate it. And I swear to you, I won't bother you."

"Now, go back to your alley..." I said, disliking how nice it felt to have him smile at me like that.

"Oh, about that, I was just kidding," he said with a laugh.

"I'm at a hotel down the street."

Before I could react, he pecked me on the cheek and disappeared in a puff of green.

Something told me I was going to regret letting him back into my life.

Eighteen

"The pact says five miles. That doesn't mean you have to go to class with me."

James had been waiting downstairs when I left for class, a large cup of coffee in hand. Luckily, it was Tuesday, which meant Sam wasn't with me. I wasn't sure how I was going to explain all this to her.

"I merely wanted to bring you some coffee and thank you again for letting me into your clan," he said.

"I thought you weren't going to bother me," I said, hating how good the coffee tasted.

"Bringing you coffee is bothering you?" he asked with a laugh.

"Your presence is bothering me," I said. "And why are you walking with me to class?"

He didn't answer, his eyes brimming with excitement as we walked through the campus. "Would you still be angry with me if I magicked my way into the school? It looks like so much fun."

I glared at him. "I thought this was a *temporary* arrangement? One week."

"It is. Just wanted to get a rise out of you." He grinned, that damned twinkle in his eye so familiar and infuriating. "You still wear your emotions on your face. It's fun to push your buttons."

"*Stop saying that*," I snarled. He'd said that the night he said he loved me, the night he'd first kissed me.

"C'mon, Lexie, it was a joke."

"It wasn't funny, and neither are you. You realize I could've died in that ring—"

"Not from where I was standing," James replied. "And how many times do I have to tell you things got out of hand—"

"Intent means nothing, James."

He stopped and grabbed my arm. "I'm truly, humbly sorry that my idiotic plan backfired and caused you distress. I'm sorry I let you think I betrayed you for the past six months. I'm sorry that I caused you pain."

"Are you sorry that—" I shut my mouth. I didn't want him to apologize for sleeping with me. That would mean it hadn't meant anything to him, and I hadn't healed enough to be able to handle that.

"I'm sorry for everything." His eyes softened and threatened to drag me under again. But I wouldn't let that happen a second time.

"Apology not accepted," I snapped, ripping my arm out of his grip.

"I deserve that," he said, staring at the space I'd vacated. "Have I mentioned how cute you are when you get mad?"

I stopped and fish-mouth gaped at him for a moment. "Don't start with me."

"It's just an observation," he said, shoving his hands into his pockets. "You haven't changed one bit."

"I've changed a lot. I no longer trust backstabbing assholes like you."

"And yet…you agreed include to me in your clan for a week," James said.

I cleared my throat, more to clear the memories from my head. "I'm starting to regret this agreement. I should be able to just nullify it. Kick you out."

"Yes, you can," James said with a smile. "But you haven't, which proves my point."

"Which is what?" My cheeks were burning at this point, and damned if I didn't hate my face for being so obvious.

"Um, hey, Lexie. You okay?"

I nearly dropped my coffee in surprise, and I was pretty sure I would have had my magic not caught it before it slipped through my fingers. Sam, obviously coming from breakfast, watched James and me with narrowed eyes. Had she heard our conversation? I hadn't been very quiet, especially as my temper got out of hand.

"Hey, Sam," I said, wrenching my gaze away from her. "This is…um…James. James, this is my roommate, Sam."

"And who is James?" Sam asked.

"Nobody," I said. "Old friend."

"Well, am I nobody or an old friend?" James asked, laughter in his voice.

"You were just leaving, if I recall," I said. "Bye. And don't think I've made a decision yet."

"Yeah, you have," he said with infuriating certainty. His gaze landed on my lips for a moment, and I froze—was he going to kiss me in front of Sam? But he decided against it, instead saying, "I'll see you around, Lexie."

I watched him disappear down the sidewalk, torn between wanting to follow him and figure out what he was up to and wanting never to never see his face again.

"So, that's your ex, huh?" Sam said with a knowing look.

"Yeah," I said with a glare at his retreating back. "How could you guess?"

"Girl, it's written all over your face. I've never seen you so… red." She laughed when I groaned. "I don't blame you for being conflicted. He's hot."

"He's a backstabbing traitor."

"Whoa," Sam said. "That's some heavy talk. I mean, he probably deserves it. But heavy." She eyed me. "And curious that you're giving him the time of day."

"I'm…" I struggled to find the words to describe what I was doing. But even if I could've told her the truth, I didn't really know what I was doing. Or I did, but I didn't want to admit it. Perhaps all of the above.

"Just don't make the same mistake twice," Sam said, placing a gentle hand on my arm. "Cause you look like you're about to. And the whole thing with your dad…"

"I know, I know, I know," I said, shaking my shoulders. "I'm not, though. I know exactly what I'm doing—with both of them."

"Oh yeah? And what is that?"

"Making sure they're not…doing anything…" I trailed off, cursing my lack of quick thinking. "Evil."

She burst into laughter. "You're a trip, Lexie Carrigan."

I was a trip, because I had the power to undo what I'd done, and there I was, sitting in class and ruminating over it, instead of taking action. After all, as James had rightly pointed out, I was technically a Clanmaster. They had all kinds of powers over their clansmen, most of which I'd never really tapped into. Gram could summon and compel. So yeah, I could compel James to speak as long as he was in my clan.

But I had a feeling he'd still figure a way out of the truth. He was sneaky like that. So if I wanted answers, I'd have to find them myself. And for that, I'd have to follow him.

After my class let out, I sent my books and things back to the room and found a quiet space to concentrate. I asked my magic to find James, and it couldn't, which I expected. So I closed my eyes and compelled my magic to move as Clanmaster.

"Find me James Riley."

And then, like a homing beacon, I saw him, crossing the Key Bridge.

I transported myself to a small park close to the bridge, behind a pair of bushes and ran to the front of the bridge, squinting in the sunlight. There was a brown-haired man walking with purpose about halfway across the bridge, and I was pretty sure that was him. I followed briskly, making sure to keep him in sight, but with enough distance between us that he wouldn't notice me.

He walked off the bridge then took a sharp turn into the city. I could get closer to him here, with the crowds of business people and tourists, but I kept losing him in the crowd. I'd ping him again with my magic and he'd reappear on my radar. Finally, he turned down a side alley then disappeared, so I concentrated hard on his signature again. And it was…

Right behind me?

"You have all the subtlety of an elephant."

I jumped out of my skin at James's voice behind me. He wore a look of annoyance, but there was something else there. Something painful.

"How'd you know I was here?" I asked.

"You're making no attempt to hide your very unique magical signature," he said, dully. "And I felt your magic poking me every five minutes, Clanmaster."

"Well!" I flushed, not realizing I was putting off something significant. "Maybe tell me the truth and I wouldn't have to follow you around."

He exhaled. "I need you to leave."

"And I need you to tell me the truth. What are you even doing here?"

"It has nothing to do with you. Please leave.'

"No. Not until you tell me what you're doing."

"Don't you have class?"

"Sure, but I can get notes from someone else."

He growled in frustration, something I'd rarely seen from Mr. Cool. "Lexie, go home. Trust me when I say you don't want to be here."

"Oh yeah? Who are you meeting? Cyrus? A band of evil magicals?"

A girl appeared in a bright yellow cloud. A pretty girl with dark brown skin and silky hair, with eyes that shone bright when she spotted James.

"Hey, baby," she purred then stopped when she saw me. "Who's this?"

"Yeah, who is this?" I said to James, trying my best to ignore the flash of jealousy.

"Lexie, this is Meagan," James said. "We've been seeing each other for a while."

"Oh." I blinked. This was…not at all what I was expecting. But at the same time, it was exactly what I should've expected. James had slept his way through half my class, why would I expect him to be any different now?

"Meagan, this is my sister, Lexie," James said, giving me a look that asked me not to contradict him. "She's the one I'm here in D.C. visiting."

"Oh, right." She smiled, and she actually looked like a nice person. "It's nice to meet you."

"Mm-hm," I said, feeling incredibly stupid for several reasons. "Well, I guess I'll be going."

"That would be a good idea," James said, his eyes filled with guilt. Perhaps because he'd been caught. "See you around, sis."

I transported myself back to my dorm, not even checking if Sam was there or not. I fell onto my bed, surprised at the emotion welling somewhere in my chest. James had been flirting with me, hadn't he? Or was that another part of his game? It did fit.

Turning onto my back, I was ashamed that I'd fallen for his stupid crap again. I was supposed to resist his charms, and I thought I had. So why did my chest hurt so damned badly at the thought of him with someone else?

Oh, because he'd flirted and kissed and sweet-talked his way into getting exactly what he wanted out of me. Inclusion in my pact. I still had no idea why he needed it, but I was suddenly much less curious about it. A smarter girl would've nullified the agreement, but apparently, I was just dumb enough to linger.

The door opened, and Sam came wandering in. "Oh hey, I didn't expect you to be back so soon. Are you feeling better?"

"No."

"What's wrong?" Sam said. "Fever? Cold?"

I sat up, frowning. "You ever know who somebody is, and yet…you just hope that maybe they aren't as bad as you know they are?"

"Like your boy, James?" She shook her head. "What did he do?"

"He's seeing some other girl," I said numbly. "But using me for…something. Help with getting a job. But he's seeing another girl." I sniffed and glared at the ceiling. "Like…ask her to get you a job. Why even bother me?"

She put down her backpack and slumped into her chair. "I saw him today, too."

"Okay…" My pulse quickened. What had he done this time?

Sam stared at her hands, as if embarrassed. "I was getting coffee after class, and he was there. I started talking to him about some stuff…"

Oh no… Had James told her about magic? About me? What could he have possibly had to talk about with Sam?

"I swear I wasn't trying anything, but the dude asked me out.

Knowing I was your roommate. Asked me right out." She shook her head. "I was upset for you, but…I guess you know what kind of a guy he is."

Especially after what I'd seen with him and *Meagan.* "Yeah, I do."

"I told him to get lost, although I was much meaner." She grinned. "I don't think he's met a California girl before. He seemed surprised at my vocabulary."

"Yeah, he's…well, he is who he is," I said, sitting down. Was I actually a little disappointed James hadn't talked to her about magic? Or was I disappointed that he was exactly the kind of person I thought he was?

"I'm sorry, if you were thinking you two were getting back together," she said. "Because if you are, I would seriously reconsider that. He's definitely playing the field."

"I knew that," I said, lifting a shoulder. "I didn't think we were getting back together. I was just…tolerating his presence for the time being."

"You may have *thought* that, but your face says something different." She threw an arm around me. "Okay, so tell me exactly what happened between the two of you."

"He…knew my dad pretty well. Enrolled at my school my senior year. So, of course, I hated him at first. But then I guess, we kind of got each other? Like he and I had the same way of looking at the world. I don't even know when we became friends or when I… fell in love with him. I knew it was a bad idea, but it happened anyway."

"So what happened?" she asked quietly. "Did he cheat on you?"

I swallowed, considering my words. How to explain it in nonmagical terms? "He did something that put my sisters in danger."

Sam sat up. "And why are you giving him the time of day?"

"Because..." Dammit. This was even more difficult than talking about Gavon. "Because he says there's more I don't know."

"Like what?"

"I don't know. Stuff." I hated myself and I hated this.

"It sounds to me like you're still in love with him, and you're looking for reasons to forgive him for something unforgivable," Sam said. "And I mean, I can see why. He's the first guy you really fell in love with. And you're so closed off that you don't really have a lot of friends."

"Thanks..."

"I mean that in a constructive way," Sam said. "I mean, even now, I can tell you aren't telling me the whole story. And that's cool, it's your story to tell. But I also know that you know I'm right. If he did anything to hurt my family, I wouldn't even give him a second look."

I didn't know what to say to that, so I just stared at the ceiling, wishing I had someone I could be honest with and trying my damndest to not miss James.

"I mean, aren't you supposed to be going out with Dave this weekend anyway?" she asked. "Why are you even bothering with this idiot?"

"Because I'm an idiot."

"Lexie..." She gently patted my shin. "You are not an idiot. I mean, if you stay pining over this boy, you will be. But Dave is a nice, *normal* boy. One who'll hold open doors and pay for food and won't do anything shady. Promise."

182

Nineteen

I didn't want to go on this date, but Sam was right. I would only be an idiot if I wallowed and made the same mistake again. James, smartly, hadn't shown his face. And as far as I was concerned, he was dead to me. He could use my clan's magic for the next six days, then disappear.

So, Saturday morning, I arrived bright and early at the Smithsonian metro stop. I had woken Marie up early to figure out an outfit, but she'd merely pointed at her closet and slept on. I went simple—t-shirt, jeans, and tennis shoes. After all, it was just a museum, not a fancy restaurant.

The sun blinded me when I walked out of the metro stop, but I paused to take in the scenery. The National Mall was so much larger than I'd thought, and landmarks I'd only seen in photos rose on my left and right. I stared at the Capitol building for a moment, reminding myself of where I was.

"What are you looking at?"

Dave had arrived, sporting a pair of dark jeans and a plaid

shirt. He looked kind of handsome, and for a brief moment, I was a little tongue-tied. Maybe this wouldn't be as bad as I'd thought.

"I'm just being an obnoxious tourist," I replied, gesturing to the view. "It's the first time I've been to the Mall. It's really cool."

"Yeah, I guess it is," he said, folding his arms over his chest and standing with me.

Embarrassment warmed my cheeks. "I'm sorry. I'm just kind of nerdy about these kinds of things."

"It would be weirder if you didn't get excited about it." He draped an arm around my shoulder. I tried not to tense at his arm around my shoulder, but failed miserably.

He released me almost immediately. "Sorry, I guess that was a little forward."

"Uh…" I flushed more, surely now a vibrant color. There was no reason why I should be uncomfortable with such an innocent gesture, I mean, we were on a *date* for crying out loud and I was definitely attracted to him. "I mean…"

"I promise I won't bite," he said, his accent noticeable. "And you can leave me at the flag exhibit if you hate me."

I cracked half a smile, relaxing a little. "I don't think that'll happen."

"Good."

With that super awkward beginning to our date out of the way, we continued toward the museum. This whole place was still pretty impressive, but the American History museum had been on my bucket list for some time. I craned my neck, immediately wondering if Gavon had ever been in here. This was his type of place. I glanced at Dave, deciding that might be an okay conversation as long as it didn't stray too far away from the normal.

"My dad loves history," I said, my voice sounding weirdly out of place. "I should take him here one day."

"Yeah? Is he back in Florida?"

I swallowed. "N-no. He…uh…travels a lot. For business. So I see him regularly." *Nice save, Lexie.*

"Oh? What does he do for a living?"

"Er…" *Crap.* "It's kind of complicated to explain."

Dave laughed. "When most people around here say that, they mean their parents work for one of the three letters."

"Three letters?"

"CIA, FBI, NSA…"

"Oh right…" I chuckled nervously.

"Sounds cool. You seem really fond of your dad."

"Yeah." I smiled.

"You said your mom died, right?"

This question was still uncomfortable to answer, but I did my best to keep it out of my voice. "Passed away when I was born. My dad talks about her a lot," I said, taking care to avoid the part about him being gone for most of my life. "I obviously never met her, but he says I'm a lot like her. So that's kind of nice…" Was I rambling? I felt like I was rambling.

"Man, I don't know what I'd do without my mom," he said.

"I bet it's hard being away from her," I said. Yes, change the subject! "You said your whole family was back in Texas, right?"

"Yeah, but I see them pretty often. They travel a lot too."

"Oh good," I said, starting to feel like the conversation was pretty normal. If I could face Cyrus in a duel, I could hold a conversation with Dave and not freak out about it. "I'm sure you're glad to have Sam local so you have someone to hang out with. She seems really nice."

"She's a peach," he said. "I really like that group. We get along well, you know? Like minds. I think you should hang out with us more often. I think we're going to Baltimore next."

"I could probably take a train up there," I said, though I'd probably just transport myself. "I've never been to Baltimore."

He made a noncommittal noise as we walked into the atrium of the history museum. He plucked a brochure off the front table and handed it to me.

"Where do you want to go first?" he asked.

I quickly scanned the options, my gaze landing on something I hadn't expected. An exhibit on the early colonial settlements in Salem.

"That one."

Sure, I knew it was probably all about the nonmagicals, but I might find some nugget of information. It was set up complete with an old house they'd moved from the village that looked kind of like the ones in my grandmother's village—from what I could remember of it anyway. Each placard had a long discussion about life in the olden days.

"This is pretty wild," Dave said, looking at the old laundry tub and washboard. "I can't imagine doing laundry by hand. Have you used the dorm machines yet?"

I shook my head. "Not yet. Probably need to soon."

He chuckled. "One of my friends said they used to leave their laundry in the machines and come back to it wet on the floor."

"Oh yeah?"

"You gotta watch it. People get real short about their underwear."

I laughed then pressed my lips together. I was just about to say that I went home to do my laundry, but that would require an explanation. We fell into another awkward silence after that, and I struggled to come up with a topic of conversation that wasn't centered around magic.

"So what is it about history that you like so much?" he said, as we stood in front of an exhibit about the clothing of early settlers.

"I don't know," I said, thinking. "I like the story behind it, I guess. That everything that is right now is because of something that happened in the past. It's all connected."

"Yeah, I guess it is," he said, nodding. "I just can't keep all the dates straight. That's why I went into engineering."

"And what do you like about that?" I asked.

He gestured with his hands. "I liked building stuff. Getting dirty and figuring out how stuff works, you know? When I was a kid, they were building a bridge. I used to count the beams every time we drove by it. Just fascinating how it all comes together."

"Yeah, that is kind of cool. I suppose that's kind of like…" I closed my mouth abruptly. I was about to say it was like charms, which I was terrible at.

"Kind of like what?" he said.

"Um…nothing. Sorry, lost my train of thought," I said, flushing. Well, now he definitely thought I was an idiot.

"Happens to me all the time," he said with an endearing

smile. "I think it's a sign of exceptionally smart people."

I barked a laugh. "If you say so."

We kept walking to another part of the exhibit, this one with journals encased in plastic boxes, talking about how the inhabitants of Salem used to manage their stock. The journals looked similar to the ones I'd had my nose in all summer long. Still, I couldn't help my cry of surprise when a familiar name appeared on a ledger behind a plastic box.

"What is it?" Dave asked, peering over the box.

"Uh…my ancestor," I said. Well, it wasn't a lie. John Chase was my ancestor, and this was, apparently, his journal. But how was that even possible? I would've thought that the magicals kept all their artifacts together. How could this journal have ended up in a museum instead of, say, Gram's basement?

I wished Dave wasn't staring over my shoulder so I could summon the journal and look at it in more detail. Then again, the security guards and cameras might have a problem with that. I squinted hard, sensing that there was something on the page— something magical. I didn't know if nonmagicals could see magical translations, but I also didn't want to test it. Instead, I pulled my phone out and snapped a photo, sending it to Gavon.

John Chase's journal @ The American History Museum.

"I don't get it. Who's your ancestor?" Dave asked, squinting at the book. "This guy, Chase?"

"Yeah," I said, cursing my luck that I'd come across this book when I was out on a date. So much for putting aside magical interests.

"Okay, I gotta know what the deal is with this thing," Dave said with a smile. "You practically jumped through the glass."

I scrambled for an excuse. "My…uh…grandmother does a lot with genealogy, and my dad does, too. Just something to add to our collection. She still lives in Salem."

"Ah, well, that makes sense," he said with a nod.

"What does?"

"You have a Yankee look about you."

I had to laugh at that. If only he knew. "Let's see if we can find more of my ancestors around here."

I found several more mentions of John Chase, and his daughter Johanna who'd succeeded him, but no mention of the Separation or any of the magical war that had occurred just down the road. But I hadn't really expected to see much of that. Finding Chase's journal seemed like a lucky fluke, and I couldn't wait to get back and find out what was behind the words on the page.

My phone buzzed with a text from Gavon.

Can you get a closer look?

I cast a look at Dave, who was peering at a case.

Can't, out with a friend.

I can see that.

I looked up, my eyes bulging out of my head. Gavon waved at me from a bench on the other side of the exhibit. His gaze slid to Dave, then he nodded approvingly.

I could've died.

"Um, I'll be right back," I said to Dave. "Give me a minute, okay?"

I left the exhibit, hoping Gavon would take the hint. I found him standing in front of the front desk, casually perusing the literature and sporting his Georgetown Dad shirt. I would've pegged him for a tourist anywhere.

"How can you just transport in the middle of the room like that?" I asked.

"Look Away charm cast just before I land," he said, putting down the pamphlet. "Who's the guy?"

"He's a nice, normal nonmagical boy from Texas named Dave," I said. "That's all you need to know right now."

"Oh, really?" He wore the sort of obnoxious Dad-smile I hadn't had the pleasure of experiencing for most of my life.

"*Stop*," I said with a loud whine. "I don't know. He asked me to go to a museum with him. I don't even know if it's a date or not."

"Oh, it's a date," Gavon said with a nod. "He definitely likes you."

"Fine, it's a date. So why are you here?" I said, casting a nervous glance back at the exhibit and hoping Dave just thought I had gastric distress. That was preferable to having to explain why my father was following me around a museum.

"Because you texted me a photo of a journal I'd never seen before," he said, holding up the journal I'd just been ogling behind plastic. "And I thought it merited investigation."

"I hope you left a replica behind," I said, shaking my head. "They get kind of mad when you steal things."

"Of course, Lexie. This isn't my first museum," Gavon said, flipping through the book. "There's definitely a translation charm on here. I doubt anyone would need five hundred sheep in one day. It may take me a bit to get through it though."

"Good, so go do that."

"Are you trying to kick me out?" he asked, smirking. "Don't

want to introduce your old man to your boyfriend?"

I grimaced, thinking of James, and that I conveniently hadn't told Gavon he was still hanging around. I hoped James would have the good sense to avoid the area while Gavon was here. Perhaps his magical radar worked a little better than mine did.

"Fine, fine," Gavon said when all I could do was make noises. "I'll leave you to your date. But I did want to let you know that Josefa has been reaching out to some Clanmasters. We might have a meeting scheduled with some of them in a few days."

"About what?"

"Updating the Danvers Accord."

My brows shot up. "Are you serious?"

"Don't get your hopes up," he said with a patient smile. "We've still got a long way to go. But it's a nice first step. The more Clanmasters we can get on our side, the better. I thought you might want to come with me. Josefa definitely asked you to."

"Am I allowed to?" I asked.

"Have you been going to any more meetings you aren't supposed to be?" Gavon asked.

"Just going to class," I said. I wasn't lying—although even in my own mind, I knew that was skirting the line of truth.

"Good." He kissed my forehead. "I'll let you know when Josefa gets them together. Have fun on your date."

I groaned as he disappeared in a puff of purple. True to form, every nonmagical in the room was looking the other way when he did it.

"He's gotta teach me that trick," I muttered, turning and walking back into the exhibit.

We spent most of the day wandering around the museum, and when we got hungry, he bought me a hot dog from the stand outside. He held open doors, asked me questions and listened patiently for my response. We laughed and had discussions about different things, although he didn't have as firm a grasp on current events as I did. He didn't try to kiss me, but he did give me a long hug when we parted at the metro.

I transported myself back to the dorm, spending a moment staring at my reflection in the mirror before returning to the dorm. I'd almost wanted to disappear into my magical pocket, but I had a feeling Sam was eager to hear everything.

True to form, she nearly knocked me over when I walked into the room.

"*Tell me everything!*"

I held my hand against my chest, taking a moment to draw down from the surprise. "About what?"

"Your date, silly!" she said. "I want to know everything. Where'd you go? What'd you talk about? Did you kiss?"

"Oh, um…it was good," I said with a smile.

"Good?" She sat down on the bed. "So you don't like him?"

"I mean, he's…" I chewed my lip. "He's fine."

"Fine. Fine? He's a damned catch is what he is." Sam shook her head. "So you don't think you'll go out with him again?"

"I didn't say that," I said. "I mean, he's really sweet. I just…"

"You're still hung up on your ex, that's what your problem is."

But that wasn't the problem, not really. For as much as we talked, as great as the conversations were, every other one featured me keeping quiet about large portions of my life. Dave didn't know about magic—and as hard as I tried, I just couldn't picture myself telling him.

Twenty

The next morning, I got a text from Gavon, asking if I was up for going to Spain. It was definitely preferable to hanging around the dorm and answering questions from Sam. Or wondering what James, who I still hadn't heard from, was up to.

Gavon was waiting in his usual spot on a park bench near my dorm, reading the book he'd lifted from the Smithsonian. He glanced up when he saw me, and the smirk on his face that said he had some good news to share.

"This is a very interesting journal," he said. "Belonging to one Abigail Chase, not John."

"Abigail was…" I wracked my brain.

"John's potion-making daughter," Gavon said, and my eyes widened. "Now, don't get too excited. I haven't gotten very far into it, but it appears to be a journal during the process of creating the potion. But Abigail was killed before the potion was ever completed, so it may be nothing."

"But it may be something?"

"It very well may be," he said, and the journal disappeared from his hand. "But for today, we'll be focused on something else. Trying to convince the Clanmasters that they should update the Danvers Accord."

"Not...trying to nose into stuff I'm not supposed to, but..." I swallowed. "Isn't that what that Trent guy was talking about?"

"Not particularly," Gavon said. "They want to do away with the Accord. We want to expand it to include magicals like you and me. Although based on the way magic works, the Accord won't apply to us, but to any children you or your sisters may have." He sighed. "But as I said, we'll need complete agreement from all the Clanmasters. Including your gram."

"Fingers crossed she'll answer my letter then..."

We transported back to Spain, walking the rest of the way into the Clan Vargas village. Josefa was standing outside talking with her sister. She waved excitedly as Gavon and I walked past their barrier and came to greet us with a hug and kiss. I didn't understand a word out of her mouth until I remembered to cast the translation charm again.

"Thank you so much for putting this on," Gavon said, clasping her arms with a smile. "I can't tell you how much it means to me that we're moving forward."

She looked behind me and frowned. "Gavon, darling, where is that potion-maker? I thought for sure you'd be bringing her this time."

"She had to work," Gavon said. "Shall we?"

Josefa led us into a small room with a table. There were several older men and women already seated, and none acted as if they'd met Gavon before. In fact, a few were eyeing him as if they weren't quite sure what to make of him.

"Clanmasters Raimundo from the Bordeaux region of France, Katja from Finland, and Cynna from Macedonia," Josefa said, pointing to each of the magicals seated around the table.

Gavon bowed his head. "Guildmaster McKinnon of the New Salem Warrior's Guild."

Their eyes swept to me, and I cleared my throat. "Lexie from…"

"My daughter," he said with a twinkle in his eye. "Currently attending Georgetown in the States."

They murmured their approval, and I stared at my hands until the attention passed.

"Thank you for letting me speak with you today." Gavon spoke in English, but perhaps the rest of the room had their own translation charms. "As Clanmaster Vargas might have told you, I came to this world in 1989, purely by accident. My world was the same one that John Chase had created in 1692 after the Two Years' War. Unknowingly, I introduced a new element into this world, one that hadn't been seen for almost three hundred years. My daughters and I aren't bound by the Danvers Accord." He formed an attack spell in his hand and held it in front of them. "Alexis and I have Warrior magic, and my other two daughters have Healing and Potion-making magic."

"It's a miracle, is what it is," Josefa said.

"As a father, my first priority is my girls, but I also have concerns about the Guild. There are five hundred souls there— mostly Enchanters and Charmers. This world is without sun, without a sustainable source of food. When I'd made the tear, we were dying off from magical rot." He paused, probably for effect. "The point is, the sins of our ancestors have been paid for. Keeping the inhabitants of New Salem in their world forever seems too harsh. Along with my daughter, I'd like to petition for an addition to the Danvers Accord. Not to change anything," he added hastily, "but to apply the same restrictions to those in New Salem."

"And why would you give up such a wonderful gift?" Cynna asked.

"Because it's the right thing to do. And…" I didn't miss the split-second look in my direction. "We all know there are those who want to do away with the Danvers Accord in its entirety. I'm worried that if word got out—truly got out, that there are magicals who have specialties, it could be a free-for-all. Instead of just my daughters and I, you'd have your magicals flocking to New Salem to create children like Lexie. Ones without any restrictions."

"Is that really a danger, though?" Josefa asked.

"I believe it is." Another look toward me. "As Guildmaster, I'm willing to sign any accord that guarantees the safety of my Guild. But what I need is help gathering the signatures. Finding the clans who originally signed it. And perhaps convincing a few that this is the best course of action."

"I think it's a marvelous idea," Josefa said. "Clan Vargas gives you our full support."

"I don't know," Raimundo said. "Is it really worth drudging up all this work? Irene was pretty clear about him—"

"Irene is a bitch," Josefa said, and I choked on my spit. "Sorry, love. I forgot she's your grandmother."

"Hardly," I wheezed. "Just glad to know someone else agrees with me."

"Irene is…looking out for the best interests of her clan, which doesn't always coincide with what's best for her family," Gavon said gently. "And I believe, if shown the true risk a group of unbound magicals poses to her and her clan, she could be persuaded."

"What kind of risk are we talking about?" Cynna said.

"Lexie, will you show them your magic, please?" Gavon said.

"W-what?"

"Just an attack spell, no need to send it anywhere."

I held out my hand and formed a spell, the purple of my magic reflecting on the faces of those around me. There was a noticeable retraction.

"Lexie is the product of myself, an inhabitant of New Salem, and my wife, who was a member of Clan Carrigan. While Lexie's a good kid with a good head on her shoulders, others may not be. Are you willing to risk that more magicals won't find out about the tear and want the same powers for their kids?"

Cynna gestured to Gavon and myself. "Then why don't we simply close that tear you made? Problem solved?"

"Except for Gavon and his family," Josefa said.

"Then we'll lock them inside too."

My mouth fell open, but Josefa was quicker. "I would like to see you try. You saw the power the girl has. Her father has just as much. Would you like to go head-to-head with them?"

Cynna sat back, chastened.

"This is the best possible outcome," Josefa said with a firm nod to Gavon. "We can welcome the members of our long lost magical family, and make sure nobody with this kind of power is allowed to walk free in our lands."

Katja, who'd yet to speak, leaned forward. "How, exactly, do you propose we do this?"

"There needs to be some kind of a guarantee," Raimundo said. "Some sort of stick to the carrot. Is there any way we can mend this breach you've made?"

Gavon sighed, lines of frustration on his face. "Theoretically. We've been searching for that very solution but have so far been unsuccessful."

Josefa leaned forward. "Gavon, have you asked your potion-making daughter to help?"

"Unfortunately, we don't have the original potion Johanna used. It's still in Irene's care. And so far, she has been unresponsive to our overtures. But even if she were to give us the potion, I brewed it once before and was unsuccessful." There was the faintest sound of desperation in his voice. "Is there no way you'd consider amending the Accord without a potion to close the tear?"

"I'm afraid not, Gavon," Cynna said. "It's good business sense. Especially, as you've said, there are those who might not sign onto the Danvers Accord."

Gavon sat back, frowning.

"We'll continue to socialize the idea," Josefa said, more to Gavon than the rest of the room. "We'll reach out to other Clanmasters with news of what we've seen and your proposal. You two continue seeking a resolution to New Salem. Together, we'll find a way to make everyone happy."

"That went well, right? You got them to agree?" I asked Gavon as we left Josefa's house.

"I got them to think about it," Gavon said, frustration evident on his face. "They will agree when we finish the potion and can close the tear. So I'm afraid we're back to the same place we were before."

I chewed my lip. "Nicole could—"

"Nicole hates the very ground I walk on. It would do us no good to continue to badger her," Gavon snapped. After a moment, his shoulders drooped. "I'm sorry. I shouldn't involve you in that."

"I mean, I'm kinda involved. She's my sister and you're my dad." I exhaled. "And she's also an adult. She can put aside whatever problems she has with you. We need to figure this out, and she's the only one who can help."

"Nicole has every right to feel the way she does, and it's not my place—or yours—to try to fix what's been broken. I don't want to get in the middle of your relationship with your sister, so it's best to leave that where it is."

"Dad," I said, stopping. "This is bullshit."

He turned, raising his brows. "Excuse me?"

"You need answers, Nicole has them. Why don't you just *ask* her?"

"Because I know what the answer will be, and I don't really want to put myself through hearing it," he said. "One day, Lexie, you will have children. And I hope you never understand how it feels to know they despise you. It is not pleasant."

"Then let me work on her," I said. "Give me Abigail's journal and I'll see what she can do with it. I know there's a lot of hurt going around, but if I can get over it, so can she."

He stared at me for a long while then procured the journal. "Be very careful with this. I still feel like there are more charms on it to break."

"I will." I held the book to my chest, as if it were a precious jewel. "And I think you underestimate Nicole."

I stood in the bathroom in my dorm, preparing the long speech I was going to give to Nicole to get her to come around. I would point out the benefits, that when she and Guy had babies, they wouldn't have the wildly unpredictable magic like mine. Also, we could prevent another Cyrus—or the man himself—from coming for our family.

Along with a lot of flattery and maybe even a few bottles of wine.

Deciding I was ready, I transported myself into the living room.

"Nico—"

Loud voices drowned out my call, and I clammed up immediately.

"Nic, I don't understand why you're acting so weird. It's just dinner with my folks."

"I don't feel like going! That should be enough for you."

I froze, realizing I'd unintentionally barged into the middle of a *very* loud argument between Guy and my sister. Panicking, I dove into the nearest closet, holding my breath, not sure what to do next. Part of me knew it was better to go back and wait for things to calm down—but part of me wanted to know why they were fighting.

"It is, but you weren't up for going last week either. Or with me to the concert the week before. Are you trying to tell me something, because if you are, I'm obviously not getting it!"

"I just haven't been feeling great," Nicole said after a minute, but there wasn't much behind it. "It's not you."

"You love me, right?"

A long sigh. "I don't know, Guy. Maybe we should cool it for a while. I feel like things are moving way too fast, and…I just don't know what to do with all of this."

"Fine. Call me when you figure it out."

The door slammed behind him and Nicole's soft sobs echoed from the kitchen. Now I was *sure* I couldn't stay—she'd be furious at me for eavesdropping. But I couldn't just leave her there, not when she was obviously upset.

So instead, I whipped out my phone.

Hey, are we still on for dinner tonight?

I frowned when I got the response: *Not tonight. Not feeling great. Love you.*

Knowing I was faced with an impossible choice, I headed back to Georgetown, promising myself I'd come back down in the morning.

Twenty-One

I think I've got a virus. Don't want to get you sick.

That was the text I got when I asked Nicole if I could meet her for breakfast. So, of course, I texted Marie and told her to call me when she could.

"Oh, what?" Marie said, appearing on Sam's bed in a puff of white and yawning. "It's so early, Lexie."

"I think Nicole and Guy broke up," I said, turning in my seat.

"What?" Marie sat up. "Are you serious? Why? Did he cheat on her? Beat her? Do I have to kill him?"

"No, she broke up with him."

"Oh, damn," Marie said, sinking back on the bed. "Well, if it's what she wants…"

"But is it? She's really happy with him."

"Obviously not, if she broke up with him." Marie cracked open an eye. "And how do you know they broke up? Did she tell you?"

I cringed. "Not really. I came by to ask her to help me with a potion and I overheard them fighting. Then…I panicked and hid in a closet."

"And you're supposed to be a Warrior," Marie said with a shake of her head. "How's Nicole?"

"She's telling me she's sick now," I said, scrolling through my phone. "Which is a lie, of course. She just doesn't want me to see her all weepy. She's really upset about it."

"She'll get over it," Marie said.

I slapped my hand on the desk. "Seriously, Marie?"

"*Seriously*. If she broke up with him, she has her reasons," Marie said, narrowing her eyes at me. "And you just want her to be in a better mood because you want to ask her something. You can't fool me."

"That's not…entirely true," I said, flushing. "If she's breaking up with Guy, obviously, I don't want to make her angrier."

"Because it has to do with Dad?"

"*Stop* reading my mind," I said.

"That was just an educated guess," Marie said, swinging her legs over the bed. "Also, this room is really sad and tiny. Do you really share it with another girl?"

"Yeah, I do," I said, ignoring her commentary. I liked our dorm. "And yes, Dad wants her to help us figure out how to close the tear. He thinks a potion will do it, and since she's the only Potion-maker alive…"

"Nicole and potions, already a volatile combination. Add Dad and you're asking for trouble." She tapped her finger against her chin. "Then again, her issue with potions comes *from*

Dad, so maybe it's all connected. Either way, you're probably going to have to get her good and drunk before you ask her. She'll probably get super pissed, but she'll forget about it."

"As always, Marie, you are just full of helpful ideas."

"So what's going on with that boy?"

I froze. "James?"

"No, the one you went on a date with?" A smile curled around her face. "But oh-ho, is that ex-boyfriend of yours back?"

"N-no…" I tried, but based on Marie's smirk, it was useless to lie. "Fine, yes. But not really. He just needed some help. I gave it to him. That's it."

"Uh-huh," Marie said. "What kind of help?"

"Are you going to tell Dad?"

That earned me a Cheshire smile. "The question, Alexis, is why haven't you? Didn't we learn this lesson already?"

"I did tell him…kind of…" My shoulders sagged under the weight of my own half-truth. "I told Gavon when James first showed up. He told me that James shouldn't have come to me, and I should tell him to go away, basically. But he also said they were working together on something, so I know it's nothing bad."

"Oh, well, of course," Marie said with a bark of laughter. "And what did your boo want from you?"

"To be added to our clan," I said, flushing even more. "He said Cyrus is after him, and if he's part of our clan, and by clan I mean, you, me, and Nicole, then he gets those same protections we have. So I told him he could, temporarily."

Marie shook her head. "You are just so stupid. You know that, right?"

"Well, I found out what he's doing, at least," I said. "He's dating some chick. He promises me there's more to the story, but…meh."

"Was she cute?" Marie asked. "I bet she was cute, wasn't she?"

"Are you really asking me this?" I said with a scowl. "C'mon, I'm hurt enough as it is."

"Then *why* is he still temporarily in our clan?" Marie said. "Kick his ass out!"

"That would be the smart thing to do," I said. "Maybe I'm just a glutton for punishment. But if he's telling the truth, and Cyrus is after him…" I swallowed. "I haven't seen him since. So maybe—"

"So maybe he's just using you," Marie said. "Which is just *so* much better."

"It's a week," I said, knowing how idiotic I sounded. "A few more days."

She made a noise. "And what about that Texan you're dating? Dad says he's super into you?"

"T-Texan? How does he know he's Texan?" I jumped to my feet. "Did he talk to him?"

"I believe you told him," Marie said. "What's the big deal? I looked him up on Facebook. Pretty cute. And definitely comes without all the baggage that other guy does."

I slumped into my chair. "Dave's nonmagical. And that's kind of…well, it's kind of a nonstarter for me. We went out on a date and I can't even tell you how I felt about him, because I was too busy censoring myself."

"Then don't censor yourself. Just tell him you have magic."

She shrugged. "Easy."

"Easy, sure. I also haven't texted the guy in three days—hadn't even thought about him. I'm sure that's a fantastic sign."

Marie shrugged. "Can't help you there, kiddo. Just like you can't help Nicole. You both are going to have to come to your own terms with the things that make you the way you are. I'll just be here to drink wine and clean up the pieces."

Marie might not have wanted to help Nicole, but it was important somebody did. Because she was making a giant mistake, and there was no need for that.

Since it was late, I transported myself outside of Guy's house. His lights were still on in his garage out back, and I found him working under the open hood of an old car, accompanied by the occasional bang of metal against metal and a curse.

"Working late?" I said.

He jumped, banging his head on the hood and squinted around the corner. "Lexie? What are you doing here?"

"Had a feeling that something was wrong with my sister," I said, crossing my arms over my chest. "So I got a flight down."

"That was nice of you," he said, leaning against the engine. "Wasn't that expensive, though? You've only been there for a few weeks. Already homesick?"

"Just concerned about Nicole. But since she won't tell me what's wrong, thought I'd come ask you."

"Ah, that's our business." Even as he shot me down, he offered his charming smile. "But I love that you care so much about your sister."

"Yeah, well, if you hurt her, I'll kill you," I said, taking a seat on the stool nearby. "And I mean that. But…it sounds like she's the one pulling away. Did you ask her to marry you?"

"Oh no, no." He shook his head. "I'm smarter than that. I just…I want to know why she's being the way she is. I know it's got something to do with your father, but she won't tell me the truth." He looked at me. "She says you and your dad are getting along now, right?"

"For the most part," I said. "But only because I want to. Nicole doesn't, and that's okay."

"I just wish I knew what he did," Guy said.

"Disappeared for a few years," I said, wishing I could tell him the whole story. "He had his reasons."

"They were shitty reasons, probably. You don't just leave your family. Especially your little kids." He wiped his greasy hands on a nearby towel. "And I get that you want to have a relationship with him, but have you considered that it may not be the best for you?"

"Yeah," I said. "Trust me, I think about that a lot. But this isn't about me, this is about Nicole. Are you guys gonna break up?"

"I hope not, but if that's what she wants." He shrugged, but I could see sadness there, too. "I just get the feeling she's hiding something from me. And I told her, whatever it is, I don't care. But that just set her off." He chuckled. "Won't make that mistake twice."

"She'll come around," I said.

"But if she doesn't," Guy smiled sadly, "you're always welcome in my shop. You and Marie. I still gotta teach you how to change the oil in a car, remember? Everyone should know how to do that."

I smiled, not having the heart to tell him I'd probably never own a car. "Can't wait."

"Lexie!"

I froze, wishing I could transport myself away, or maybe turn back time fifteen seconds.

"What are you doing here?" Nicole asked, her face somewhere between surprised and livid. "And can I have a word with you? Just a small word."

Guy waved at me, sympathy in his eyes and a smile on his face as I followed Nicole with a gallows-like dread. Oh, if only I knew how to track magicals, I might've known she was coming.

"What the *hell* are you doing here?" she seethed once we were far enough away so Guy couldn't hear. "And how did you explain it to Guy?"

"Said I caught a flight, 'cause I thought something was wrong."

She licked her lips, crossing her arms over her chest. "And how did you know something was wrong? I said I had a virus. And here you are, talking with Guy."

"I…might have overheard you guys fighting yesterday."

"Overheard?" she said. "Were you…*eavesdropping*?"

"I didn't mean to!" I said, but even I knew that wasn't an excuse. "I was stopping by to ask you something else, and I just…"

"Well, you have me. What do you want?"

Now was absolutely not the time to go there, but I was already on thin ice. Why not fall all the way in? "Gavon and I —"

"No way in hell."

"Nicole, just listen," I said, summoning the book. This was going to take some work, but I hadn't expected her to shut me down before I even got the words out. "We need help on a potion, and you're the only one who knows how to do this crap.

"I'm not just here to brew potions for the two of you," she snapped. "You've already proven yourself adept at it. I, for one, would love to see you with purple spots."

Damn it, Marie. That had been a secret. "This isn't a healing potion. It's…well, Dad—"

"*Gavon.*"

"Fine, *Gavon* is trying to close the tear. I thought that if we could recreate the potion that made New Salem in the first place, maybe it could seal it up, too."

Nicole's lip twitched. "Will he seal himself inside, too?"

"No, Nicole. But…he said that he'd always hoped you would help him. Because you're so good at potions."

That earned a sardonic laugh. "He's said that before."

"I know it's a lot to ask, but I kind of feel like we're out of options."

"Then find another one," she snapped. "I'm not doing it."

"There are no other ones, Nicole. You are literally the only one."

She looked to the side, perhaps considering it. But when she turned back to me, there was resignation on her face. "I haven't brewed a potion in ages, Lexie. I wouldn't even know where to start."

I summoned the journal, holding it between my hands. "This is the recipe. Maybe you could take a look at it?"

Nicole hesitated, staring at the book as if it were speaking to her, then took a step back. "Lexie, I'm under a lot of stress right now. I can't add this to it."

"Nicole—"

"Just go," Nicole said. "I don't want to see you right now."

That had gone well. Why I continued to make such idiotic decisions about my friends and family, I had no idea, but I was getting quite annoyed with feeling like I was always in trouble with everyone. I arrived back at the dorm and stormed to the room, falling face-first into my bed and groaning.

"That good of a day, huh?" Sam asked.

"Fantastic," I said, lifting up and looking at my desk. I furrowed my brow. There was an envelope sitting on top of my history book.

"Hey, Sam?"

"Mm?"

"Did you put this here?" I asked, walking over slowly.

"What? The envelope?" She frowned. "No?"

"O-oh, sorry. I must've. Forgot." I swiped the letter up as if it were explosive and a thousand ideas of what it could be ran through my mind. *Alexis* was written in long, loopy script, which worried me more.

I scurried out of the dorm as quickly as I could, just in case the letter had some magic in it.

Alexis,

I have received your letter requesting a meeting. I don't wish to meet with your father; however, circumstances have arisen that it make it prudent to do so. Please reply to this message with a time and date.

Irene Carrigan

I sucked in a breath, confused and exhilarated at the same time. What did she mean by "circumstances?" I wished someone would just be *honest* with me.

Summoning a pen from my dorm, I hastily wrote down *Tomorrow at 6pm* and watched as the ink sizzled on the page before settling. I assumed that meant the paper was charmed. I'd have to ask Gavon to teach me that one.

Gavon!

I pulled out my phone and tapped out a text.

Gram wants to meet tomorrow at 6pm. Can you make it?

A few seconds later, *Of course. See you then.*

Twenty-Two

"Circumstances have arisen," I mumbled as I pulled on my jacket. It was about as bad as a "we need to talk" text. The mature thing would've been to come out with it and tell me what was happening, but no. Circumstances. Thanks, Gram, for being up front.

Gavon hadn't offered any insight as to what she might mean, either. I was preparing myself for a fight between the two of them. We were meeting her in Salem at a coffee shop I had vague memories of, which became clearer the more I thought about them. Although I was sure once our meeting was over, Gram would re-strengthen the barrier around her clan and the memories would become hazy again.

"Ready to go?" Gavon asked when I met him outside my dorm.

"Yeah," I said, joining him as we walked tc our usual hiding spot to transport. "Are *you* ready?"

"Mm." He shivered. "I'm not looking forward to this

conversation. Last time I spoke with your gram, it didn't end well."

"What happened?"

"I asked her to reconsider your place in the clan, and when she didn't, I had a few choice phrases for her," Gavon said with an uncharacteristic blush. "I was a little angry and might have gone overboard. I believe I called her a selfish narcissist who cared more for her own standing than her grandchildren."

"Oh, come on, Dad. You can do better than that."

"Fine, I called her a Grade-A bitch."

"There it is."

"Might be best if you took the lead today," he said with something of a sheepish look. "I'm not sure I can be nice where she's concerned."

"I'll do my best."

We transported into a small alley in the center of town, and took our time leisurely strolling toward the coffee shop where Irene wanted to meet. Gavon wore something of a nostalgic look on his face.

"Have you seen any more of that boy?" Gavon asked, tearing his gaze away from the local library.

I froze. "Boy?"

"The one you went on a date with?"

Date…date… Dave. "No, I haven't. Been a little busy."

"He hasn't called you or anything?" Gavon frowned. "Maybe he's waiting for you to call him?"

"Maybe, or…" I swallowed. "Maybe he just got the impression I wasn't interested."

"Are you?"

"I...I don't know. He is nice and kind, but there's something that keeps…" I wanted to say, "Keeps making me feel like he's going to pull the rug out from under me and I'll end up dueling for my life." But considering Gavon was a partial reason for that fear, I didn't want to go there.

"You're young," Gavon said. "Just have fun. If you don't like him, end it and focus on school. If you do, keep dating him. It's really that simple."

"Oh yeah?" I smiled. "And what about you and Mom?"

"I liked dating her," he replied with a wink. "Although it took me a *long* time to convince her to marry me. Years. She wanted to go to college, to explore the world."

"Yeah, I know all about your *exploring*," I said with a disgusted look.

"We didn't start sparring until she was pregnant with you," Gavon said with a nudge. "As you saw with those kids at the school, the ability to cast attack spells is significantly dampened under the Accord. I wouldn't have dared get into the ring with her otherwise."

I toyed with my fingertips, thinking. "Do you think…if Mom was alive, Gram would still hate us so much?"

He clenched his jaw, and I almost regretted my question. But I was still trying to understand this whole familial hatred thing. Was it just because of Mom, or was it something else?

"I can't say for sure, of course," he began slowly. "But Irene never liked me—never liked what I represented. Fought valiantly to persuade your mother not to marry me." He laughed. "That just made her want to do it more, I think. When Nicole was born, Irene was relieved. But when Marie came along and was able to wield magic almost from the get-go…Irene began to suggest containment spells. And I was *not* going to allow that to happen to my kids."

"Uh…" I said, pointing at myself. "You let it happen to me."

"That's because I wasn't there to manage your magic myself," he said. "And believe me, if there was any way it could've been avoided, I would have. But Jeanie's magic was…not strong enough to handle yours."

"But it was strong enough to handle Marie's?"

"Yes," he said. "Healing magic is less powerful than Warrior magic. And besides that, Marie already knew she had magic—there wouldn't have been any benefit to keeping it from her. Jeanie could use containment spells when she was out of the house until she was old enough to know better."

"Marie said Jeanie resented us," I said. "Do you think that's true?"

"I think she resented me, and with very good reason. In her mind, I'd gotten her sister killed then disappeared. She was a kid herself, and I'd placed this great responsibility on her. But there was no one else I trusted. And no way I could've raised you girls while still maintaining my Guildmastership—and keeping Cyrus away from you."

"Imagine if I'd grown up with Gram," I said with a shiver.

"She never would've taken you," he said. "Because it would've meant she would've raised you without magic—presumably never telling you, if she had her way. And then she wouldn't have been able to become Clanmaster, and *nothing* would have kept her from that."

"Such low opinions you have of me. Shall I share some of my

own?"

Irene looked about as old and severe as the last time I'd seen her. There was a palpable crackle of energy between her and Gavon, and I figured I might as well de-escalate the situation before Gavon sent her flying across the coffee shop.

"Hi," I said. "Thanks for agreeing to meet with us. Hopefully this won't take too long."

Irene hadn't taken her eyes off Gavon, and the color in her pale cheeks rose. "I see you've taken a renewed interest in your daughter. I'll remind you what happened the last time that occurred."

"I'll also remind you that I'd hoped you would train her so I wouldn't have to," Gavon said before I could reply. "You knew Jeanie couldn't."

"And I informed Jean that I'd prefer the girl never to know about her magic."

Gavon's eyes flashed. "I wouldn't have let that happen."

"I'm right here," I added casually. "And we have stuff to talk about, so why don't you both cool it?"

"Haven't taught her any manners, I see," Gram said, bristling. "I've heard from Celeste Davis that the two of you are causing trouble with the young magicals."

"Uh...that wasn't us," I said. "That was some guy named Trent. I just...showed up there."

"And helped my clanmember sneak out of her house at seven in the evening?" Irene asked, eyebrow raised.

That, I had no good answer to. "It was her idea!"

"I'm sure," Irene said, her hawklike gaze turning to Gavon. "So surprising to see your children pass blame to someone else."

Gavon's eyes flashed. "She's also your grandchild, Irene."

"True as that may be, my clansmen are *off limits* to whatever activities you and your daughter are involved in," she said. "I've informed Celeste of your history, and she's keeping an eye out for you. Anyone caught cavorting with those magicals will be expelled."

"I apologize," I ground out. "It was out of line for me to help her sneak out. I won't bother them again."

"Very well," Irene said, adjusting her shirt. "Your letter indicated you needed some information."

"We'd like to borrow the journal with the potion that created New Salem," I said.

"And as I recall, that potion failed to do anything of value," Gram said to Gavon. "After you wasted several years of dithering with it. Why so eager to close the tear now?"

"I've been eager to close the tear for eighteen years," he replied, coolly. "Simply retracing our steps to see if I missed anything."

"Forgive me if I don't believe you," Gram said. "Since you lied to Ashley and our clan for your entire marriage to Mora."

"I didn't lie—"

"You promised you would fix the problem, didn't, and both my daughters died because of it."

Gavon's nostrils flared and his cheeks took on a reddish hue.

"Back to the topic at hand," I said, a little uncomfortable that my father had no response for that. Perhaps because I knew there wasn't any lie there. "Dad and I have been retracing his steps, as he said. Maybe there's something in Johanna's journals he missed the first go-round. It would be nice if we could see them just to check."

Gram reached into her purse and retrieved an old journal, placing it on the table. "You are aware, I presume, that the man who killed my daughters has been quite busy lately."

My heart stopped cold, but Gavon simply took the book. "I am aware, hence my hurry to close the tear."

"You're aware?" I said. "What the hell is he doing?"

"Don't concern yourself with it," he said with a patronizing smile. "We're close to closing the tear, and then it won't be a problem."

"Don't *concern* myself with it?" I said. "Dad, he—"

"Is not a problem because you are protected," he said. "Your pact remains very strong, and he can't come within five miles of you or your sisters. Promise."

"Your promises mean little, Gavon," Gram said. "You should know that by now, Alexis. He promised your mother he would keep New Salem away from her, too."

"Cyrus slipped my attention once, but he won't do it again," he said, the color rising in his cheeks.

"It seems he's slipped your attention a number of times," Gram said. "Perhaps you should renounce your Guildmastership and deal with the problem directly."

I turned to Gavon, not sure what I was expecting from him. But the disgruntled look of frustration—and maybe even a little guilt—was surprising.

He cast a look in my direction and cleared his throat. "I'm saving that option until there are no others left."

"And how many will die until that happens?" Gram asked.

"*Okay*!" I said, stepping between them before the sparks

really started flying. I wasn't sure I wanted to see Gram vs. Gavon, because I wasn't sure I wanted to watch my grandmother get her ass handed to her (or maybe I did). "This isn't helping. Gram, stop being a pain in the ass. Dad, stop instigating."

Gram rose from her seat. "Deal with the problem, Gavon, or you might find your entire family gone."

And with that, she turned on her heel and walked out of the coffee shop.

We sat in silence for a few moments before Gavon picked up the journal. "That went better than I thought."

"Did it?" I said. "You could've been a little nicer."

"I was being nice."

I licked my lips. "So Cyrus is…doing stuff over here? Doesn't that concern you?"

"Exceedingly," he said, picking up the journal. "That's why I'm glad we now have this."

"And you aren't going to tell me what he's up to?" I said. "I mean, *I* could fight him. I almost won last time. Maybe—"

"No, Alexis," Gavon said swiftly. "I'm not going to ask that of you. Not now, not ever. This is not your problem to solve."

"But it is," I said. "I mean, if I can help—"

"You are helping," he said, plastering a fake smile on as he handed me the book. "You're going to help me read through this."

I sighed. "I'm not a kid, Dad."

"Yes, you are. You aren't even eighteen. You should never have had to deal with what you've dealt with and I would never forgive myself if you had to deal with it again."

Then why don't you just challenge him? Round and round we went. And for the first time, I found myself agreeing with Irene's assessment, which made me very uncomfortable. "But we have this journal now," I said after a moment. "So that's good, right?"

"Maybe," Gavon said. "Any…luck in convincing your sister to help us?"

"Oh, right." I winced. "She might not be talking to me right now. Might've approached it a little too…quickly."

Gavon muttered something under his breath, and I could've sworn it was "told you so."

Twenty-Three

I didn't go back to Georgetown, not when I had all these feelings boiling inside me. Instead, I returned to the sparring beach. I hadn't been there in months, what with school and tear research and all the other stuff that had been taking up my life. But now, the smell of salt water invaded my senses and I inhaled deeply, letting my blood pressure return to normal as I processed all I'd just learned.

Gavon's hesitance was understandable, but if he didn't think he could handle it, then why not just let me take care of it? It was frustrating as hell to know I could help but wasn't being allowed to. And his reasoning for keeping me out of it was… well, not all that convincing.

I looked up at the bright moon overhead, wishing I had someone to talk to who understood.

"Hasn't changed one bit."

James stood next to me, his hands in his jeans pocket as the wind whipped his hair across his forehead. It must've been the sea air, because I felt nothing but calm at his presence. It was a weak moment, I fully recognized that, but for just a few precious moments, I let myself be weak.

"Can Gavon defeat Cyrus?" I asked.

"What are you talking about?"

I let the sound of the waves wash through me for a moment. "Gavon said he's afraid to renounce his Guildmastership because he isn't sure he can beat Cyrus. Is that true?"

James crossed his arms over his chest. "They're pretty evenly matched, in my opinion. But Cyrus may have the edge. Gavon's been preoccupied with other things lately. May be out of shape." He tilted his head. "Why do you ask?"

"Because I wanted to know if he was telling the truth," I said, sitting back on my hands.

"Gavon won't lie to you," James said softly.

"He has. And he won't tell me what you two are working on. What's going on with the Danvers Accord? Is Cyrus trying to undo it? Is he—"

"And see, here I thought you were hoping to never have anything to do with Cyrus ever again," James said. "I thought you were so angry with me for dragging you back into that world."

"I'm angry with you for putting my sisters in danger."

"And what do you think you're doing by poking around in this?"

I opened then closed my mouth.

"This may be hard for you to believe, but not everything revolves around or needs to include you," he said.

"Says the man currently using my pact for protection…"

And just like that, my weakness evaporated. "What do you want? Need another favor?"

He turned to me. "Another week, if you don't mind."

"Why don't you ask your girlfriend? Meagan?"

"Because Meagan's clan doesn't have the protections against New Salem that you do." He was still staring at me, but I forced myself not to meet his gaze. "And so far, I haven't done anything to bother you. In fact, I've been making sure to avoid you, so I don't intrude on your life. *You're* the one who followed me that day, and I tried to spare you from it. I haven't bothered you or your sisters in any way."

The urge to tell him he *had* hurt me was strong, but I didn't want to give him that satisfaction. "I suppose not."

"The timing of this thing is a bit out of my control," he said. "I think it's soon, though. Then I'll be out of your life again, for good."

"Well, you can have another week," I said, not bothering to look at him. "Now go away."

"I didn't come here to ask a favor. I come here when I need to think," he said. "Why are you so upset?"

"I'm upset because you're here."

"Liar. You were upset before you knew I was here."

I closed my eyes. "I've just had a bad string of days lately. Needed to blow off some steam."

"Mm…" His eyes sparkled. "You want to have some fun, then?"

"I am *not* sleeping with you again," I said with a disgusted look.

"No," he said with a hearty laugh. "But it's been a while

since I've sparred and I feel antsy. We could go a few rounds. I'd like to blow off some steam, too."

I forced myself not to look excited by the prospect. "Is this a trick?"

"Only if you've gotten rusty since I last saw you," he said, that damned charming smile glinting in the moonlight.

"I'll show you rusty," I grumbled, transporting to the other side of the beach and my customary spot.

"Ready?" he called.

I formed a spell in my hand, the bright purple magic violent and beautiful at the same time. I was as mesmerized as the first time I'd ever seen it, a young fifteen-year-old girl with no idea what she was getting into.

The green spell whizzed toward me, and I released my own ball toward it, knocking it into the ocean.

"Are you daydreaming over there?" he taunted, another fireball ready.

"A bit," I confessed. "But let's do this for real."

We moved like dancers across the dark space, energy crackling and roaring as it touched and exploded, the sand spraying with each impact (human and magic), the cool, salt air blowing on my face as I moved effortlessly through our unchoreographed dance. The rush of danger as his magic came toward me, the knowing that I could block or avoid and then return fire. This feeling of being limitless and invincible. This was who I really was. A Warrior on the battlefield, pushing the limits of my magic and my mind. Devising plans and recalculating on the fly as circumstances changed. This was the sort of thing Dave or Sam couldn't understand. This was why I would always be different from them.

I fell to my knees after a moment, panting heavily with exertion and grinning ear-to-ear.

"Ready to call it quits?" James said, his voice breathy and all kinds of alluring. White sand covered his forehead and cheek from where he'd landed, but his eyes sparkled with excitement.

"Yeah," I said, slowly coming to my feet. I summoned one of the few remaining healing potions I had under my bed in Nicole's apartment and popped the cork, drinking it down. "That was pretty fun."

"Warriors need to get their exercise, or else they get cranky," James said, sucking down a potion of his own. He grimaced at the taste and then summoned another.

The moon was half-full, casting a white glow over everything. My heart skipped when his shoulder brushed mine as he sat down beside me, reminding me of the few precious days when everything had been perfect. When we'd kissed more often than talked, when he'd been so vulnerable and scared with me. When he'd held me after my sisters and I had fought. Before he'd ruined *everything*.

He turned to me, and even in the low light, his green eyes were vibrant and beautiful. His mere existence, faults and all, was everything I'd been missing these past few months. And that was what made him so very dangerous.

I wrenched my gaze away from his, trying to steady my breathing and not give away just how much he got to me. One sparring session and all my carefully laid landmines had gone dormant. I forced myself to relive the moment he'd appeared in shackles. His voice when he admitted what he'd done. No matter his reason, there was no excuse for it. Even as my heart cried out for there to be.

"So what's Cyrus up to these days?" I asked, forcing myself to sound hard and uncaring.

"He's…under control," James said. "I wish I could tell you more."

"I honestly don't believe that." I looked at him. "What about Meagan? Why are you dating her? And if you're dating her, why are you here with me?"

"I'm not just dating her. I'm dating a bunch of magicals from different clans," he said then grimaced and looked away. "That's not very helpful."

"Other than to hurt my feelings," I admitted quietly.

"I'm sorry that you had to see that," he said. "I didn't want you to find out like that."

"You just didn't want me to find out at all, I'm sure."

"She's part of what I'm trying to do," James said. "And one of three girlfriends I currently have. None of them mean anything."

"That's just so typical you," I said. "Using girls like tissue paper. Why did I ever like you in the first place?"

"Because you know the real me, just like I know the real you," James said. "I'm just sorry things have happened they way they are."

"You don't understand, do you?" I said softly. "It's not enough to tell me you're sorry. It doesn't *fix* anything. I'm still broken. I'm still… I'm still hurt. You can make all the amends in the world, but there's always going to be what you did." I sighed. "Even if I forgive you, even if I want to move past it, there's always going to be the scar. There's always going to be that small bit of me that remembers. And if you really want to try making things better, you've got to start with telling me the *truth*."

"How many ways can I tell you I *can't*?" he said, his eyes flashing. "And don't blame your massive hang-ups on me. You were chicken before we ever started dating. The only person keeping you from making relationships is you. And it's not like I don't understand, because I do, but one of these days, you've got to stop hiding behind your magic as an excuse and just be vulnerable with people again."

I rose, caught between wanting to stay, wanting to throw a fireball at his head, and wanting to collapse in a ball of misery. He was in love with me; well, as much as I didn't want to be, I was still in love with him. But just like with Gavon, I couldn't forgive him. Not yet.

"And what the hell did you even have to talk to Sam for?" I said, changing the subject. "What *possible* reason could you have for asking her out?"

"Is that what she said I told her?" He laughed. "She's a lot more interesting than you give her credit for."

"She's very interesting. But you'd better stay away from her. She said she'd murder you if she saw you again. Nonmagicals have guns, you know. If she snuck up on you, she could…"

James laughed, and it just made me angrier.

"Here's an idea, Lexie: why don't you just ask her yourself? Or better yet, why don't you just *tell* her you have magic?"

"I can't just go around telling people I have magic," I said, flushing.

"You're not bound by any agreements. The only thing keeping you from telling them is fear."

"And what if they freak out? What if they call the government and have me arrested and sent off for science experiments?"

"You are, hands down, the most frustrating individual I've ever met."

"Yeah, well, guess what: so are you!"

To my surprise, his warm hand covered mine on the sand. I felt his gaze on me and forced myself not to meet it. "I'm sorry, Lexie. The last thing I want to do is hurt you."

"But you do." I removed my hand. "And you have. So what you want and what you do seem to be two very different things."

"I'm hoping all this will be over soon so I can tell you everything."

"Telling me everything won't fix it."

"Then how did you fix things with Gavon?' he asked. "He paid for your school and you forgave him?"

My face grew warm. "That's not what happened. The school was a *start*. We've been working on building our relationship all summer. It's not like he just shows up out of the blue to disrupt my life. He texts, we talk about stuff. And he certainly doesn't lie to me and go around breaking my heart every chance he gets."

"You so sure about that?" James asked. "He hasn't told you what we're doing, has he?"

"N-no…but only because he doesn't want me involved," I said.

"And yet…didn't I hear something about you walking right

into the thick of it?" he said with a smirk.

My face burned. "So you're having conversations about me, hm? Just you and Gavon, discussing how both of you ruined my life? Maybe I should ask him what you're up to."

"He won't know, either," James said, but there was a touch of nervousness in his voice. "I'm sorry."

"For?"

"Making you angry again."

"Apology not accepted," I said.

"We could go for round two, and you could beat me up some more," he said. "I'll even let you get a few shots in."

But even sparring had lost some of its luster now. It made me feel so perfect—so right—to be using magic, to be here on this beach with James. But as with everything James touched, it was now tainted. The one good thing I had left in my life—the one tether I had left to the person I was—was now as full of conflicted emotions as everything else.

"I just want things to be normal again," I whispered, resting my chin on my knees. "Whatever normal might be. I don't want my sister to be mad at me. I don't want to feel like I'm hiding big parts of myself. I don't want to come here and think about all the things you've done to hurt me. I just want…"

He slid his hand across my cheek, where a tear had fallen. Then, he swept his lips across mine, and for a brief moment, I let myself believe in him, even though I knew it was a recipe for disaster.

"One day," he whispered, a hair's breadth from my lips. "I will make this right. But for now, thank you for a remarkable evening."

And then he left me on the beach, more confused than ever.

Twenty-Four

I didn't enjoy kissing him, and I definitely wasn't licking my lips to remind myself of the taste of him. I arrived back at my dorm in a haze of frustration and confusion, so palpable that even Sam didn't ask what was wrong. I slept better than I had in weeks, though I woke up thinking about James and the way he looked at me, and it just put me in a bad mood.

"Where were you yesterday?" Sam asked as I sat up. "And is that beach sand on the floor?"

"I was at a volleyball court yesterday," I said, the only thing I could think of. I didn't have the energy to work up a decent lie.

"You okay? You've been kind of quiet lately," she asked. "Dave says you haven't returned any of his texts."

Had he even texted me? I couldn't recall. That poor boy. "Family trouble."

"Your dad?"

"No, my sister Nicole." I sat up. "She's been seeing this really great guy. He drove me up from Florida to move me in. Crazy about her. And she's trying to break up with him because she's just…I don't know. So I tried to get involved and now she's pissed at me."

"Hm…kind of like how Dave took you out to a history museum even though he failed like every history class he ever took?" Sam said, tapping her finger to her chin. "And you're still obsessed with your ex, so you won't give him the time of day?"

I glared at her. "It's different. And I'm not obsessed with James." I'd only woken up thinking about him, and yeah, I'd kissed him, but I was certainly not still in love with him. "Nicole was older when my dad left, so she hasn't yet forgiven him."

"Smart."

I released a frustrated growl. "Sam, you don't know the whole damned story, so why don't you just quit making assumptions?"

"Fine," she said, holding up her hands in surrender. "I don't have a sister, but I'd think that the best thing to do is just to talk to her. She can't stay mad at you forever. Go apologize and see what happens."

"Or we could just stay mad at each other forever."

"You could do that, too." She rose and walked to the door, carrying her shower caddy. "But it seems like a waste of energy."

Once she was out of the room, I summoned my magical pocket and transported into of it, curling into a ball on my large, squishy chair and releasing a loud breath of relief. Maybe I was just cranky from sparring, so I summoned a large cup of coffee and sat for a long time, sipping and stewing in my anger.

My coffee gone, I still wasn't interested in being social, although I could see Sam wandering around on the other side of the magical pocket. I went to the stack of books that Sahil had given us that I was still working through. But sitting atop the stack was the journal we'd gotten from Irene. Strange, I would've thought Gavon would've read through it. Settling back in my chair, I thumbed through the yellowed pages.

Johanna's thought process was incredible, and her notes as succinct and detailed as Gavon's. With her sister Abigail, they worked methodically, changing one or two ingredients in her recipe and documenting the results. Most were "no change," but when she found something that worked, she kept it in the ingredients list until she hit another wall. Not wanting to waste time, I turned to the very end of the book, finding half the pages blank. I worked backward until I found the last page, where the potion that had created New Salem rested.

There was something so surreal about it—so simple about its ingredients. But it hadn't just been the potion, it was the infusion of magic from over a hundred and sixty magicals that had given it potency. And it had taken just one to rip a hole in it.

It seemed impossible, but Gavon had spoken at length about the power of Potion-makers. The right combination of ingredients made by the right magical could create and another could destroy.

And all that power resided in my sister.

I still thought it was stupid she wouldn't help us. This was bigger than her and Gavon, bigger than all of us. If she could help us solve this puzzle, so much would change. We could move forward. Her vendetta meant nothing in that.

But to convince her of that, I needed to swallow my pride

and apologize.

I transported down to Florida, finding her apartment empty, but that wasn't unusual. It was mid-morning (had I really slept in that late?), so she was probably at work. I transported to the bathroom in the pharmacy where she worked and made my way out, walking through the rows of beach apparel and medicines to get to the back.

Nicole was behind the counter, speaking with an older woman. She looked up and caught my eye and her expression darkened, but she put on a good show for the woman. There was a line, so I sat and waited until it dwindled. My class wasn't until the afternoon, and this was important. I'd just do my homework by magic (sorry, Jeanie).

Finally, she disappeared from behind the counter and came out the back door.

"What are you doing here?" she asked.

I shifted from one foot to the other. "Got a minute to talk?"

"No, I'm not on break yet," she said, glancing at another old couple as they walked through the front doors. "But...we do need to talk. I'm sorry for what I said."

"No, I'm sorry I got involved. I didn't mean to eavesdrop, but I was worried and—"

"You don't need to worry," she said sharply. "What happens between Guy and me is none of your concern. We're just going through a patch right now. It's fine."

It most certainly wasn't, but I didn't want to push. "I also wanted to talk about...what I wanted to talk about. Gavon, and the potion—"

"Lexie..." She groaned. "This is ridiculous. I can't help you."

I pushed the journal into her hands. "Yes, you can. Just… look through it. If it doesn't make sense, fine. But I have a feeling you'll be able to get a lot more out of it than we can."

"Lexie, I would help, but I honestly think you're barking up the wrong tree, there," Nicole said. "I don't have much knowledge on the subject. I can make healing potions, and that's about it."

I chewed my lip, struggling to find the right words. "Nicole, you're the only one who knows anything about this stuff. Please, just look at it, okay?"

She looked back at the counter, where the line of people was starting to grow. "Fine. I'll look at it. But don't expect much."

So I read the journal.
I smirked, unsurprised to get the text later that night. *And?*
I have a lot of questions.
I chewed my lip. Was that a good thing or a bad thing? *Questions for Gavon?*

She took a long time to respond. *Yes. He can come by before dinner on Sunday. But he can't stay.*

That she was even letting him in the house was a miracle— that she was inviting me back to Sunday dinner was pretty surprising, too. *Will do.*

Sunday evening, I arrived at Nicole's apartment, bracing myself for a fight. Nicole was sitting at the kitchen counter, an open bottle of wine half-empty in front of her.

"When is he getting here?" she asked.

"Soon, I think." It was a few minutes until six, and he was usually pretty punctual.

"Tell me about this potion," Nicole said, playing with her glass. "The one at the end."

"That's the potion that made New Salem. D—Gavon made it once before, but it didn't work. And he thinks that since you're a Potion-maker, you might be able to tell us what he did wrong with it."

"What? Like I have some sort of innate power I don't know about?" Nicole snorted and chewed on her nails. "Yeah, right. I think he's just looking for an excuse to talk to me again."

"I mean, he always wants to talk to you, but this is… We need your help."

She tensed when a puff of purple appeared in the center of her kitchen. Gavon wore an apprehensive look, his gaze sweeping from the journal to Nicole in one motion.

"Hi, Nicole," he said softy.

"So, this potion," she said, nodding to the journal on the table in front of her. "Is this the one you were making in the basement?"

"You remember that?" he said, eyes widening.

"Of course I do," she said. "And I also remember that it had *nothing* to do with closing the tear."

I turned to Gavon, but he looked as confused as I did. "How so?" I asked.

"That potion won't close anything," Nicole replied, gesturing to it. "It's a potion to create, not to mend. There's a difference."

"There…is?" I said with a look to Gavon. He seemed about as confused as me.

"Of course there is," Nicole said, picking up the journal and angrily flipping to the last page. "Void Lily? Frankincense?

They're all things that grow, maintain. The Domdafosie will help in the self-sustainment. This isn't one that sealed the world. That was a whole different thing. So why the hell would it be used to seal up a tear?"

"Because…" Gavon was at a loss for words. "Because I thought maybe that if we used the same potion, we could re-seal it?"

"And *why* would you think that?" she said, scathingly.

"I thought that, too," I said meekly. "Nicole, we have no idea what you're talking about."

"He does," she said, nodding to him. "Because he's the one who told me about all this potion-making stuff."

"I never taught you any of this," he said, fighting a smile. "We left off on identifying lavender and thistle, if I recall. What you're describing, that's…just your magic working, I believe."

She flushed bright red and looked at the counter.

"Do you…" He carefully considered his words. "How would you close the tear?"

"I have no fucking idea," Nicole snapped, and then pointed at Gavon. "But I bet you anything he knows, and he's just dragging his feet. The same way he did with Mom."

"I learned that lesson very dearly," he whispered. "Thank you, Nicole. You've actually been very helpful. If you think of any potions that could be useful…I would appreciate the assistance."

"Yeah, well," she demurred, looking anywhere except Gavon, "I didn't do much. I mean, it doesn't make any sense. Why would you use frankincense to mend?"

"I don't even know what that is," I said. "Or that it's not

used to mend."

She shrugged. "Maybe naming random plants is the one magical thing I can do."

"You have plenty of magic, sweetheart," Gavon muttered.

"Don't call me that," Nicole snapped. "Is that it? Can I go back to pretending you don't exist?"

He opened his mouth to respond, but then took a moment to collect his thoughts. "Thank you again. If you think of anything else…" He shook his head, then disappeared in a puff of purple.

Nicole buried her head in her hands. "That sucked."

"I'm sorry," I murmured.

"Did you…really not know that frankincense wasn't used to mend?" Nicole whispered. "Like…I don't know why I think that's just common knowledge. And I swear he's the one who told me."

I hesitated, unsure if I should share. "We met a woman who knows you. Josefa? She's the Clanmaster in Spain. They had a strong Potion-maker line. Dad…Gavon said he wanted to bring you there, so you could be around more people like you."

"But they aren't like me," Nicole said. "You heard him: I'm the only Potion-maker alive."

"It couldn't hurt to go see them," I said. "Josefa keeps asking about you."

"I don't know, Lexie. I've been pretty happy in my magic-less life so far."

"I shouldn't have even brought it up," I said. "I'm sorry."

"No, I'm sorry," Nicole said, resting her head on her hands again. "I've just been on edge these past few weeks, haven't been sleeping. This house has been too empty lately."

"Do you want me to spend the night?" I asked. "I don't mind."

"No, I just… I don't know." She wiped her wet eyes.

"What's going on with Guy?" I asked, gently stroking her hair.

She shrugged. "Nothing to tell. Guy and I have been fighting a lot. I just feel like… Being with him is great. But then…"

"Do you still love him?" I asked.

She exhaled a long breath. "I do love him. He's…he's everything I ever wanted. He's kind, he takes great care of me, he listens to me and cares about what I think. But then we get close to these conversations, especially when he wants to know more about Mom. When I think about actually telling him everything… It's so terrifying. What if he walks out the door?"

"He's not going to," I said.

"I thought Gavon wasn't going to, either." She shook her head. "Why am I even trying? You two are best buds again."

"We're not," I said quietly. "We're working on our relationship because I want us to have one. But even now, when he talks about how proud he is of me, all I want to do is tell him that he could've been there my whole life. But…" I sighed. "I also know he did what he thought was best at the time. He didn't have a lot of options."

"I know you want things to just turn out for the best," Nicole said, toying with a lock of my hair. "But sometimes, people are exactly who you think they are. And trying to see anything else is just asking for trouble."

"Gavon turned out for the best," I said softly. "Or at least, he's trying to."

"And sometimes even the best isn't good enough." She pressed her hands to her stomach. "I know you and Gavon have been able to let the past go, but I can't. Not with everything I've been through. Not with all this hurt I've been carrying around for years."

I had nothing to say to that, nothing that would fix the problem. So instead I asked, "Want to get take-out and watch crappy TV?"

<h1 style="text-align:center">Twenty-Five</h1>

I fell asleep on the couch next to Nicole, waking up at three in the morning and forgetting where I was. I magically put her to bed, glad she was finally getting a good night's sleep. Then I transported back to my dorm to continue sleeping, but I just couldn't.

Nicole would take some more work, but something told me she was the key we were looking for. The way she'd rattled off ingredients like that—and I fully believed that Gavon had had nothing to do with her knowledge. At least that level of detail. After all, they hadn't spoken in almost eighteen years.

How's your sister? Gavon had texted me sometime the night before.

She'll survive.

I'm sorry I made her so upset.

Again, I found myself at a loss for words. Theirs was a relationship I didn't want to get in the middle of anymore.

I think she could help us. Any word on the Danvers thing from

Josefa?

Irene's been in contact with most of them, so they won't meet with me. But I'm working on an alternative way to talk to them.

A second later, I got another text. *Go to bed.*

I couldn't sleep now, not when the wheels were turning in my mind. After quietly slipping out of bed, I transported into my magical pocket and turned on the light, hunting for the journal on the Separation. I flipped through to the end, where there was a full list of all the Clanmasters who'd signed to the Accord.

I created a new spreadsheet on my laptop and used magic to add all the names into it. Obviously, I could mark off the current Clanmasters of Carrigan and Vargas, but the rest were a little more difficult to piece together. In another spreadsheet, I listed all the clans I knew about—which totaled just the ones Josefa had introduced me to.

So we had…five clans. Of the two hundred signatories.

Going back to the search engine, I searched for the first Clanmaster on the list and—surprisingly—might've gotten a hit. It was on one of those genealogy sites, and when I clicked on the name, it brought up a man who'd lived in Charleston, South Carolina by the name of Grenard in 1704. The entire family tree was listed, all the way down to 1970, thousands of names and dates. But were these people magical, or was it just a coincidence?

This would take a lot longer than I'd thought.

I spent the next few days working through the genealogies of the clanmembers I could find, and I didn't get very far. Of the two hundred signatories, only twenty had anything on a search engine, and as with Grenard in Charleston, I didn't know if they were magical. I supposed I could just visit each of them, but how would *that* work?

"Hey, I'm Lexie and magical. Are you in a clan? Can we talk to your Clanmaster?"

Sure, that would just work perfectly.

The other magicals I knew about were in Vegas and at the Arlington School. But Marie, of course, was less than helpful:

Can you go back to the Vegas magicals and find out which clans they belong to?

Why?

For the project Dad and I are working on.

Go yourself. I'm busy.

"Gee, thanks, Marie. So sorry to disturb your tanning and whatever else you're doing."

I could go to the Vegas place by myself, but…I didn't really want to go by myself. Not after I'd made a fool of myself and was asked if I needed remedial magical training. So perhaps I'd wait on that.

Which left the Arlington School. Conscious that Celeste hated me, I couldn't just walk in the front door and start talking to kids. But maybe if I asked to speak with her, she'd listen. Or maybe I was barking up the wrong tree. Either way, it felt like being helpful without getting into too much trouble.

After class, I transported across the river to an alley near the magical school and adjusted my clothes. I'd summoned a blazer and black pants from Nicole's closet, just to give myself a little bit more of a professional look. This was a business meeting, after all.

And then James walked right by me.

I thought for a moment I was seeing things, but after tripping over the garbage cans and other boxes in the alley and scrambling toward the street, I found him again, walking right into the Arlington School.

"What the hell…?"

Was he going to see another girlfriend? And if so, why was Celeste letting him in the front door? Did she not know who he was?

I crossed the street after him, curiosity getting the better of me. The hostess at the front gave me a once-over, but didn't stop me as I hurried to the back of the restaurant and through to the school. There, as before, the rooms that lined the atrium were filled with kids practicing their magic. But I'd lost James.

A puff of brown appeared in front of me—the snooty man was back.

"I believe Celeste was pretty clear that you are not to be here," he said with a sneer. "We know who you are."

"So move me," I said, raising my chin. I didn't have much confidence in his abilities, although I wasn't trying to get into a fight with Celeste. "Or better yet, can I make an appointment with your director? I have some things to talk to her about."

He rolled her eyes. "Appointment, sure."

"I'm serious." I adjusted my jacket. "*I'm* not the bad guy here."

"Sure you aren't." He pulled out his phone, pretending to check it. "Her schedule is filled for the next three months. So if you can wait that long…"

"I'm sure she doesn't have an opening like…right now," I said. "She's *so* busy."

"She is, in fact. With a magical with the same kind of powers that you have," he said, frowning as he looked at his phone. "No idea how he scheduled that one."

"Maybe *magic*?" I said. Why didn't I think of that? "If you're looking for a bad magical, he's the worst. I'd be worried about Celeste being in danger. You should take me up there."

He studied me for a long while then seemed to believe me. "Fine. I'll show you upstairs. But no funny business, you understand?"

He transported to a room three floors up with lush carpeting that smelled new and sculptures on stands around the room. Everything smelled and looked like money here. But at twenty grand a student, Celeste could afford such niceties.

"Stay here. I'm going to go check on her." He rapped on the door and cracked it open.

I spotted a familiar mop of brown hair and pushed by the man into the office.

"What is the meaning of this?" Celeste said, rising from an exquisite desk that looked hand-carved. "You! I thought I was very clear that you aren't allowed here."

"So why are you meeting with *him*?" I said, nodding to James. "Do you know who he is?"

James spun around in his chair, giving me a look of pure venom. "I'm here discussing a sizable donation to the school, *Alexis*. Nothing else that concerns you. Haven't we had this conversation before?"

My fingers sparked with magic as my heart raced. "James is

from New Salem," I said to Celeste. "Same as my father."

"I'm aware of that," Celeste said, surprising me. "Jonathan, you can let her in. Miss Carrigan, please."

Numbly, I stumbled into the room, unsure if this was a trap or something else entirely.

"She doesn't need to be here," James said, sounding somewhat strained. "Send her home."

"It sounds like I owe her an apology, as well as my thanks," Celeste said. "It's because of you, Alexis, that we finally have a name for that magical—"

James made a noise, and for the first time, I noticed the light sheen of sweat on his forehead.

"Trent?" I said.

"Yes," Celeste said. "He used to be one of Irene's, although she's refusing to admit it. But now that we have his name, we can find his signature. And then we can find out—"

"Celeste," James choked out. Was that blood coming from his nose? "Lexie should go."

"Not yet," I said, turning to Celeste. Whatever James was struggling with had nothing to do with me. "What are you two meeting about? Besides this endowment which is probably just an excuse. And what's going on with Trent?"

"Trent's been recruiting children—"

Something slumped hard to the ground beside me. Spinning, I registered James' comatose body on the ground.

"James!" I cried, running over to him. His skin was clammy and pale, as if he had the flu. I looked at Celeste, who seemed as bewildered as I was. "What's wrong with him?"

"He said he was under some kind of agreement not to

divulge certain things," she said, kneeling beside me and pressing her hand to his forehead. "This looks like a magical pact."

"You said you were meeting to discuss trouble," I said, gently stroking his forehead. "What kind of—"

He convulsed, and another dribble of blood fell from his nose.

"You should get him out of here," she said. "Get him a healing potion. And if I were you, I would stay far away from whatever he's wrapped up in, unless you want to kill him."

"Marie!" I cried, appearing in her living room. "Marie, are you here?"

I had no other options, as contacting Gavon was out of the question. Marie would be able to heal him, I was sure of it, and then I'd have some answers.

"What the…" Marie walked out of her bedroom, her face covered in a mud mask. "Lexie, what the hell is happening?"

"I don't know, but can you heal him?" I said.

"Heal who?" Nicole popped around from behind her, also wearing a mud mask.

Just perfect. "What are you doing here?" I asked.

"What are *you* doing here with…*him*?" Nicole blanched when she saw who I was dragging toward the couch. "Lexie, what the hell?"

"It's a long story, but he's really sick." I turned to Marie with pleading eyes. "I don't know what happened, but can you heal him?" His color had improved, but only a little.

Marie made a noise and stomped over, kneeling down beside him. "What's wrong with him?"

"I have no idea. I was…following him. He went to that magical academy to talk to someone there," I said. "Then he just kind of…collapsed. I don't know what happened."

"I do."

I froze. The very last person (well, almost the last person) I wanted to see had materialized in the middle of Marie's living room. Nicole made an annoyed noise, but didn't say anything as Gavon swept toward me, shaking his head.

"Lexie, why can't you just leave well enough alone?" he said, kneeling beside me. "He's been hit for a loop, but he'll be fine. Marie, you can give him a little healing magic, but you won't be able to do much." His gaze darted to Nicole for a moment, and I thought he might ask her to help, but instead he said, "I'll need a few minutes to gather some supplies, but I can make a potion that should bring him back."

"What's wrong with him?" I said.

"It's a very long story, one I guess I'll tell you when I get back," he said, standing up. "Along with a long, very interesting talk about why you can't seem to keep your nose out of things you don't need to be involved in."

My mouth fell open; Gavon rarely used that tone with me.

"I didn't…"

"Exactly, you didn't," Gavon snapped. "I'll be back in a moment."

He disappeared once more, and shame for something I didn't understand enveloped me.

Twenty-Six

"Good job, Lexie," Marie said, breaking the tense silence.

"Wait, do *you* know what's going on here?" I said, rising.

She sputtered for a moment, which was enough to tell me she didn't. At least Gavon was being consistent.

"So…what in the actual hell is going on?" Nicole asked. "Why is the boy who tried to get Lexie killed in your house? Why are we helping him at all?"

"Because she's still in love with him," Marie said, pressing her hands onto James's face. They glowed while she healed him, but he didn't wake.

"That's not why," I said, although my face burned. "I wanted to know what he was up to. He and Gavon were working on something, it seemed, but neither of them were being very forthcoming about it, so—"

"So you decided to be nosy," Nicole said. "Haven't you learned your lesson yet?"

"I'm not a child, so stop talking to me like I am one," I

barked.

"You let Gavon talk to you like that."

"That's because…" I shook my head. "I wasn't trying to do anything nosy this time. I was going to the Arlington School of Magicals to try to find more Clanmasters to talk to. He was there, talking with the director. This just happened."

"Talking about what?" Nicole asked.

"I didn't get a chance to talk to her. James started convulsing. But she said it was about some trouble with her kids —"

James groaned from the table, and I jumped to my feet.

"What are you doing to him?"

"She's doing nothing. You, on the other hand, need to stop talking," Gavon said, reappearing with a cauldron and other materials in the kitchen. "James has been bound to a very specific pact, one that forbids him from discussing or divulging anything about it or anything it pertains to."

I blinked. "All this is from a pact?"

Gavon nodded and carefully ladled some clear liquid into one of Marie's measuring cups. "Any discussion around or about the pact results in severe bodily harm to James. For the time being, let's not discuss it."

"But he can discuss it with you?"

"He's forbidden to discuss it with me, too,' Gavon said. "I was able to glean some particulars, based on context, before it became too much for him."

I bit my tongue instead of asking the thousands of questions that had suddenly arisen in my mind. A pact? One he couldn't tell Gavon about? Something that would inevitably kill him if he did?

This had Cyrus written all over it.

But instead of asking, I remained quiet next to a seething Nicole. After we'd been sitting in silence for at least half an hour, Gavon finished his potion and brought a cup into the living room. With nurse-like care, he lifted James's head and opened his mouth, pouring the potion into his mouth. James coughed but swallowed most of it, and almost immediately, the grayish tint to his skin turned pinker. His eyes fluttered, and he looked around, his brow creasing.

"James, can you hear me?" Gavon asked, his tone even.

James's gaze landed on Gavon and the color drained from his face once again. He glanced in my direction for a split second before turning back to Gavon. "Yes, I can hear you."

"What year is it?"

"Twenty-seventeen," he said, his lips barely moving.

"What's your name?"

"James Malcolm Riley."

"Are you well enough to stand? Use magic?" Gavon asked, rising himself.

"Yes."

"Then get back to work," Gavon replied, all traces of concern gone. "And I don't want to hear about you bothering Lexie anymore, understand?"

He nodded and disappeared in a puff of green.

"I mean, technically, I was the one who bothered him this time…" I said, breaking the awkward silence in the room.

"And you'll leave it alone if you'd like to continue at Georgetown," Gavon said. "I have given you one warning. This is your second. On the third, your tuition will be cancelled. Am I clear?"

I nodded, looking down at the floor.

"So what? We're all just going to ignore that Lexie brought the kid who put our lives in danger to Marie's house?" Nicole asked, leveling a glare at Gavon. "Color me so surprised you two are working together."

Gavon straightened and offered her a smile. 'Hello, Nicole. Am I allowed to speak to you again?"

She narrowed her eyes, crossing her arms over her chest. "Yes, to answer my question. You're just letting him walk out of here unscathed?"

"He transported, but yes, because his only mistake was involving Lexie, which I expressly told *both* of them not to do," Gavon said.

"And kidnapping us," Nicole added.

"Apparently there were extenuating circumstances," I chimed in, but withered under Nicole's stare.

"I think it's time for you to go," Nicole waved her arms. "Both of you."

"Yeah, it's my house," Marie said, sitting on the couch. "And it's time the two of you had a conversation. A real one."

"I have nothing more to say to him," Nicole said. "I helped him with the potion. That's enough for a lifetime."

Marie sighed, but Gavon held up his hand. "It's fine. I understand and I'll see myself out." He paused then looked at Nicole. "But, congratulations."

Nicole's face went white. "What the hell are you talking about?"

"Yeah, what the hell are you talking about?" I said, looking between him and Nicole.

"You can't sense it?" Gavon asked me.

"Sense what?"

"Nothing!" Nicole cried, but it was drowned out by the sound of glass breaking. Marie's balcony door lay in pieces on the ground.

"W…what just happened?" I said, glancing between Nicole, Gavon, and Marie, who was shaking her head as she rose to fix the glass.

"Nicole's pregnant," Marie said as the door reassembled itself. "What did you say, Nicole? Six weeks?"

I could scarcely believe my ears. "Did this happen before or after you broke up with Guy?"

"I don't see how that's any of your business," Nicole said, glaring at Gavon. "Or *his*."

But Gavon was wearing a look of concern. "You ended things with that mechanic? Why? I liked him—"

"*You* don't get a say in anything," Nicole said. "I thought you were leaving?"

"It's my house, and I say he can stay," Marie said. "It's his grandchild."

"It most certainly is not," Nicole said, and the glass shattered again. "Son of a bitch. How is this real life?"

"Dad?" I said, looking at Gavon.

"Well, strictly speaking." He cleared his throat. "Nicole's unique, of course, but the Danvers Accord magicals, when they become pregnant with a child from New Salem, as your mother did, take on those powers for a brief time. If I were to make an educated guess, Nicole is benefiting from that as well."

"So, like…" Marie stood. "If I got knocked up, and I was having a Warrior, I'd be able to spar and use attack spells?"

"Probably not," Gavon said. "Your Healing magic is potent, as is Lexie's Warrior magic."

"But my Potion-making magic is nonexistent, so I get to be a freak of nature for a few months," Nicole said, sitting down on the couch. "Great. Just great."

Gavon took a step forward, but I put my hand in front of him. "Maybe it's best if you go. I'll…fill you in on the rest later."

"All right," he said, although he looked pained to agree. "We aren't finished with our discussion about James. But please, *please*—"

"No more digging," I said. "I promise."

"Good girl." Gavon kissed me on the forehead. "Take care of your sister."

He disappeared in a puff, and I turned to the couch, where Nicole had buried her head in her hands and Marie was comforting her.

"This is a disaster," Nicole said, finally lifting her head. Her cheeks were streaked with tears and her lips were red and puffy. "This is a disaster."

"It's not a disaster," Marie said, patting her on the back. "You just call up that man of yours, tell him to marry you, and be done with it."

"You forgot the part where I have to tell him I have magic and so will this…this kid." She shook her head, her face screwing up with unshed tears. "I wish Mom was here. It's so weird. I haven't missed her in years. I mean, I was only four when she died. But now… God, all I want is to have her back. I don't know what to do. I'm so scared."

"Don't be a chicken," Marie said. "I know it's hard, but you have to see how much Guy cares for you. Why are you afraid to be with him?"

She quieted, working through her words as she stared at the table in front of us. "If I tell him…everything. That means it's real. Not what happened but…we're real. He and I are real. And that just really…makes me nervous. Because I'm not sure I could survive if I let it get that far and then he…"

Then he leaves like Gavon did. She didn't need to say it, because I'd felt the same thing. Even as far as my father and I had come, I still carried that fear in the back of my mind. James had, of course, exacerbated it.

"He's not going anywhere," I said calmly. "Especially not now."

"You can't guarantee that," Nicole said.

"Yeah, but…what good is living if you spend your entire life afraid people are going to let you down?" Marie said gently. "At some point, you have to put yourself out there. And I can't think of a safer guy to do that with."

"It's not even just the emotional stuff." Nicole held out her hands, which had begun to glow white. "Things have been flying around, and now I can do this. Is this an attack spell?"

"No," Marie said, a grin on her face. "I won."

"Won?" Nicole said, sniffing back. "Oh, is this…healing magic?"

"Hah!" Marie jumped up and did a dance. "You and Dad

have your little Warriors club, and me and this little nugget are going to have the Healers club. Just you wait!"

"I…never thought I'd see Marie excited about a baby," I said to Nicole.

"Well, it's not my baby, so of course I'm excited," Marie said, coming to sit back down. "And I can already tell it's going to be a powerful little sucker."

"Great," Nicole said with a groan. "How…how am I supposed to handle that? I don't have magic—I don't even know the first thing about it. And I don't have anyone I can go to for help."

"I'll help," I said. "Marie will help." Gavon would too, but I didn't mention it. "Do you want me to move back home? Transport to and from college?"

"Not a chance," she said. "You can zip home if I need you."

"Absolutely," I replied with a smile. "Any time. Day or night."

"I'll hold you to that when the baby needs a midnight diaper change," she said, taking my hand.

I squeezed her hands. "You're gonna be a mom, Nicole. A great one. I mean…you basically raised me."

"I didn't, not really," she said.

"You raised me, too," Marie said. "As much as I hated you for it, you raised me. And you are going to be a great mom. Just need to loosen up a little and stop being so scared of everything." She patted Nicole on the hand. "And I'm going to have so much fun teaching that little bugger how to heal."

"Stop calling my child a bugger," Nicole said, pressing her hand to her stomach.

I rested mine on top of hers, closing my eyes and searching for this thing they were talking about. And then I felt it, as clearly as if I'd been staring at it all along. Was this what everyone was talking about with the magical radar? It wasn't something that just jumped out at me, but now that I noticed it…I couldn't understand how I hadn't seen it before.

"I'm…excited that you guys know," Nicole said, squeezing my hand. "And you're right, I honestly had no idea what it was like when you got magic, Lexie. I feel like my whole body is tingling."

"You get used to it," I said with a laugh. "Just as long as you don't blow up your nightstand."

"Well, I guess it'll only last for a few months, right?" Marie said.

"I…honestly don't know," I replied, scratching my chin. "That would've been a good question for Gavon."

"Don't." Nicole shook her head. "Just don't."

"Like it or not, he's *kind* of the expert," Marie said. "And it is technically his—"

"Don't say it."

"Okay, we won't say it," I said, sharing a look with Marie.

"And *promise* me whatever Gavon was talking about, whatever that boy is wrapped up in, you'll just leave it alone," she said. "There's not a lot I agree with him about, but I think we both want you safe."

"I promise if you promise to tell Guy," I said. "You deserve to have him be with you during this process. And I bet he'll surprise you."

"You know, seeing Gavon today reminded me what it's like

not to have a dad around," Nicole said after a moment of silence. "Especially when he started calling me his sweetheart. Like I'm four years old again and he's taking me to learn about potions." She made a face. "It's not about me anymore. It's about the baby." The grimace turned into a soft grin, and a little light shone in her eyes as they filled with tears. "I'm gonna be a mom."

I squeezed her hands. "Your next one will be a Warrior, right?"

"I'm not even two months along. Don't rush me into a second pregnancy." She wiped her cheeks. "And I can't transport or anything like that yet, so somebody's gotta get me back to Florida."

Twenty-Seven

I took Nicole back home with a promise that we would talk much more about everything over dinner on Sunday, and she promised that she'd work up the nerve to tell Guy, but wouldn't commit to a date to tell him. We hugged, something I needed after the day I'd had and she probably needed just as much, then I transported back to my dorm.

But I wasn't even back before I recognized that magical signature—the little voice in the back of my mind that said Gavon was nearby. Steeling myself for another lecture, I descended the stairs, preparing for the worst.

Gavon sat on the park bench, his arms crossed against his chest. He wore a serious look, his gaze pinning me to the spot when I walked through the door.

"Why was James unconscious in Marie's apartment?" he asked across the courtyard.

"Why are any of us anywhere?" I replied with a nervous laugh.

He made a noise and stood up. "You do know that the grounding spell can be used up until the child no longer requires the parents' support. And you're locked in my care until you graduate from Georgetown."

"Oh." I stared at the ground. "Is that why you paid for my school?"

"No, just an additional benefit to for giving my too-nosy daughter the education she needed." He stopped in front of me, clasping his hands behind his back. "Do you enjoy fearing for your life in a sparring ring? Is that what this is about? Because I was under the impression those sorts of events tended to leave a mental scar on you. But all of your investigation and sneaking around seems suggest otherwise."

"Dad, just tell me the damned truth. What the hell is going on? What are you and James up to?"

"We aren't up to anything," he said. "What did he tell you?"

"He said you were working together on something. Couldn't tell me details. Same way you told me to let that symbol thing go. It just sounded too coincidental. Can you tell me now what kind of pact James signed? Would it hurt him?"

He sighed, pinching the bridge of his nose. "James signed a pact that essentially forbids him from divulging either the details of the pact or what prompted him to enter into it in the first place. It's why he decided to kidnap your sisters in an idiotic attempt to get my attention. He couldn't form the words, so…" Gavon gestured into the air. "Here we are."

"Oh…" I frowned. That certainly accounted for all his choked words. "But I assume he made the pact with Cyrus."

"That would be a wise assumption, yes," Gavon said. "Have I

answered all your questions?"

"Not even a little," I said. "I hate you guys sneaking around behind my back."

"Nobody is keeping anything from you, Lexie. We're just trying to protect you," he replied. "Well, I am, in any case. I can't understand why James would even *be* around you after I explicitly told him to leave you alone."

Well, I was already in trouble. Might as well just come out with it. "He asked me to…temporarily add him to my clan so he'd have the same protections as we do. Against Cyrus."

"That doesn't make any sense," Gavon said, shaking his head. "And I also don't understand why you didn't think that was something I would like to know."

"I didn't want to get you involved," I said, tempting fate. But he was pissing me off and I was tired of being lectured.

Gavon raised a brow, complete with that singularly paternal look.

So I backtracked. "You know *eventually* this crap ends up dragging me in whether I want to or not, so I might as well be prepared."

"I'm so very tired of having this conversation with you."

"Yeah, well, me too," I said.

"I just can't understand why you would trust James so blindly," Gavon said. "Not that I think he's up to anything, but considering your history—"

"I swear I don't love him anymore, if that's what you're trying to say."

The words flew out of my mouth before I realized what I was saying. I could practically see them hanging in the air, laughing as they vanished into the ether.

"I'm sorry, what?"

Did I go all-in? Backtrack? Disappear into a puff of smoke and never show my face again? That last option seemed the best, although Gavon had a nasty habit of finding me.

I cleared my throat as my face grew as warm as the sun. "I meant, he's not my friend. I know who he is. But you said you were working together. And he said he was desperate, so…"

"You said love, darling."

I sighed, closing my eyes and wishing I could disappear from that spot. Or at the very least, reverse time and the words that had just come out of my mouth.

"Did you…did you really love him?" Gavon asked after a painful few moments.

"I thought I did," I answered, trading one shame for another. "I mean, I fought it. Hard. I knew he was a really bad person, but at the same time, we were just so similar it was hard not to." I swallowed and continued my truth parade. "And now, with college…I guess part of me liked having him around. I know who I am with him—myself. I don't have to pretend I'm someone I'm not."

"Lexie, I know you're adjusting to college, but you're an adult now. You can't keep blaming your stupid mistakes on being lonely. You know better." He ran a free hand through his hair. "I don't understand why you don't just *listen* to me."

"And how the hell can I do that when I don't even trust you?"

The words came out softly, but they landed like a ton of bricks. I had been dancing around it for weeks now, this explanation for my behavior. I'd fooled myself into believing Gavon would be the father I'd always wanted him to be. The sad part was he'd been everything I wanted and more…and it still wasn't enough to erase all that had been between us.

"I'm sorry you feel that way." I didn't need to look at his face to know just how deeply I'd cut him.

"Me too," I murmured. "I don't want to feel this way. I want to be able to trust that when you tell me you're taking care of it, that you don't want me involved because you're protecting me, that it's the truth. But I can't. Not after everything that's happened. Not after the lies. After spending two years of my life thinking that you were the sort of monster who'd let me die. That kind of scarring doesn't disappear, no matter how many times you prove yourself to me."

He didn't say anything, and I wasn't brave enough to look at him in the face.

"And it's not just you, I don't even trust myself. I haven't in years. I feel like every decision I make is the wrong one, the one that's going to get me in trouble, and yet I second-guess that decision. Because I trusted you implicitly, didn't even question why some strange guy showed up and just happened to have magic. And I should have. If I was smart, I would've turned around and walked back to the house." I sighed, and two tears slipped down my face. "So now, whenever my gut tells me to do something, I just…don't trust it."

He'd been silent for a long time, so I chanced a look up at him and wished I hadn't. His eyes were wet, and his cheeks bore a few track marks.

"I'm sorry," he said quietly. "I'm just…I'm sorry that I

didn't do better for you."

I averted my gaze. I felt no better after saying what I'd said, and knowing I'd hurt him cut me somewhere deep. But at the same time…it was the truth. And it just sucked.

"I should be getting back," I said, rising and wiping my cheeks. "I'm…sorry again."

I appeared in the dorm bathroom and, exhausted, trudged across the hall into my dorm. I hated this feeling, like I was all alone in the world again. Like I was suddenly thrust into adulthood, and there was nobody there who'd rescue me from it. It was, if possible, scarier than being in a match with Cyrus. Then, I had confidence in my magic. Now, it was just me. And I wasn't sure I could hack it by myself.

I walked into the dorm room, waving lightly to Sam who was sitting at her computer, before falling face-first into my bed.

"You skipped again," Sam said with a clipped tone. "As your roommate, it's imperative that I inform you that skipping class —"

I smiled into the pillow. "I've already had like fifteen lectures today. Please don't give me another one."

"Oh yeah? What about?"

My natural instinct was to clam up, to lie, and to be evasive. But I was just really tired of trying to keep it all straight.

"My dad is pissed at me. He and James are working on some kind of project, and neither of them want to tell me what it is. I accidentally ran into James at the Arlington School for Magic, and apparently I made him sick, so he collapsed, and I had to bring him to my sister so she could heal him. My *other* sister,

Nicole was there, and apparently *she's* pregnant, and she broke up with her boyfriend 'cause she's too chicken to tell him the truth. And oh yeah, she hates my dad, who showed up because Marie texted him. So, there we all are, one happy damned family while James is dying because I couldn't leave well enough alone. My dad gives me a lecture about how if I don't stop bothering the two of them, he's going to stop paying for my college, and then, oh *then*, I tell him that I used to be in love with James, as if that wasn't awkward enough." I banged my head on the pillow. "Basically, I just realized that I don't trust anyone, my father, my sisters, or even myself. And I told him so, and I really hurt his feelings. So now I feel like the world's biggest asshole, my dad is hurt and mad at me, and I'm just…I wish I could go back to being a kid and not have to deal with all this crap."

Silence rang out in the room and I chanced a look at Sam, whose brown eyes were so wide, I could see the whites from across the room.

"Let's take that one more time," she said slowly. "So… *what?*"

I sat up and exhaled. Well, Gavon had said there was no harm in me telling my roommate. And if she freaked, I could probably just have Gavon whip up a memory charm. At this point, I kept making the wrong decisions, so why not try the exact opposite of what I thought was the right thing to do?

"Sam, I have magic."

"Well, no shit. But what the hell was the rest of that mess?"

Twenty-Eight

I blinked, sure I'd misheard. "What do you mean, *no shit*?"

"I mean, obviously you have magic," Sam said. "So do I. But I didn't follow one word of the rest of it. So please, enlighten me to the insanity that is your world because it's so much more interesting than my biology homework."

My mouth hung open and I stared at her, something buzzing in the back of my mind. And then I recognized it—that small sense that I'd always felt with Sam. The same feeling that I sensed with Nicole's new baby. That kernel of… magic.

Sam was magical.

"Holy shit." I stood up. "Are you serious?"

"Yeeeeah. Kind of wondering why you hadn't said anything." She giggled, although she looked a little embarrassed. "I mean, at first I thought you might not know. But then I thought maybe it was some kind of thing where you didn't want to talk about it cause of your weird family—"

I blinked dumbly, still trying to wrap my head around what I was hearing.

"Then, maybe I thought you couldn't tell me because of all those weird restrictions about magic and nonmagicals. And then I guess I just figured you'd tell me when you were ready. I kept poking your magic. Dave did, too, but he said you didn't react to it."

I nearly fell over. "*Dave* has magic, too?"

"Oh yeah, the whole group does," Sam said with a laugh. "Remember? I said we all met at fifteen? I thought for sure that would've tipped you off. That's why Chris thought you didn't know about magic—because you didn't even flinch when we said that. But Dave was sure that you did, but there was some reason you weren't telling us."

I slapped my hand against my forehead. This was surreal, and it was hard to wrap my brain around all the implications. I'd been wandering around this stupid city for weeks, looking for the very thing that had been under my nose this whole time.

"So I don't understand," I said, rubbing my face. "How come we got placed together in this room? It couldn't have been a coincidence, right? None of the others on the floor have magic?"

"Nope," she said. "I chalked it up to fate. But my mom thinks maybe there might be a magical at the registrar's office? Or maybe—"

"Or maybe someone was trying to teach me a lesson."

This seemed like the kind of thing Gavon would do. It just made my heart hurt more from the fight we'd just had.

"Who?" Sam asked.

"My dad. He'd rather I *learn* then flat-out tell me something.

It's like a few weeks ago, we were in Japan, and did he charm the thing? No, I had to figure out how to do it myself." I felt tears coming to my eyes again and I couldn't stop them from falling. "And I just told him I didn't trust him. I'm a big idiot."

"That you absolutely are not," Sam said, handing me a box of tissues.

"I can't even tell a magical from a nonmagical," I said, blowing my nose as the tears fell harder. "My roommate is magical, and I didn't even know. *We* live together!"

"Okay, we obviously need a drink," Sam said, standing. She opened her palms and a bottle of wine appeared in a puff of pink, along with two glasses. She transported the other glass to me, magically uncorked the bottle, and poured a velvet-looking red wine. "Cheers."

"To idiots who can't see the forest for the trees," I said, clinking my cup against hers.

"This is fucking awesome," Sam said, climbing up to sit next to me in bed. "I don't have to hide around you anymore."

"I can't believe you were hiding in the first place," I said, wiping my cheeks and sipping the wine. "I can't believe I didn't notice."

"My mom and dad were so confused," she said with a laugh, and I groaned loudly. "They kept asking me to outright tell you, but I had a feeling. It's like you were holding back. And I'm not about to poke when someone doesn't feel like sharing."

I took another sip to swallow my shame. "So…your parents, what are they really like?"

"What do you mean?"

"I mean, are they really a lawyer and doctor?"

"Um, yeah?" She made a face. "Why wouldn't they be?"

I ran my finger along the rim of the glass. "I don't know. I guess I still don't know what a magical does when they grow up."

"They do whatever pays the bills, dummy," she said. "Like becoming a lawyer or a doctor or an astronaut or a baker or whatever else they can do to make money. What I'm planning to do, I still have no idea. But it's like we said, we're just a few weeks into our freshman year. We don't have to know what we're gonna do."

"Yeah…" I said, leaning back into my pillow. "Do we still have to walk to class on Mondays or can we transport?"

"Girl, yes. I am not getting those freshman fifteen." She took another sip. "Besides that, I don't know about you, but transporting in bathrooms is so gross. I mean, I don't like bathrooms in general. I go home if I have to go. Public bathrooms are for nonmagicals."

I furrowed my brow. "Are you…serious?"

"Yeah." She made a face. "Don't you?"

"No!" But the idea was so hysterical, laughter bubbled out of me. Before I knew it, we were both howling, wiping tears from our eyes. After the heavy day I'd had, it felt good to laugh.

"What other weird stuff do you do?" I asked.

"What weird stuff do *you* do?" she said. "Weird is in the eye of the beholder."

I supposed that was true. "I just go home on Sundays to have dinner with my sister. And…I guess I travel around the world with my dad. Or I used to."

"Yeah, so…" She refilled my glass with more wine. "Let's

hear about your crazy life, hm?"

I took a long breath and then I told her everything. From the day I learned about magic to meeting Gavon for the first time, all the way through James arriving my senior year and Gavon paying for school. I spoke until my voice was hoarse, at which point I took a very welcome drink of the wine.

"Wow," Sam said, having climbed up on my bed to drink with me. "Just...wow."

"I told you it was complicated."

"You're telling me," she said, summoning the bottle and refilling my cup and hers. "So your dad is really from an alternate dimension?"

I nodded, then hedged. "Not really. It's more like a big magical pocket."

"What's a magical pocket?"

I was about to explain, then decided against it, summoning my pocket and opening the door, leading her inside. She released a loud cry of surprise and then spun around a few times.

"Whoa, okay, you definitely know more about magic than I do," she said. "Are all these books magical? Is this that library you were talking about?"

I nodded, growing a little sad. "My dad gave them to me. We've been collecting for ages. He helped me make this pocket so..." I flushed. "So I'd have a place to hide when I wanted to get away—"

"From your nonmagical roommate?" she said with a chuckle. "I couldn't figure out where you'd run off to. I felt you around, but you weren't *around*."

"I was in here," I said, conjuring another chair for her to sit in.

"This is much nicer than our dorm furniture…" Her eyes lit up. "Oh great, we can charm our furniture now! I've been trying to get the mattress to be less lumpy."

"I…have no idea how to do that," I said. "Me and charms don't really get along. I usually set things on fire."

She laughed, obviously not believing me. "You're hilarious. With all that magic you've got?"

"I'm serious!" I said. "You should've seen me the first time I tried to take notes magically. I erased the entire chalkboard."

Her eyebrows flew upward. "You mean you can use magic in front of nonmagicals?"

I opened my mouth, unsure. "Yeah. Remember how I said my dad's from New Salem? That means all those magical laws don't really apply to him. Or me."

"So what does that mean?"

"It means…" Again, I hesitated. "It means I don't have magic like you. I've got Warrior magic. So I can shoot attack spells—enough to hurt and even kill people. I've had magic since I was a baby, although my grandmother locked it away until I was fifteen. And…yeah, I guess I can use magic in front of nonmagicals."

"Wow," she said, shaking her head. "That sounds amazing. I can't even say the word in front of a nonmagical. I guess that explains what James was talking about then…"

I narrowed my eyes. "James? What does he have to do with anything?"

"Remember when I said he asked me out?" I nodded. "Well, he was really asking me to introduce him to his Clanmaster. And he was in this coffee shop, talking about magic and all that stuff, right in front of the nonmagicals." She smirked. "Of course, I was too busy telling him to screw off to really pay attention to what he was saying at the time."

I smiled. "What else did he say?"

"He told me I should tell you I was magical," she said, looking down. "And I guess I was getting kind of close to doing it, since you weren't paying attention to what I was putting out."

"Why did he tell you to tell me?"

"He said because you were kind of nervous,' she said. "And it was your dad's fault, mostly, but he'd exacerbated it by making a mistake a few months ago."

I picked at the chair. "Did he say what he did?"

"No, and I didn't ask," she said. "Because it was clear from how you were talking about him that he's a manipulator, and he was trying to get something out of me. And I hate him on principle 'cause he's your ex."

I shook my head, Gavon's warning clear in my mind. "You know what? I don't want to know. I'm done with him. He's the reason my dad got so mad at me. I didn't even mean to run into him at the Arlington School—"

"Oh, are you enrolling?" She puffed out her chest. "I'm a graduate. Six years I went there. That's actually where the group met."

"I'm not enrolling. He just happened to be there, talking with the director, and then he collapsed." I rubbed my face, trying to wipe his pale, lifeless face from my memory. "So I took him to my sister's apartment in Vegas—she's a Healer. And my other sister was there, she's a Potion-maker. Marie called my dad, then it all went downhill." I took another sip, recalling Gavon's face when I told him I didn't trust him. "All downhill."

"It's all right," Sam said. "The good news is you and I are now in the open with each other. And while I don't have any weird magic or strange family history, I do have a chemistry lab in the morning, so let's finish this wine so I can get to sleep."

I cringed. "Yeah, that's right. I have Latin in the morning, too."

She climbed off the bed and grinned at me, summoning her pajamas from the closet and magically dressing herself in a cloud of pink. "So I know your dad roomed us together to teach you a lesson or something, but I'm honestly really glad we're roommates."

"Yeah, me too."

And as I settled in to bed, I tried not to think about all those little signs of love Gavon left in my life. And how perhaps I'd been afraid of the truth for absolutely no reason at all.

Twenty-Nine

It was my turn to get an up-close-and-personal look at how another magical lived. And as with the magicals in Las Vegas and the Arlington School, there…wasn't much difference from how we were living before. We got up, went to class, spent hours in the library, did homework and…pretty much went about our lives. It seemed so incredible that I'd been expecting something different when the secret was out, but life went on as normal. Except, of course, we now summoned breakfast instead of walking to get it.

There hadn't been any abnormal intrusions lately either. I hadn't seen James since Vegas, and although I'd sent a couple texts to Gavon, I hadn't received a response—except for a smiley face when I told him Sam was magical. I didn't like this radio silence thing, but I hoped that one day he'd just show up on the park bench again.

But with Sam there to talk about all manner of things—magical and not—I finally was starting to find my footing.

"You are coming to trivia tonight, right?" Sam asked.

"Of course," I said, summoning the gift certificate I'd won a few weeks before. "So…everyone in the group has magic, right?"

"Yep. They're all from different clans, all over the country."

I stopped, pursing my lips. "They are?"

"Yep! Like I said, we all went to the Arlington School." She stopped. "Why?"

I picked up my notebook of Clanmasters—the one I'd been writing in when I ran into James at the Arlington School. Maybe I could find a few more masters for Gavon to talk with, and then we'd get our relationship back on track.

Later that night, we walked (yes, walked, to my annoyance) into the trivia bar, where the group greeted us with their usual vibrancy. In this crowded room, it was hard for me to focus on their kernels of magic, but I supposed now that I knew what I was looking for, I'd probably be better at finding it.

Chris gave me the once-over. "Glad you finally decided to be social with us."

"Hey, Lexie," Dave said, flashing me a wide grin. "What Chris is trying to say is we're glad you could join us."

"Me too," I said. "And…I'm really sorry I didn't say anything sooner. I honestly didn't know and—"

"It's all right," Dave said with a wave. "Sam filled us in on the major highlights."

I shared a grateful smile with Sam. It was kind of nice to have a friend who had my back. We followed the boys to the table in the very back.

"Magic?" Dave said as soon as we sat down. "Magic, magical, magic, magic."

"Spells. Spells and sorcery," Chris said, then nodded. "Think we're good."

I blinked. "What are you doing?"

"Gotta make sure the nonmagicals can't overhear us," Dave said, settling in beside me. "You know how you get a frog in your throat whenever you talk around them?"

"Sure…" I sipped my wine, and Sam snickered into her glass.

"So, Lexie," Chris began. "Spill. What's your deal?"

"My…deal?"

"Yeah, how come you didn't tell us you had magic?"

"Because she couldn't tell that you had magic," Sam said. "As I said."

"No, but I don't get it. How can you not tell that someone has magic?" Chris said, scratching his chin. "Like…were you raised in a barn?"

"*Chris*," Sam huffed. "God, why do I like you?"

"Good question," I said with a good-natured smile.

Even Dave choked on his water. "Is this a new, feisty Lexie?" he asked.

"Maybe," I said, retreating into myself again. This felt good —sitting in a group with them, being comfortable enough to shoot back like in a sparring match.

"So enough about Lexie," Sam said, catching my eye. "Why don't you guys tell her about yourselves? Like, really about yourselves?"

"Like what?" Chris asked.

"Like what clan you guys belong to," I said then turned to Sam. "I've never asked you which one you're in."

"Clan Grimes, mostly in the Pacific Northwest," she said. "But my mom used to be in Clan Driver, which is Dave's clan. That's how we knew each other."

"And I'm Clan Carrigan," Chris said.

Somehow, I wasn't surprised. Maybe it was the holier-than-thou attitude. "Yeah, me too." I paused. "Kind of."

"Are you?" Chris said. "You do look kind of familiar. But I've never felt magic like yours before."

Maybe he hadn't seen my epic explosion at Thanksgiving a few years before. Or Irene had wiped it from the clan's collective memories. "The Clanmaster is my grandmother."

Chris made a face. "Irene said her daughters died in a fire like twenty years ago."

I chuckled and shook my head, taking another sip of water. "Whatever she says."

"And Vicky and Amanda, they'll be here in a bit," Sam said, blessedly turning the conversation. "They're part of Clan Vargas."

"Really?" I said with a smile. Josefa would be so happy to hear I was meeting her clanmembers.

"Does Irene know you're alive?" Chris asked. "Did your dad leave when your mom told him about magic? That happens, too."

I snorted at his obvious digging. It was clear Irene wasn't very forthcoming. "Yeah. Irene knows I exist. Both my parents were magical. My mom died when I was a baby. We grew up outside the clan."

"Did you know about magic, then?" Dave asked.

"When I was fifteen."

Chris leaned across the table. "So why didn't you say anything?"

"Being magical is the least complex part about my family history," I said, pinching the bridge of my nose. I'd already shared it all with Sam. I didn't want to go over it again.

Luckily, I was saved from that particular fate as the twins arrived. They bypassed Chris and Dave, and sandwiched Sam and me, clearly eager to get the details about my big reveal.

"Josefa sends her regards," Vicki said with a grin. "And she wants to know when your sister is coming to visit her."

"I'm…working on her," I replied. "But I can't believe you guys are Clan Vargas. Small world. Do you know Martin?"

Amanda rolled her eyes. "He'd be cute if he wasn't so addicted to video games. But he's got a friend, Cisco, who's all kinds of dreamy. Pity he's nonmagical."

"Wait," Sam said, turning to me. "You've met their Clanmaster?"

"Yeah, it's part of that project my dad and I are working on," I said. "Just a couple times."

"She *loves* you," Amanda said.

Vicki shook her head. "She loves your sister more. She said something about how she's good with potions?"

"She is, sort of," I said. "Do you guys brew?"

"Oh, nothing worth writing home about." Amanda said. "Not like Josefa says we could do in the old days. Maybe we'll get back there again."

I opened my mouth to ask what she meant, but Chris had stood up and was waving someone over. Now that I knew what a magical kernel was, I felt it almost immediately. Perhaps because it was one so very familiar to me.

My heart skipped a beat as James and I locked gazes. He looked honestly surprised to see me there, his mouth falling open and his eyes widening.

"Whoa, Lexie," Sam said, placing a hand on my shoulder. "Chris, where did you pick this guy up?"

"We've been talking for a while," Chris said. "He's pretty cool. Has the same kind of weird magic that Lexie does. Thought they might know each other."

"We do," I said, narrowing my eyes at him. "Can I have a word with you, please?"

"Oh, but the game is about to start!" Dave said, and I didn't miss the look of uncertainty he gave James. Well, he needn't have worried.

"We'll just be a second," I said, not even bothering to plaster a smile onto my face as I dragged James out of the bar by his shirtsleeve.

I didn't speak until we were outside, releasing him and letting my blood boil as I stared at him.

"Lexie—"

"So, I promised Gavon I would avoid you, and here you are, hanging out with my friends," I barked. "What gives?"

"I didn't expect you to be here," he replied. "I thought you were still avoiding the truth about your friends."

"You know my magical radar is messed up!" I said, stomping my foot for effect.

"It's not messed up, you just think that because you can't see what's right in front of you half the time," he replied in that casual way that drove me insane. "Like all your friends being magicals."

I narrowed my eyes. That was true, but I wasn't about to admit it to him. "What are you doing here? Can you even tell me without having a seizure?"

"You know I can't," he said quietly.

"You know, *I* can't help but feel there's a mountain of things you *can* tell us, but are choosing not to," I said with growing anger. "Starting with why you decided to appear back in my life. Gavon said you didn't need to use my pact."

He was quiet, gathering his words before he spoke softly. "I did need your pact, but I can't tell you why. But, if I'm being honest…when I saw you out with that guy, I couldn't stand it."

My eyebrows lifted to my hairline. "Are you…serious? You're telling me you showed up on that park bench, lied about needing to be in my pact, because…" I shook my head, amazed that James could still leave me speechless. "Because you were jealous that I was on a date with someone else?"

He exhaled, and the tops of his cheeks turned pink. "Yes. No. I mean, I did need your pact. So it's both things."

"Are you…" I couldn't even find the words to describe the range of emotions that coursed through me. Anger, at his stupidity. Anger at him for being so selfish. Anger that he didn't have a better reason. Anger that if he hadn't gone and screwed everything up in the first place, I would still be his girlfriend and we wouldn't have had to go through this crap.

Okay, so it was mostly anger.

"And those girls you're dating?" I asked slowly.

"I told you, they didn't mean anything. I'm trying to…do the thing I can't tell you about," he said, his face growing redder as he strayed closer to the truth. "I still…Lexie, I still love you. And I'm sorry that things have happened the way they have but —"

I felt nothing at his words. "And did you think that if you just showed up, telling half-truths and lies, that I'd forgive you? That we'd go back to making out on the sparring beach?"

"No. I mean…maybe." He grinned hopefully, which melted at the scathing look I gave him. "I don't know. I thought I'd gauge your reaction and see. It was stupid, but…"

"Yeah, it was stupid!"

"I know," he said. "And I'm sorry. But…this thing I'm doing is exhausting. And I was so lonely. And you…" His eyes finally met mine, sending me a step backward at just how green they were. "Lexie, what we had last year was the best time of my life. I wanted to experience a bit of it again, even for a moment."

"Did it ever occur to you that I hate your guts?" I began slowly. "That your half-assed apology didn't mean anything to me?"

"I tried, Lexie. You know I'm sorry—"

"Stay away from my friends," I said. "I don't know or care what you and Gavon are doing, but they have nothing to do with it. Back off."

He released a loud blast of air. "Just…don't go anywhere with them tonight. As a personal favor to me."

"No, the only favor you get is inclusion in my clan," I said. "Now, get lost."

Thirty

It felt good to tell off James, and yet, all I could see were his eyes. Not when he said he loved me, but when he said our year was the best of his life. Because deep down, I agreed with him.

But that didn't mean I excused *any* of his behavior.

My hands shook when I walked back inside—my entire body felt like it was vibrating, actually—and I wished I had that bottle of wine.

Vicki and Amanda made room for me, and I sat back down, reaching for a slice of pizza and eating my feelings.

"You okay?" Sam asked.

I raised my gaze to hers and lifted half a shoulder. "Fine, I guess. He's gone."

"Sam said you used to bang him," Chris said.

It took all my willpower not to send him careening across the bar, but the glare I leveled in his direction was just as fierce. Chris, to his credit, recognized the threat and retreated into his chair.

"So, um…" Dave began quietly. "What did he want?"

"Nothing," I said, forcing a smile onto my face. "What question are we on?"

The trivia game went on, but my heart wasn't in it, so we got third place. It was hard not to sink back into my thoughts, or hear James in the back of my mind. But I forced myself to focus on Dave, who was being extra sweet and asking me questions about my week between the trivia.

"You were saying your Latin class helps you with magic?" he asked.

"Yeah," I said, pulling myself out of another funk. "My dad has a few books written exclusively in it, but I think the etymology aspect is the most interesting. Like where to words come from? I can see a lot of what I learned in French."

He nodded. "I guess I've never read a magical book before. You'll have to show me. Sam says you've got quite a collection."

She caught my eye and winked. "It's pretty incredible what this chick has on hand."

"Yeah, maybe we can go there for our next date." Why the hell not? There wasn't any reason I shouldn't actively date this handsome, rugged, magical Texan. Sure, he couldn't spar with me, but we could find plenty of things to talk about. And I was suddenly incredibly uninterested in Warriors.

He grinned. "Actually, I had some place else in mind. Are you busy tonight?"

"Tonight?" I checked my phone for the next morning. Wednesday's classes didn't start until noon. "Yeah, I'm up for it."

"Y'all want to come, too?" Dave said to the rest. "It's a big gathering of magicals. One of my cousins told me about it. Like a concert or something."

I chewed my lip for a moment. James had said I shouldn't go with them, but…Dave was harmless. And James was an asshole —probably just jealous that I was seeing someone else. "Where is it?"

"Out in the middle of nowhere," Sam said. "Seriously, Dave can't even tell us where it is."

"Why not?" I asked.

"Because it's one of those chain border spells," Dave said. "Alice said it's like a ticketing system, said she can bring up to ten people."

"I have to write a paper," Chris said.

"Yeah, I'm not really feeling up to it tonight," Shea said.

"Look, if it's lame, we'll just transport out," Dave said. "But Alice was really excited about it, and asked me to bring friends. It'll be over in an hour, tops." He grinned at me. "And if it's *really* lame, I'll take you out to dinner on Friday night."

I gathered my courage. "You could just do that anyway."

He smiled. "But let's do this thing tonight, okay? You said you're looking for more magical friends. There will be a bunch of them there tonight."

And probably from different clans, too. I wouldn't be able to talk to them all, but I bet I could get some more names for my book.

"Why not?" I said with a shrug. "Sam?"

She looked unconvinced. "I mean, it sounds kind of stupid. And I have class early tomorrow." She looked at her phone. "Oh, fine. I need to quit being such a damned old woman anyway. Let's have a ridiculously collegiate night."

After assembling in the back alley of the trivia place, we followed Dave's particular orange-colored magic to a spot somewhere in the wilds of Virginia. At least that was how it felt when we all showed up in a dark forest, the only lights coming from people's cellphone cameras. There were a ton of people here, all of them magical.

"Great, are we about to be murdered?" Sam asked.

"Very funny," Dave said. "Look, there's my cousin!"

Alice was a blond girl a few years older than us, and she introduced us to the rest of her friends and cousins, all from the same clan as Dave. As predicted, they gave me the weird once-over, but didn't ask me about my magic.

"What's happening?" I asked Alice. "What's this big thing?"

"It's like a concert or something?" she said with a shrug. "A friend of a friend invited me. There's some kind of charm involved—you only know about it if you're invited."

"Cool," I said, remembering something similar with that group of magicals who'd been busted by their parents. I hoped this wasn't the same thing. "Why the secrecy?"

"Because our parents and the Clanmasters are totally against this," Dave said with a grin.

My stomach dropped. So much for harmless. "Do you know anything about the Danvers Accord?"

He brightened. "Oh yeah, the pact that keeps us from specialties?"

"Of course you know what it is," I said, the bad feeling growing into something like stupidity. Had I just walked into another one of those meetings? I could tell Gavon it was in the pursuit of finding more magicals, but he hadn't bought that before. Maybe I'd just tell him I was out on a date. After all, it was clear my taste in men was downright godawful. How appropriate that the nice magical boy had dragged me into this mess once again.

"I take it you know Trent, then?" Dave said. "This is his show. Alice is the one who invited me, though. I haven't been to a meeting since school started."

I groaned. "Are you serious, Dave? These guys are idiots. There's no undoing the Accord. There's no way to bring back specialties or to do any of the stuff they're talking about."

"*Thank* you," Sam said, pulling her jacket tighter around herself. "I think all this talk about breaking the rules and doing magic in front of nonmagicals is ridiculous."

"I went to talk to these guys," I said. "They're flinging poor excuses for attack spells at each other. It's not...I mean, the Accord has been in place for three hundred years. It's not going anywhere anytime soon."

"That's not what I'm hearing," Dave said. "Look, maybe it's all bunk, but I've gotten pretty good at making that spell."

He formed a bright red ball in his hand. It was more powerful than those I'd seen in that little gathering, but it was still nothing compared to mine. But I decided against breaking out my magic just yet.

"I mean, some of what they're talking about is crazy," Dave said with a laugh. "I don't believe half of it, but it's nice to meet some new magicals. Alice is the one who's really into it."

I cursed under my breath and pulled out my phone, but

there was no service. And when I tried to send out a magical signal or even transport away, I found I could do neither. Something was tethering me to this place, like I was stuck on some kind of magical flypaper.

I tried not to panic. It wasn't as if I was helpless. I could also be worrying for nothing. But that little voice in the back of my mind was pretty much screaming that I had, yet again, walked into something I shouldn't have.

"I'll be right back," I said, hoping I didn't look concerned.

"You aren't leaving me alone here," Sam said, threading her arm through mine. "Something about this place gives me the willies. And I can't transport out of here."

"Yeah." I squeezed her arm reassuringly. "I'm sure it's nothing to be worried about."

From what I could tell in the darkness, there were those in the crowd who seemed worried, but many more who seemed excited—even eager. They stood in groups, talking in hushed voices with grins on their faces. I spotted several familiar faces, most of whom I'd seen at the meeting that had been busted, and a few more I recognized.

"There's the guy from the Arlington School for Magicals," I said, nodding to the sour-faced man who'd been Celeste's gatekeeper.

Sam followed my line of sight. "Oh man, I hate that guy."

We continued walking through the crowd, Sam pointing out various magicals who'd attended school with her, and me making a mental note of which clans they belonged to. My mind kept jumping back to Gavon and my goal of the Danvers reunion, but there weren't Clanmasters here. Just clanmembers.

From everything I'd read, members couldn't really do much.

"Lexie, hey!" Kailey, the girl from the Arlington School, waved emphatically at us. "Who's your friend?"

"This is Sam, my roommate," I said. "What are you doing here? I thought you were grounded?"

"I snuck out," she said with a smirk. "One of my friends transported me here."

"You look familiar," Sam said, squinting. "Do you go to Arlington?"

"Yeah," she said. "I'm in the fifth years."

"Right, I graduated last year," she said. "Do you know what's going on?"

"I do," she said cryptically. "But you guys will just have to find out when it starts."

"Yeah, I don't like the sound of that," Sam said. "Let's find the guys and get the hell out of here."

We made our way back to Dave and Chris and for the umpteenth time, I checked my cellphone for service and tested my ability to get a magical signal out of the area. But as before, nothing.

Now, even Chris was starting to get nervous, shifting his weight from foot to foot. "This whole thing had better be worth my time, Dave. Because I have two reports and twenty pages to read for my physics class tomorrow."

"Just do it magically," Dave said.

"I *can't*. My mom told me if she caught me cheating on homework, she'd quit paying for school."

"Poor Chris, has to answer to his mommy," Dave teased.

"Look, I don't know about you," Sam said, "but all of this is giving me super bad vibes. And I can't transport out—can't even get a text message. I want to go home."

"Me too," Chris said. "Lexie?"

"Yeah, all of this looks like trouble," I said. "Maybe if we walk far enough into the forest, we could get a signal or break free of the magical barrier."

Sam made a noise and huddled tighter to me. "That is the *last* thing I want to do, walk through some scary, dark forest. If whatever this is doesn't kill us, the redneck nonmagicals will."

I had to laugh. "Don't worry, Sam. I can protect all of us from whatever's out there."

I felt a presence behind me, and for the second time that night, knew exactly who it was, even before the rough hand grabbed and spun me around. He was white-faced, both from anger and maybe even a little worry as he pulled me away from the group.

"Didn't I explicitly tell you *not* to show up here?" he seethed.

"Oh, is this like with Meagan?" I said, prying his grip from my arm. "You don't want me to see you screwing your way through every clan in the US?"

"Lexie, this is the thing your dad wanted you to avoid," James said.

"*No shit, Sherlock!*" I screamed. "But oh no, I wanted to go out on a date so I could get *you* off my mind—"

"You are not blaming this on me," James cried, his tone quieter than mine, but no less forceful. He pointed at Dave accusingly. "I told you not to go with him anywhere, and you did the opposite of what I said!"

"Because you're a *liar!*"

"Okay!" Sam said, stepping between us as purple sparks flew from my fingers. "Both of you need to take a chill pill. So, James, what's going on here?"

He opened his mouth to respond, but no sound came out. A magical hush had fallen over the crowd, silencing the conversations. Even as I tried to speak, no sound came from my lips. Sam wore the same look of confusion, opening and closing her mouth. But I felt a tug toward the center of the gathering.

Trent stood on a makeshift platform, gazing out like some kind of preacher at his disciples. Now I was really starting to get nervous, and wished that I'd had the foresight to text Gavon my whereabouts. Maybe he'd be able to find me, like he had before. I just hoped he didn't think I'd done this intentionally; I could pin all this on Dave. Or James. Or both of them.

Maybe I should just stop dating altogether.

James stood at my shoulder, gently pulling Sam and me away from the crowd, but as he did, ghostly shadows appeared in the trees. Not shadows—magicals. They were boxing us in. And sure, I could release a few fireballs, but since I was there…maybe I could finally find out what the hell was going on.

"Thank you for joining us here today," Trent said with a sweeping gaze around the audience. I intentionally hid behind Dave, hoping my aforementioned "strange magic" didn't give me away. So far, he hadn't seemed to notice.

"I'm so pleased to see so many of you here," he said. "Tonight, I hope, will be the first night of the rest of your lives. A life where we no longer have to hide who we are. A life where we can return to the old ways of magic-making. Where we can restore the power and glory of magic to its rightful place."

I resisted the urge to snort, mostly out of respect for Dave, who was nodding in sincere appreciation. If what Trent had told me was true, then all these kids were in for a massive disappointment. But what I couldn't understand was how he'd been able to attract so many.

"Tonight, we will go on a journey together. By your arrival here, you've signaled that you're ready to take the next step with me. We will transport together to our new home."

"Shit," James mouthed.

Something hooked around my navel, pulling me forward.

Thirty-One

Screams echoed in my ears, but the sensation ended as soon as it began. I, along with everyone else, had landed in heaps on the ground in a dark room. As my senses came back to me, I felt…magic. More than I had before. The energy danced along my skin, seeking out my own underneath and reminding me of New Salem.

"Oh man, what the *hell*!" Sam croaked, rubbing her throat. "Well, glad I have my voice back."

"What happened?" Chris moaned, sitting up. "Dave, what did you do to us?"

"I don't know," he said, sitting up. "I didn't know any of this was going to happen."

"Lexie, are you okay?" Sam asked.

I nodded, but what had begun as nerves was now all-out panic. I still had no cell service, I still couldn't transport out of whatever room we'd been deposited into. James, who'd landed in a heap next to me, had grown even paler than before.

"Lexie…" he said, looking nervous. "Do you know where we are?"

"Whoa! Look at that!"

A girl's cry drew my attention to the left, where a guy stood holding a dark brown ball of magic. But it wasn't the meek, mild fireball of the post-Danvers magicals. It wasn't quite up to my level either, but it would certainly hurt.

"Holy…crap…" Sam said, holding up a fireball in that pretty pink color. Hers crackled and sizzled, much stronger than anything I'd felt from her before. Dave's red fireball and Chris's green one were similar in power.

"I was afraid of this," James whispered, coming to his feet. "The Danvers Accord doesn't apply in New Salem."

It took me a minute to register what he'd said. "New Salem? As in…we are in New Salem…*right now*?"

"Yes," he said. "That feeling? That was a complex transport charm—not even sure how they managed it with so many people. And there's no magic out of here either. That's how the pact works. Once you get in, you can't get out."

I released magic into the air, and it landed—hard—against something. "If we can't get out, how did we get in?"

"Variation on a containment charm," James said. "One that takes advantage of verbal chain pacts."

"Verbal…" I closed my eyes. "So when we agreed to come to the concert—"

"You were agreeing to all the fine print," James said. "Hence why I told you not to go. So now we're trapped in this room until the pacemaker lets us out."

"And who would that be?"

James nodded to the front of the room. "I'll give you one guess."

And of course, as soon as I had that thought, none other than Cyrus appeared in the center of the room. "Ah, my dear friends. Welcome to your new lives."

James grabbed me and forced me to my knees again. "Listen very carefully to me, okay? I want you to stay hidden. I'm going to try to find a way out of here. I'm pretty sure there *are* no ways, but maybe…" He shook his head. "Whatever you do, don't let Cyrus goad you into breaking the pact you have with him, all right? As long as it exists, he can't hurt you."

I nodded, too shocked to do anything else but trust him. What kind of pact was so powerful that it could trap a bunch of unsuspecting young magicals?

"My name is Cyrus Fairchild. You are all in a place called New Salem, the separate world created over three hundred years ago when John Chase banished my ancestors."

An uneasy energy washed through the room; perhaps they were all starting to realize they were trapped, as I had.

"You're here because you've expressed a desire to live more freely, to return to the old ways of the world. And here, you will be free to do that. Live amongst magicals without any barriers. Return to specialties."

"Except my magic is exactly the same," a teenager with a British accent said, coming to stand. "It's more powerful, yeah, but we were promised specialties. Warrior magic."

"Because of the Danvers accord, you won't gain the true powers of a Warrior," Cyrus replied casually. "But with training, you will be able to wield your magic effectively here. And in a generation, you'll be able to bring those powers back to the real world."

My heart skipped a beat as Cyrus's full plan became clear to me. He'd brought these magicals here under the pretense of giving them more powers, but in reality, he was just trying to make more…of me. More kids of the Danvers Accord magicals and New Salem magicals.

No wonder Gavon had been so focused on closing the tear recently.

Everyone else was too busy chatting with each other to pick up on that nuance yet. Cyrus walked through the crowd, smiling and pleased that he'd been able to fool them all.

That was…until he laid eyes on James and me.

"Ah, Alexis, James." Cyrus actually didn't look pleased to see me. He turned behind him and Trent appeared, bowing his head in shame. "I thought I was explicitly clear that Miss McKinnon—"

"Carrigan," I snapped.

"—wasn't to be included."

"I didn't realize she was here. She must've snuck in," he whispered. "I'll find out what happened—"

"Never mind," Cyrus said. "They're here now. And since Miss Carrigan is here, it must mean that I have no intention of harming her. Which, of course, I don't." His gaze slid to James. "But I'm curious how you're here, James. And why you aren't currently…well, dead."

"Loophole," James said, smirking. "If you told her yourself, our pact is rendered null and void."

Cyrus narrowed his eyes. Maybe James had outwitted him.

"How did you even get in here?"

"I was invited," he replied simply.

"Forgive me," Cyrus said with a chuckle that had very little humor in it. "But there was a very clear direction that neither you, nor Alexis, nor *Gavon* were to be informed about any of this. And my pacts are very well written."

"Well, see," James said, clearly enjoying that he'd gotten the better of Cyrus. "That direction was rendered null to anyone within five miles of Lexie's pact, as poor Trent found out when she crashed his party a few weeks ago."

Trent glowered in my direction and my mouth fell open. Was he talking about when Kailey had invited me to that last get-together? She'd seemed surprised she could talk to me about it at all.

"So all I had to do was become a temporary member of Clan Lexie, and I was able to score not one, but *several* invitations."

I pursed my lips at him, caught between amazement at his brilliance and annoyance that most of those invitations had been after he'd wooed girls all over the country.

"Very smart of you," Cyrus said, nodding. "But it appears your scheming is all in vain. You're still in this room, which means you can't get out to warn your precious Guildmaster. And you are hopelessly outnumbered."

"Outnumbered by what?" I said with a scoff. "These pathetic magicals? They may be a little stronger now, but they aren't anything compared to me."

Cyrus surveyed me, a smile appearing on his face, unnerving me. "You know, it's a good thing you're here, Alexis. I can show all my new friends just what I'm talking about.'

He moved closer and my skin tingled with disgust as his voice rose in volume to address the room again. "This, my friends, is Alexis. Her father, Gavon, is from this world. New Salem. Almost thirty years ago, he created a tear between our world and yours, introducing a new element. Alexis is the result —a magical with abilities not seen in your world for almost three hundred years. Merely as the product of a magical from New Salem and your world." His eyes sparkled as he looked at me. "A demonstration, if you please."

"No," I said, leveling my glare at him as James shifted next to me. "Like hell you'll trick me into a sparring match again."

He laughed, and it raised the hairs on the back of my neck. "My dear, this has nothing to do with our pact. Don't you see? I've moved beyond your family. My goal is now the entire world."

"The world?" I snorted. "Good luck with that."

"In light of our extensive history, and the pact you've mentioned," Cyrus said, after a moment. "I will allow you to walk out of this door. No retaliation to you or your sisters. As, of course, I'm still unable to bring them to harm, presuming the pact remains in place."

"Lexie, who the hell is this guy?"

Clinging to Chris, Sam stood behind me next to Dave, Alice, and the rest of the magicals. Amanda, Vicki. Kailey. Magicals from clans all over the world now looked to me to save them.

"What about them?" I asked Cyrus.

"Oh, they stay," he said. "And we'll make another new agreement that you won't breathe a word of this to anyone, including your father, your lover, or any of the others."

I flinched at the word 'lover,' but recovered quickly. "I'm not leaving them here. Not so you can breed them."

"Hang on, *what*?" Sam said, looking between me and Cyrus. "Breeding?"

"You heard him," I said, raising my voice so the rest of the group could hear me. "He said you wouldn't get your powers now, but in a generation. The moment you walk back into the real world, you return to the magic you had before. You go back to your life. But have a kid with a New Salem magical, and they end up like me."

"But I'm eighteen," Sam said, stepping away from Chris a little. "This all sounds well and good, but I'm not ready to have kids yet."

"You'll be happy here," Cyrus said, dipping into a sugary-sweet salesman voice. "It's what you wanted, after all. A place to practice your magic, a place to spread your wings and truly be yourselves without the confines of that pesky Accord. Magicals can be magicals."

"I don't give a crap about that," Sam said. "I want to go home."

A chorus of agreement rose up around us, which made me uneasy. Cyrus was nothing if not thorough, and he wouldn't have brought everyone here if he didn't have a well-thought out way to make them stay.

"Cyrus, this is ridiculous," James said. "You aren't keeping them here, and you can't make them stay. They haven't signed any pacts and you can't force them to."

"Oh, can't I?" he said, his voice taking on a singsong cadence. "Then strike me, if you're so eager to get involved."

I looked at James. I couldn't get into it with Cyrus, but he could. So what was he waiting for? Was he not sure he could defeat Cyrus? Did I have to do everything around here?

Then again, I wasn't sure I could win, either.

"If you're wondering why your lover remains paralyzed," Cyrus said, gesturing to the magicals lining the room. I'd barely noticed them before, too preoccupied with my friends and Cyrus. But they were numerous, perhaps numbering over a hundred, all wearing black robes and unfriendly expressions.

"Who are they?" I asked.

"A little experiment I've been running these last few years. The magicals have been restless on your side, chafing against the bounds of the Danvers Accord. This group is the second I've brought to New Salem. These other magicals are the first."

"Willingly?" I said.

"Of course," he replied. "I just had to show them the power of Warrior magic and they couldn't sign up fast enough. I gave them instructions and sent them back out into the world to find more. Trent, here, brought back this group." Cyrus gestured to the man behind him. "And how do you feel? Powerful?"

"Very much so," he said, with almost cult-like glee.

"These magicals here may not have Warrior magic, Alexis, but even you can tell they can do some damage. One or two, maybe not. But twenty of them have been under my steady training these past two years." He shrugged. "Care to test my teaching?"

"These guys don't scare me, and neither do you."

"They should," James muttered under his breath. "You can't fight a hundred magicals by yourself, Lexie."

"Good thing I've got you here, then," I snapped. "Their magic is pathetic—"

As if testing me, three fireballs came toward me at once. I only just put up a barrier spell to deflect them. Together, they were as powerful as any of my own.

"Just a small test," Cyrus said. "The offer is still open to walk out the door."

"I'm not leaving my friends," I said, catching James's eye. He seemed to have come to the same conclusion. We had no options—no good ones, anyway. Leave Sam, Dave, and the rest of these poor magicals to be trapped in this world. Fight Cyrus and his goons and risk death or worse.

I opened my palms and formed two attack spells, appreciating how beautiful and powerful they seemed in this room, especially after seeing what my enemy could produce.

"Wow," Sam breathed behind me. "That's...your magic?"

"Jeez, Lexie," Dave said.

"I guess we're really doing this, huh?" James said. He opened his palms, his magic a vibrant green next to my own. The sight of them side by side gave me a little confidence, especially when he looked behind us to those gathered and asked, "Any of you know how to create a barrier spell?"

"N-no?" Sam said, and Dave shook his head.

"I can," Chris said. "Irene made sure we knew how."

"Do you think that barrier is enough to protect them?" I asked under my breath.

"No, so we'll need to draw their magic," James said. "But Cyrus isn't going to risk killing any of them. He's been planning this for too long."

"Right." I looked at Chris, flashing him a smile. "Erect a barrier around everyone who isn't trying to kill us. James and I will…" I smiled at him, surprisingly thrilled at the prospect of getting into it with these guys.

"Do what Warriors do," he said with a grin.

Thirty-Two

The first attack spell came toward me, and I sent it back with twice the power. The magical didn't know what hit him, flying backward and landing upside-down against the wall. I cringed a little, but there was no time to dwell. Two more came in its place, then five more—then more than I could count. It was all I could do to bat one away before ten more took its place. And when they hit, they stung. One didn't feel too bad, but when five slipped through at once, I fell to my knees, wheezing.

"C'mon!" James said, surrounded by a green ball of barrier magic. "Now is *not* the time to be timid."

I jumped to my feet, glancing behind me at the barrier spell, keeping the scared young, magicals safe from errant attack spells. I caught Sam's gaze and she nodded at me.

"This is who you are, Lexie," James said, knocking another one. "So don't hold back."

I shrugged and my magic grew brighter in my palms. He was right; this was me. And who cared if I was different? Right now, different was saving our asses.

"There it is," he said with a grin. "Let's show these guys what Warrior Magic does, hm?"

Cyrus's laughter strengthened my resolve. I surrounded myself with a magical barrier and allowed their magic to hit it with wild abandon. But that tactic didn't last long, not with the constant pressure of magic against it.

So I used the last bit of barrier to protect me as I concentrated on the twenty or so magicals who'd surrounded me. Then in one movement, I released twenty attack spells, sending them into unconsciousness. But that strategy didn't work so well, not when there were twenty more to take their place.

"Quit wasting your magic," James snapped.

"I'm not wasting shit," I barked back.

But it was true, I was already winded. Perhaps I should've been sparring on the beach more.

"You look a bit roughed up, Alexis," Cyrus said, standing off to the side, observing. "Perhaps you and I can settle this like old times."

"You'd like that, wouldn't you?" I said, wiping my lip. "Was that your game? Exhaust some of my magic with your little minions, then goad me into breaking the pact?"

"Oh, no, no. This was all your decision," he said. "As usual, you thought to play the hero, and now you've got yourself in too deep, waiting for your father to come save you. And this time, you've gotten poor James into trouble as well. When *will* you learn?"

"This *wasn't* my fault," I snapped.

"It never is, is it?" Cyrus said, shaking his head. "As it stands, you've more than proven my point to your brethren. I'm sure, after seeing the ease with which you wield Warrior magic, they'll all be clamoring to join my cause."

"Or not," James said, turning behind him. His brow furrowed. "Lexie, where is—"

"This one?" Cyrus said, Sam appearing beside him with a whimper. Behind me, Chris and Dave cried out, but the barrier was still intact. "Your magic, while improved here, still lacks the basic strength that comes with Warrior magic."

"Let her go," I said, as James brushed my fingers with his.

"Don't do anything stupid," he muttered.

"I think I've proven my point," Cyrus said, his hand lingering near Sam's face as he formed a small attack spell in his hand. "You cannot win here. I don't wish to kill one of the magicals, but you've given me no choice." He smiled. "And I don't believe, in your weakened state, that either of you would be capable of defeating me. So I am giving you one *last* chance. Walk out the door, or your friend dies."

I caught James's eye and he nodded. I could tell he was tired, from the sheen of sweat on his forehead to the way his magic hung around him. But there was no other option—I couldn't just leave Sam here. I had no doubt Cyrus would kill her the moment I let her out of my sight—or worse.

"Do it," James whispered. "We'll figure it out."

"I thought you said not to do anything stupid," I murmured.

"You aren't going to find another roommate like her," he said, brushing his fingers against mine again. "Besides that, together we can take him on."

I didn't believe him, but we didn't have another choice. I'd defeated him once before, and I could damned sure do it again.

I formed a spell in my hand. "Let her go, or your ass is grass."

Cyrus readied his magic toward Sam. "I am so looking forward to finally watching you die, Alexis."

"You first."

I released a blast of magic, regretting it but allowing it to move forward. But just before it hit Cyrus, a bright burst of purple appeared, knocking my spell away.

"Cyrus, enough of this," Gavon boomed, exuding all the force and fury I would've expected from the Guildmaster of an evil clan. His furious gaze landed on James and me, and I fought the urge to duck behind James.

"I swear I wasn't looking for trouble! Please don't cut off my tuition!" I cried, not caring that I'd just defeated several magicals and stood in front of my mortal enemy.

"Are you two all right?" Gavon asked, not tearing his gaze from Cyrus, who returned it with a furious insolence.

"How did you even find us?" James asked.

"I went back to the Vegas magical place, heard a couple idiots talking about this thing, so I told Dad," Marie said, appearing in-between James and me. She clamped down on our arms and healing magic crept up my arm. Another hand clamped down on my other arm—Nicole was doing her best to heal me, too. She offered a relieved smile, and I joined it.

"And I informed a few more people," Gavon said.

There was a deluge of magic—powerful magic. Puffs of every color of the rainbow appeared in the center of the room. Josefa,

Irene, Clanmasters from all over appeared next to their members, standing protectively between them and those from Cyrus's side.

"Shit," James cursed. "They shouldn't have come."

"Why not?" I said. "We need all the firepower we can get.".

"Yeah, but now *they're* stuck here, too," James said, nodding to the Clanmasters. None of them had left, contained by the same magic keeping James and me in place, along with all the others in the room. "That's the pact, Gavon. It's a chain, only breakable by Cyrus."

"Cyrus, as the Guildmaster, I command you to end this nonsense and allow these people to return to their world," Gavon said, his voice low and even.

"I don't think so." Cyrus laughed, but he was still nervous. He hadn't been expecting Gavon to show up—or had he? They'd been playing chess for a very long time, it was hard to tell who had the upper hand. "There are those here who are willing to listen, who want to stay. It would be wrong of you to make them return to their lives."

"I see no one here willingly," Gavon said. "Remove the barrier keeping them in this room. If, as you say, everyone wants to be here, then your ranks will remain as strong as ever."

"No, they won't!" Irene said, barging forward. I was surprised to see her move so quickly for someone so old. "I am in charge of Clan Carrigan, and my members will be coming home with *me*."

"Ah, Irene, good to see you again," Cyrus said. "I think you'll find that your iron-fisted rule has resulted in more than a few defections. So many magicals are leaving your clan. Many of them came to me on bended knee asking for the alternatives you wouldn't talk to them about."

"Alternatives you were more than happy to provide," Gavon replied. "Until, presumably, they realized that their powers were still limited. I doubt you had very many willing participants, then, did you Cyrus?"

"It doesn't matter," Cyrus said. "The Guild will be on my side. They'll overrule you and the magicals we have here will stay. You have no power here."

Irene's power flooded the room. "Oh, don't I?"

"I've grown tired of your voice," Cyrus said. "Please do give my regards to your daughters."

He reacted faster than I could, but this time, Gavon knocked the fireball away. He wore a look of fury, but I wasn't sure if it was because of Cyrus or because he was forced to save Irene.

"You get one," he said to Irene. "Now get back to safety before he targets you again."

"Gavon, Gavon," Cyrus tutted. "This is all wasted effort. You can't fight me, not while you're still the Guildmaster."

"Then I renounce it."

Cyrus's smile fell. "What?"

"I renounce my position as Guildmaster," Gavon said, as if he'd been waiting for this moment for thirty years. "I believe I'll bestow it on Mary. I'm sure she'll be more than willing to sign an updated Danvers Accord."

For the first time since I'd known him, Cyrus was too stunned for words.

"Now, shall we have our rematch?" Gavon asked softly. "I believe it's quite overdue."

Cyrus curled his lip then disappeared in a puff of gray—Gavon following in purple.

I closed my eyes, searching for their magical signatures. They were at the sparring arena, but…I wasn't able to transport out of the room.

"We're still stuck here until Cyrus releases us from the pact," James said.

"But Gavon—"

"Gavon didn't formally renounce the Guildmaster until he said it just now, so it didn't apply to him. His power supersedes Cyrus's."

"Magicals have too many damned loopholes. Can't we just walk out the door?" I said, frantic. I didn't like the idea of Gavon and Cyrus in a death match without me.

"Sure," James said, nodding to the front of the room, where Cyrus's magicals stood guarding the exit. "Just go through them."

I balled my fists, counting them. At least fifty remained of the ones I'd already tangled with, and even more waited their turn. Even with Marie and Nicole's healing magic, we were out-numbered and trapped still.

"We have a problem," Irene said, walking up to me. "We cannot get out of this room magically."

"Which is why I told you *not* to come," James said with a glare. "But no, I don't know what I'm talking about, right?"

"James, Gram, stop it," Marie said. "We need to focus on a plan."

"And that's coming from her, too," I said, with a meaningful look. "How can we break this pact, James?"

"It's a basic barrier spell," James said, glancing to Nicole. "Think you can whip up a potion if I tell you how to make it?"

"I can help you there," Josefa said, appearing with Vicki and Amanda in tow. She beamed at Nicole. "You've gotten a lot bigger since the last time we spoke. I know a good potion that can dissolve the barrier."

"But I don't have—"

Josefa procured a cauldron. "Come on, if you make it, it'll be much more powerful."

"Oi!" Trent appeared, clearly taking over in Cyrus's absence. "Stop what you're doing! I command it!"

"We've got to take care of these guys," James said, shaking out his shoulders. "Are you ready to go?"

"What about them?" I said, looking at the magicals and Clanmasters still waiting for direction. "We can't protect them all at the same time."

"We'll help," Irene said. "Christopher, barrier spell, please."

"But it didn't work—"

"Yours with mine will work," she said, although it was less harsh than usual. "Help your cousin buy your other cousin some time. We'll protect you, Alexis. The other Clanmasters will protect their kin."

"Thanks," I said, offering her a meaningful smile as her magic surrounded me. "So about that Danvers Accord..."

"Lexie, not the time," James said, glowing a little pink from Sam's magic. Her Clanmaster stood next to her, nodding approvingly as she cast a large bubble around the room—joined by the magic of the rest of the Clanmasters.

"Right," I said. "So we're taking out as many as we can until

Nicole's potion is ready, then try to walk out the front door?"

"Basically," James said, wiping sweat off his cheek.

"I want to help," Dave said, stepping forward. "I know how to fight these guys."

"Me too!"

A chorus of agreement rose up around us, and I shrugged. "We could use all the help we can get."

"Don't die," James barked at Dave, clearly still upset that he'd dragged us into this mess in the first place. "I'm not saving you."

"And don't…" Irene wore a look. "Don't kill them. Please. They may not be ours, but I recognize a few of them."

"We'll try," James said, when I had no response. "Ready, Lexie?"

"Why not? Round two, here we go." We walked out of the bubble, refreshed and rejuvenated, and flanked by several other magicals. "So, any chance you guys want to lay down your weapons and surrender?"

Three fireballs was my response, and we were back at it. This time, surrounded by barrier spells and aided by the well-timed weak attack spells, the magicals in the room went down a little faster. With Irene's protective magic, plus that of a few others, attack spells bounced harmlessly off my body, leaving me free to work on one magical at a time. Beside me, James was beautiful, aiming for his targets with dangerous accuracy.

Out the corner of my eye, I spotted Sam, Dave, Marie, and Nicole sneaking toward the large, iron front door. Catching James's eye, I intentionally drew the attention of the magicals closest to the door to give them some cover. And when the guards at the door wouldn't budge, I released a furious spell in quick succession, knocking them to the ground. Nicole and Sam dove over their bodies, Dave providing cover as Nicole uncorked the vial and dumped it on the barrier.

"Got it!" she cried.

The barrier collapsed immediately and a weight I hadn't even noticed disappeared from my chest. It didn't take the other magicals long to realize it either, as they started disappearing in puffs from behind the barrier. But not just from behind the barrier, either. Cyrus's army was defecting fast, leaving just a few stragglers—including Trent, who was red-faced as he charged toward me.

"You've ruined *everything*." Trent stood in front of me, huffing and puffing.

"Dude," I said with a laugh. And with a flick of my wrist, I sent him careening back into the wall. "Don't even start with me." I turned around, looking for more. "Who's next?"

"They've all vanished," James said, limping over to me. "Probably didn't want to chance it against us."

"Maybe they were as trapped as we were," I said, wiping my forehead and allowing exhaustion to swim around my brain.

"I swear to God, Lexie," Marie said, appearing next to of us and healing us again. "How many times do we have to show up and pull your ass out of the fire?"

"Thanks," I said to her and then smiled at Nicole. "And thank you. I think you just saved everyone."

"See?" Josefa said proudly. "I told you your magic was impressive. At four years old, you were incredible. Now when are you coming to visit?"

"Um…at some point in the future," Nicole said, flushing bright red. "Is everyone gone?"

I spun around, taking in the magically-enlarged room. It was now empty, save the unconscious magicals lining the wall.

A puff of magic appeared next to me—Sam and her Clanmaster. I pulled Sam into an embrace, holding her as tightly as she'd held me the day we'd met.

"I'm glad you're okay," I said, looking at her Clanmaster, who was giving me the evil eye. "Where's Chris? Dave?"

"They're all okay. Chris went back with Dave," Sam said, glancing at Irene behind me. "We're going to have a long chat about all this, starting with you teaching me how to use magic like that. *You* are an *amazing* badass! I had no idea you had all that inside you!"

I laughed, smiling bashfully, but it died when her Clanmaster made a dismissive noise.

"Your parents are going to have a field day with this, Samantha," she said, sternly. "They may even ask me to permanently lock you in your room."

"That won't work, Geri," Irene said, walking over to us. She had a few bruises on her forehead, but neither Nicole nor Marie made any move to heal her. "With kids, you have to give them a little room to fail."

"Oh yeah?" I said, glaring at her. "When did you come to this great realization?"

"Since I realized half the kids you unceremoniously beat the shit out of were former members of my clan," she said wearily. "Thank you for not killing them."

I took a step back; I hadn't actually thought she was serious.

"Um...you're welcome."

"Geri, I can vouch for Ale...Lexie," Irene said. "She's a good kid, and I think she and Samantha would benefit from being in each others' company at school."

My mouth fell open. Geri didn't look convinced, but said, "We'll discuss it at home."

"See you back at the dorm?" Sam said with a hopeful look before she disappeared in a puff of green.

"Thanks for that," I said to Irene. "So about the Danvers Accord..."

"I am sure we will have a long conversation about it," Irene said, with a shake of her head. "Especially considering what we've learned about the Accord in New Salem."

"But now, Lexie..." James said, wearing a worried look. "We have to find Gavon."

Thirty-Three

There was only one place they could be, and James and I transported there without a word to one another. The dome of magic, colored dark gray and purple, loomed over the sparring arena. All that was visible inside were two blurs and fiery balls of magic. Two masters at their craft, squaring off to the death.

"This is why Alexandra never wanted you to be Guildmaster," Gavon called during a brief pause in the action. "You lack the composure to do what's right for the greater good."

"And you lack the stomach to do the hard thing. How long did it take you to avenge the death of your wife? How many times did you put your daughter in danger?"

Gavon released another angry wave of magic, sending Cyrus backward. Then they moved, nothing but magic and fury, all conversation lost.

"This is a lot less terrifying from this angle," I said to James.

"Not when you know you're next, if Gavon fails," he replied,

315

gripping the stone barrier.

"I'll go next," I said. "I've beaten him before—"

"I have a few months of pent-up anger to get out at him," James said, covering my hand with his. "And you've done enough."

"All I wanted was to go out with my friends," I said, although my attention was on his hand over mine, and how nice it felt to have him right there with me.

"Told you that Dave was trouble."

I glared at him. "And all that crap about you being jealous?"

"Was also true." He tore his gaze away from the fighting for a moment to grin at me. "But I also knew he was involved in this, and so I was doing my best to keep him out of it. And you."

"Did you really date all those girls to get an invite to this thing?" I asked hesitantly.

"Told you it didn't mean anything," he said.

"Yeah, you just slept with all of them."

At that, he laughed. "Lexie, you're the only girl I've slept with."

"You're so full of shit, James. You slept your way through my entire senior class."

"Dated, yes. Slept with, no," James said with a mock look of hurt. "You really think so little of me?"

I flushed, turning back to the furious fighting. "I still don't forgive you."

"I guess I'll just have to worm my way back into your good graces."

"Good luck with that."

"I did it before."

"Can you two quit flirting for just *one* minute and let us concentrate," Nicole said, appearing beside us with Marie. They both looked tired—Marie a little paler than usual. But they stood beside us watching the blurs of magic move.

"Look out!" James cried, throwing up a barrier spell over the four of us as a wave of magic exploded across the ring. Even with the magic protecting us, my ears rang for a few moments and dust kept smacking against James's barrier. I uncurled myself from around Nicole to squint into the dusty abyss.

"What happened?" I said.

"They…" James tilted his head forward, as if trying to see. "Come on."

We left Marie and Nicole in the barrier spell and dashed into the ring. James could see better than I could, so I held his hand as we ran onto the cracked stone. The dust had begun to settle, and I could make out a man lying on the ground.

"Dad!" I cried, running toward him.

"No, it's Cyrus," James said, slowing my gait.

My eyes adjusted to the brightening light and I made out his form. Still, lifeless.

Cyrus was finally dead.

He stared up at the sky, his ashen face frozen in turmoil. I hoped in his last minutes, he'd thought about all the horrible things he'd done, and regretted them. But knowing him, he probably just thought about how much it sucked that he was dying. Selfish prick.

A shrill scream echoed across the plain, and my heart fell into my stomach.

James and I raced toward the sound, toward Marie and Nicole who hunched over a comatose form. I fell to my knees beside them, momentarily stunned by Gavon's face. He was pale...ashen almost. The same way Jeanie had looked when Cyrus killed her.

"He's not breathing," Marie said, panic in her voice.

"There's no pulse," Nicole moaned, holding his hand. "There's no pulse. Marie, he's dead."

"He's not dead yet," Marie said, rolling up her sleeves and pressing her hands to his face. "Not yet. Not yet. Not yet."

I realized she wasn't confirming it, she was hoping for it. And my stomach dropped.

"Come on, Dad. I know you're still in there," Marie whispered as a tear streaked down her dusty face. "We still have a lot of stuff to talk about. And you've got to help Nicole with her baby. C'mon." She shot Nicole a look. "Nicole, use some of that baby healing magic and help me."

"I don't know what to do," Nicole said, her hands folded in her lap.

"Just grab hold of him," Marie ordered. "Grab hold and try to find…find some kind of life. Anything small will do. Just something to pull him back."

Nicole pressed her hand to his leg and closed her eyes, but soon the tears were falling down her cheek. Even though I didn't have healing magic, I took Gavon's tepid hand in mind, and across from me, James did the same. The only sound was the fevered whispering from Marie.

"Marie, I think he's…"

"I am *not* losing him," she snarled.

"He's gone, Marie," I whispered, putting his hand down.

"*No!*" Marie screamed, grabbing his face harder. "No, he can't be. It's not his time. He was supposed to have his happy ending."

"Marie—"

She gasped, her eyes opening. "Shut up."

She exhaled deeply and closed her eyes, her hands glowing white. Gavon's chest began to rise and fall ever-so-slightly. I picked up his hand once more, and felt a small pulse—not much, but enough to reignite hope in my chest.

"Marie, you need to stop—"

"Not yet," she slurred. "Not until…" She slumped against him.

"Marie!" I cried, catching her before she fell to the ground.

"Healing potions," James said, his voice thick with emotion. "We need to brew some healing potions."

"My apartment," Nicole said, rising to her feet, an oddly determined look on her face. "Evil guy, can you bring Gavon? Lexie, bring Marie. And…me, I guess."

We arrived back in Nicole's apartment in a buzz of activity, and I barely noticed Guy sitting on the couch until he cried out in surprise.

"What the actual hell is going on here?" he said.

Nicole paused then looked him straight in the eye. "Guy, I have magic, my sister and estranged father are dying and I have to brew a healing potion, and…well, I'm pregnant, so—"

Guy's face broke into a smile. "For real? Pregnant?"

Nicole blinked. "Did you not hear what I just said?"

"I mean," he gestured to the levitating pair in front of us, "the rest is pretty obvious. But you're really pregnant?"

She nodded. "And you don't think I'm crazy and you don't want to leave me?"

"Of course not," he said. "But only if you'll marry me."

"Deal," Nicole said. "But first I have to fix them."

"Well, that was a lot easier than you made it out to be," I muttered, following them into the living room. She deposited Marie on the couch but left Gavon in the center of the room. Then she hurried into the kitchen, her potions book appearing before her. With a furrowed brow, she quickly flipped the pages, ingredients appearing beside her as she searched.

James took a spot beside her. "Let me help. I've made potions before."

She stared at him for a moment, unsure whether to trust him, then nodded. "Fine."

As they worked, I summoned a vial of healing potion from my magical pocket. I opened Gavon's mouth and poured it down, pressing my hand to his forehead and willing him to wake up. His skin was pale and clammy, but his chest was still moving. Marie, too, looked close to death, but I was less worried about her.

"Come on, Dad," I whispered, holding his hand. "You can't die. You'd be so happy to know Nicole is brewing a potion. And we have to talk about everything. Irene couldn't believe it when you renounced the Guildmastership."

"So this is y'all's dad?" Guy said behind me.

"Yeah," I said, looking over my shoulder. "This is Gavon. He said he liked you."

"I met him a few times," Guy said, taking a seat beside Marie and holding her hand. "He made me promise not to tell Nic. Said he was just looking out for her. Seemed like he really cared about her."

I nodded. "He did. Just…made a lot of mistakes."

"Don't we all," Guy said. "So…do you mind telling me more about this magic thing? Are you guys witches or what?"

I laughed, the sound weird against my mood. "The term is magical. I'm sure Nicole will fill you in on all the details."

"Does she normally have all this…sort of levitation stuff?" he asked. "Cause if so, she did a real good job hiding it from me."

"Nah, her specialty is potion-making," I said, stroking Gavon's hand. "But your kid is going to be a Healer, so that's why she has magic now."

"Oh," he said, as if he completely understood what I was saying. "So…she's really pregnant? Is that why she's been acting so weird lately?"

"That and she didn't know how to tell you she had magic," I said, looking at Gavon again. "And, well, all this mess. With our dad and mom."

"So you flying down to visit, that was just…?"

"Magic."

"Mm." He rose, a confused look on his face. "I'm gonna see if they need any help in the kitchen."

Guy disappeared through the doorway, leaving me alone with my thoughts once more. I kept staring at Gavon, willing him to wake up and smile at me. I'd even take a lecture from him at this point. Anything that would show he was still in there.

My phone buzzed in my pocket, and I jumped, having forgotten it was even there. I yanked it out with my free hand, amazed that it had survived all of the excitement.

You okay? Sam texted.

I looked at Gavon then typed out, *Yes, barely. Back home. We'll talk later.*

My parents are talking about yanking me from G-town. I'm so upset.

I hope it's not because of me.

I won't lie, they aren't happy you're involved.

Hey, we can blame all this on Dave.

Yeah, screw Dave.

I chuckled, looking at Gavon and kissing his hand. *Cyrus, the bad guy, he's dead. You can tell your parents that.*

Except that whole place exists. My auntie was telling me there's a movement amongst the Clanmasters to close it up.

I snorted. *My dad's been barking up that tree for decades. Better to just update the damned Accord.*

We have a lot more to talk about, don't we?

Yeah.

I typed out a text, *My dad is dying* but I didn't send it. I couldn't. That would make it too real. So I placed Gavon's hand back on the couch, kissed both him and Marie on the foreheads, and walked to the kitchen where Nicole and James were arguing over a cauldron.

"No, that's not right," Nicole said, pulling the ingredient away from him. "It's gotta be this stuff."

"I've made this potion a thousand times," James said hotly. "And it's this way."

"Fine," she summoned her own cauldron. "Then I'll just brew my own and we'll see which one works better."

"Shouldn't you listen to her?" Guy said. "Lexie said she's a Potion-maker?"

"It's fine, Guy," Nicole said in a clipped voice. "If he's the expert."

"I'm just trying to save his life, that's all," James snapped.

"James," I said, intervening. "Let Nicole do her thing. I know you want to help, but she is a Potion-maker."

He threw down the bundle of herbs and held his hands up. "Fine. Do what you want."

I followed him back into the living room. He was staring at Gavon, his hair messed up and his eyes wet with unshed tears.

"Lexie, I don't know what I'll do if Gavon dies," he whispered. "I'm not ready for him to die. I know he's your father, but he raised me."

I took his hand in mine.

"I never got to tell him the truth," he said. "I wanted to so much. I just wanted him to understand, I didn't mean any of it. The last thing I ever wanted to do was to get you involved in anything. But I panicked."

"What happened…that night?"

He was quiet for a long time. "The night we slept together, I left early. Around midnight. Any longer and Gavon would've gotten suspicious about my whereabouts. And the last thing I wanted was for him to show up and see us together." He swallowed. "On my way back through the tear, I saw Cyrus leaving. So I followed him—I knew he was probably up to something. He was speaking with that guy Trent. I heard enough of the conversation to know what was happening, and I went to warn Gavon. But Cyrus had his men detain me. There were too many of them, and I couldn't get away. As you saw, one on one, they aren't really that powerful. But twenty of them?

"Cyrus said if I didn't agree to his pact forbidding me to speak of what I knew, he'd send his people after you and your sisters. They weren't bound by the edict, and they could kill whomever they chose. Cyrus said he'd just have one of his people walk into the pharmacy where your sister worked and shoot her dead. I didn't want to even risk that, so I agreed to his terms. He tapped into the power of our guild to enforce the pact. So it stood to reason that if Cyrus was kicked *out*, our pact would be nullified, too.

"So I took your sisters so Gavon would investigate and find cause to finally throw Cyrus out of the Guild. You were supposed to go to him first but…" He sighed. "This was all thought up in the span of about an hour and it wasn't very bright. But I was afraid, and I didn't know what else to do." He turned to me, sincerity in his eyes. "I wanted to tell you every single day. I'm sorry."

"Apology not accepted," Nicole said, appearing in the doorway with two mugs of something steaming. "Now get out of the way so I can give this to them."

James and I moved as Nicole handed the cups to Guy. She gently opened Gavon's mouth and poured the liquid down his throat, pausing as he coughed, then swallowed. It might've been the light, or maybe wishful thinking, but his color improved.

She turned to Marie and did the same, and my heart sighed

in relief when her eyes fluttered for a moment before she fell back into a restful sleep.

"I have another batch sitting overnight, but this should do for now," Nicole said, rising.

"Now what?" I asked.

"Now we wait," Nicole said, walking toward her bedroom, holding Guy's hand. "And try to get some rest ourselves."

Thirty-Four

There was a warm body next to me when I awoke. The last thing I remembered was falling face-first into my bed, and I'd thought I'd been alone, but…

"James?" I croaked, my breath tasting like the inside of a foot.

There was a rap at the door, and Guy poked his head in, giving James one of the meanest glares I'd seen in a while. "Keep this door open, Lexie."

I raised my head and actually laughed at him. "Are you serious, Guy? I can't even move my body."

"Yep," James said, wincing as he shifted next to me. "I'm hurting."

"O-oh…" Guy cleared his throat. "But you know—"

"You also got my sister pregnant out of wedlock, so I don't think you have any room to talk, cowboy," I shot back. Then smiled. "But I'm glad you did."

Guy gave me the goofy, boyish smile he wore when he talked

about my sister then disappeared.

"Look, Lexie," James said, turning on his side—and making me wonder if maybe I should keep my door open. "About what I said last night—"

"I'm not there yet," I said, wishing my breath smelled better for this heart-to-heart conversation.

He averted his gaze. "Do you think you ever will be?"

I closed the distance between us, kissing him gently on the lips. "You have a lot of work to do. But saving my ass was a good start."

"Can I start now?" he whispered.

"I'm not sleeping with—"

"No, no," he said, pushing himself upright. "I have something to give you."

I sat up as he procured a manila folder and handed it to me. "Gavon already paid for my school, so…"

"It's not that," he said. "I was going to wait until your birthday to give it to you, but…well, here it is now."

I ripped open the envelope, pulling out a rather official-looking document from the state of Massachusetts. I read it three times, still not understanding what it meant, and probably not wanting to.

"Remember that library we broke into?" he said.

"Where you got me arrested, yeah," I said with a scowl. "What…" The word 'deed' finally registered, and I slowly lowered the paper. "Wait a minute…"

"I had to do some digging to find out who owned it now," James said, a blush appearing on the tops of his cheeks. "I was just lucky it wasn't your mother's family or else I would've been screwed, but…"

"Hang on," I said, scanning the paper again. "What are you telling me here?"

"I bought you the old magical library in Boston," he said. "I thought you could restart it. Gavon said he'd donate his library —since he'll need a place to store it, as we're probably closing the tear."

"You bought me a library?" I said, barely registering the words. "And you want me to fill it with magical books—"

"And teach people, too. I think you'd make a great teacher one day," he said. "You could put that magical school in Arlington out of business. Probably going out of business anyway, with how many kids were targeted at that school."

"That place is huge," I said. "How am I going to fill it up?"

"I'll help," he said, taking my hands. "We can go raid Cyrus's library, too. And maybe…you and I could go searching together."

"I can't believe you did this," I said. "It's…this is…"

"So, are we okay?" James asked, rubbing the back of his head.

"Oh, we are *far* from okay," I said with a hearty laugh.

The devilish grin appeared on his face. "But you're giving me another chance?"

"Maybe."

He leaned in to kiss me again, but stopped a hair's breadth from my lips. "Your breath stinks, by the way."

"You're lucky I don't have any magic left to throw you into a wall," I said, pushing him away for good measure. "Ass."

"Come on, let's check on Gavon."

We walked out into the living room where Marie was sprawled on the couch, cupping something warm and steaming. Even from this distance, I could smell the healing potion.

"How can you walk? I feel like death," she croaked, sipping more. "And this shit doesn't help."

"Maybe you should've been practicing more," I said with a shrug.

"Don't start with me. I saved a man's life yesterday," she grunted, pressing the potion to her forehead. "I feel like I have the world's worst hangover."

"Oh, good, you're up," Nicole said, walking into the living room looking chipper, alert, and holding two mugs of healing potion. "Drink this."

I shook my head. "I don't—"

She stopped and gave me a look so terrifying both James and I sipped our drinks. It sent warmth into my fingers and toes, but also a little something extra. It was actually…more potent than the potions I made for myself.

"Holy crap, that's good," James said, taking another sip. "Wow, your sister can make a potion."

"I'm taking more in to Gavon," she said, walking out of the kitchen with another mug. "Guy, watch my cauldron. If it gets to more than a simmer, call me."

"So much for being scared about sharing magic with Guy," I mumbled, following Nicole. I didn't miss the shiny diamond ring around her finger, either.

"Can you teach me how to make this potion?" James said. "I've never had one so effective."

"Hush," Nicole said, gently rapping on the door. "Gavon? Are you awake?"

The light was off and the curtains were drawn, but there was a little light coming into the room. Gavon was lying on Nicole's bed, his skin still pale, but not as bad as the night before.

"I've brought you some more potion," she said. "Drink it up, please."

"Thank you," he whispered, taking a gentle sip. "Thank you for taking such good care of me."

"How are you feeling?" she asked, fluffing the pillow behind his head.

"I'm still in pain," he said, wincing as she gently adjusted him. "Weak. But improving. Your potions are to thank for that. You really are an incredible magical, Nicole. I'm so proud of you."

Nicole made a face somewhere between annoyed, pleased, and about to sneeze. "This was the last of it, but I'll see if I can't find a different potion to expedite the healing."

"Whatever you think is best," he said, coughing weakly. "I don't want to be an imposition on you."

"It's no imposition," she said. "You need to recover your strength."

"Please don't work too hard. You have to think about the baby."

Nicole allowed herself a smile. "The baby is fine." She pressed her hand against his forehead and he smiled. "See?"

He nodded. "She'll be quite the formidable healer. Just like her Aunt Marie. But you should limit the amount of magic you use until the baby has time to grow into it."

"I will," Nicole said, glancing at James and me. "Will you call me if his condition worsens?"

"Of course," I said, pulling up a chair next to Gavon's bedside and taking his clammy hand. "But seriously, don't go overboard, okay?"

She nodded and left the room.

"Close the door," Gavon croaked.

James rose and pushed it shut. "There. Now how are you—"

Gavon flicked his wrist and the lamp clicked on, then he pushed himself upright. "I'm fine, just need a few days to rest."

I blinked at him, looking back at the closed door. "So what's with the deathbed routine?"

"Your sister is brewing potions, and I'll be damned if my improving health ends this miracle," he said. "You two should have some of her potion, it's quite extraordinary. I think the baby's magic is feeding into it a little. I might ask her to brew a few gallons so we can keep it on hand."

"Expecting any more evil Warriors to show up?" I asked.

To my surprise, Gavon's eyes grew sad. "I still can't believe he's gone."

"You sound upset about that," I said, narrowing my eyes. "Are you?"

"Cyrus was as much a brother as an adversary," he said quietly. "His death was a long-delayed justice, but..." He sighed. "It's never easy to take a life."

"But..." I blinked. "He killed—"

"I'm very aware of that," he said. "Believe it or not, I'm allowed to have complex feelings about the situation." He patted my hand. "What is not complex is how proud I am. Of both of you."

"Gavon, I—" James began, but Gavon held up his hand.

"I have a feeling we will have a very long chat about a wide variety of topics in the coming days, none of which I think you'll want each other to be present for," he said with a knowing look to us both. "But for the moment, let's just be grateful we escaped this last brush with death unscathed."

I stared at his hand. "I'm sorry that I disobeyed you again. I honestly wasn't trying to this time."

"I know, sweetheart," he said with a soft squeeze. "This trouble would've occurred had you been there or not. As it stands, you being there was a blessing. I very much doubt James would've been able to handle all those magicals without you and your sisters." He patted me on the hand. "Rest assured, your tuition is fine."

"I just don't want you to be mad at me," I said, flushing as I felt James's eyes on me.

"I'm not," he said with a warm smile. "In fact, I'm very, *very* proud of you for handling it the way you did."

"Did you know what Cyrus was up to?" I asked. "And why didn't you tell me?"

"I didn't know the extent of it," Gavon said. "I knew he was trying to create an army of magicals, but I didn't know the how or the when." He nodded to James. "James could barely convey that information. And I knew you were no longer in Cyrus's crosshairs, and I wanted to keep you that way." He shook his head. "Closing the tear was the clearest way to resolving the issue. I thought we were close, but after talking with Nicole…"

"Couldn't you just talk to the Clanmasters?" I said. "Irene

held an immense amount of power over us. I'm sure others would've been able to keep their members in line."

"Irene had blacklisted my name to every master of every major clan around the world," Gavon said. "Hence why our letter-writing campaign had gone mostly unanswered. So I'd sent James to do the work for me. He was young enough to infiltrate the gatherings, smart enough to know when Cyrus was nearby, and nameless enough to be able to get an audience with Clanmasters I couldn't touch."

"Like the Arlington School for Magicals director?" I said, turning to look at James. "Sorry again…"

"I wanted to tell you," James said. "I really did."

"And now we have a group of magicals who know of the tear," Gavon said. "And know their magic is stronger in New Salem. Irene is going to have a field day with me."

"I can close it," Nicole said quietly, reappearing in the door with another mug of potion. "Also, you shouldn't be sitting up in your condition."

I turned back to Gavon, who'd slumped in the bed, showing her the largest (and fakest) puppy-dog eyes I'd ever seen as she handed him another mug of potion.

"You know how to close the tear? Seriously?" I asked.

"I mean, maybe not. But I could probably work on it for a bit. I looked at that journal, did a little research in some of my old potions books." Her face reddened, but she powered through. "There was something weird about the way it was written, so I kind of worked at it. Maybe there's something with the Domdafosie. Or maybe I could come up with something entirely different. But I think…I could probably figure it out."

"I know you can," Gavon said, leaning back into his pillow. "My brilliant girl."

"I'm not saying I know—"

"Nicole, for crying out loud," Marie said, leaning against the door. "Just trust your damned magic for once in your life."

Nicole flushed and smiled, looking down at her hands.

"So I guess it's time to close it," James said slowly.

Gavon nodded. "Give me a week or two to move all my books out. I hear I have a new place to stash them."

I shared a look with James, who tried not to look too pleased with himself.

"What about all the people in there?" I asked.

"The people of New Salem will continue as they have for the past three hundred years," he said, grimly. "Eventually, in a few hundred years, they'll die out from magical rot."

"That's horrible," Nicole said. "Is there nothing we can do? Can't we just add them to whatever agreement we have here?"

"Actually…" I said, clearing my throat. "I had some thoughts on that."

Thirty-Five

"Take a deep breath. It's going to go fine."

James's calming words did little to stop the butterflies swimming in my stomach, but the gentle rubbing of my shoulders did ease some of the tension there. Today, I was opening my brand new magical library—and hosting the very first New Council of Danvers meeting.

Nicole had very quickly developed a potion to close the tear —it had taken her less than a week to figure it out. That had been incentive enough for Irene to accept our proposal, opening the door for the rest of the Clanmasters. Even though Cyrus had been defeated, it was clear that magicals around the world had become too fragmented and had forgotten the lessons of the past. Not only that, but about fifty Clanmasters had become well-acquainted with what might happen when their magicals drifted over to the other side. Using their connections, Gavon and I had sent a call to magicals around the globe to come to my magical library to discuss an update to the agreement—this time, including the New Salem Warrior's Guild. Gavon had received assurances from the new Guildmaster, Mary, who was an Enchanter and who seemed incredibly fond of me when I came by to meet her.

Tracking everyone down had taken almost a year, and the combined powers of everyone in my family and friend group—especially as most of my friends were trying to complete school at the same time. But we'd finally done it.

I was now in my second year at Georgetown, having moved out of the freshman dorm into an apartment across the river. Of course, after the first night alone, I'd begged Sam to come over and spend the night then asked her to move in to the second bedroom. Her parents still didn't quite approve of me, but we'd recently had lunch with Gavon, who was nothing but charming and assured them that I wasn't a bad influence on their daughter. After all, I ran a magical library, how bad could I be?

Said library still remained half-empty, although more books were arriving with every family we came into contact with. I had big plans for the place—including massive sections on history around the world, historical books on specialties, and whatever else Gavon had in his giant library. I'd also had great fun poking through Cyrus's library, although Gavon said he'd poached most of the good books a long time ago.

Now, it would house the re-convening of the Danvers members, some three hundred years later. Gavon had helped me convert one of the small glass-enclosed rooms into a giant theater, big enough to seat the two hundred magicals we were expecting today (and then some). With Sam's help, we'd put together a PowerPoint presentation explaining what we were trying to do and how we wanted to accomplish it. I think Johanna Chase would've been proud—but perhaps a little confused about some of the animations. Gavon certainly was.

"It's about time to go," James said. "You ready?"

"Not in the least bit," I said, chewing my lip. He crossed the room and gathered me into his arms, kissing me on the forehead. Our relationship status remained vaguely romantic—the combination of our focus on gathering the Danvers Accord signatories, school, and my wanting to take things exceptionally slow. As Nicole, Marie, Sam, and even Gavon had pointed out, we weren't even twenty. Still, it was nice to have a go-to sparring partner (which usually ended with some making out afterward).

I followed him out of the stacks and into the main atrium. He and Gavon had done a great job of cleaning it up so it shone, and I could see it becoming a mecca for magicals around the world. Especially if I could get some concessions about the specifics in the Danvers Accord.

Gavon told me not to expect too much, especially where Gram was concerned, but I felt there was enough momentum to make *some* changes. Maybe relaxing the prohibition on speaking about magic in front of nonmagicals, perhaps bringing back healing as a specialty. Some that I'd spoken to were lobbying to lower the age when one got their magic. Even though we had a draft amended Accord ready to go, I had a feeling this effort would take a while.

I walked by one of the downstairs stacks and stopped. Gavon had his nose stuck in a book. My niece, Mora Jeanie, lay in a baby carrier at his feet. She was three months old now, and I wasn't sure who saw her more—her father or Gavon. Gavon's relationship with Nicole was still strained, and I wasn't sure she'd ever fully forgive him, but when the baby came, she and Gavon had at least come far enough to be in each other's lives again.

"James said people are starting to arrive," I said.

"Excellent," he said, closing the book and levitating the carrier behind him. "M.J. and I were reading up on some historical healers as inspiration."

"She's a bit young for that, isn't she?" I asked.

"Your sisters certainly weren't," Gavon said, plucking the baby out of her carrier to hold in his arms. "I'm convinced my lessons stuck, and that's why they're so good at what they do."

I cooed at the baby, reminded yet again that if we were successful, she might be the last baby with specialties. James, Gavon, and I would be the last Warriors. It was the right thing to do—the same decision that Johanna Chase and my ancestors had made. Our magic was too dangerous, and the whims of magicals too unpredictable, to allow such ferocity to go unchecked.

With Gavon and M.J. in tow, I walked into the atrium room, surprised to see it already filled with people from around the world. I recognized Sahil talking with a group of Indian magicals—his clan, perhaps? Sam had brought her Clanmaster Geri from California. And still more were arriving every second in puffs of multicolored magic.

"Well? Is this her?"

Irene stood to my left, her gaze on the baby in Gavon's arms. Gavon's face darkened considerably.

"Yes, this is your great-granddaughter," I said, trying to

diffuse the conversation. "Mora Jeanie."

Irene sniffed, and for a brief moment, I thought I saw some kind of motherly affection there. But it was gone before I could get a good look. "She'll be the last one with specialties, I assume?"

"If everything goes according to plan," I said.

"Good," she said, turning on her heel to walk away. Then, pausing, she added, "Those Healer children can be trouble at an early age, as you well remember, Gavon. Better keep a close eye on her."

"What was that about?" I said, looking at Gavon, who was shaking his head.

"Perhaps her own way of saying she's happy about the baby," he said. "You know, you might have to be the bigger person there. Reach out to her if you want a relationship."

"But do I really *want* a relationship, Dad?"

"Oh, *there* you are." Nicole pushed her way through the crowd. "You don't have to hold her all day, Gavon—"

"But I want to," he said. "We were learning about famous healers in history."

"Oh?" Marie appeared behind Nicole. "Was I in there, too?"

"Maybe one day," Gavon said. "I'm thinking of penning a book about this very interesting time in history. I have a lot of time on my hands."

"Lexie, people are getting restless," Sam said. "Are we going to begin or what?"

I looked at Gavon, who shook his head. "This is your show now, Lexie. You faced down Warriors, you can certainly handle a room full of old magicals."

I nodded and cleared my throat. "Um, excuse me—"

"Hang on," Sam said, pointing at my throat—it warmed considerably. "There you go, girl."

"Um—" My voice echoed in the space so loudly that I jumped. "Can I have your attention, please?"

At once a hundred faces turned to look at me, and my heart skipped a beat. But with my sisters, my father, my niece, my best friend, and my kind-of-we're-working-on-it boyfriend beside me, I straightened my shoulders and flashed the brightest grin I could.

"If you'll follow me into the theater, we can begin our discussions."

Acknowledgements

As always, thanks first go to you, the reader, for picking up my magical book and reading it to the end. If you've got a spare minute, I'd appreciate it if you'd leave a review on Amazon, Goodreads, or your favorite eBook store. Even a short review is incredibly helpful to an indie author like me!

Thanks go to Kristin for helping me get through the beta process.

Dani, as usual, you're the best. One of these days, I might write a manuscript with no typos. But until that day comes, I'm so grateful for your careful eye.

Thanks also go to my typo checkers, Lisa Henson and Elizabeth F.

Also By S. Usher Evans

The City of Veils

For the past three years, Brynna has been patrolling the streets of Forcadel as a masked vigilante. But one evening, she's captured by the king's guards and told a shocking truth: her father and brother have been murdered and she needs to hang up her mask and become queen.

The Princess Vigilante trilogy is a young adult epic fantasy coming in 2019 from Sun's Golden Ray Publishing.

The Razia Series

Lyssa Peate is living a double life as a planet discovering scientist and a space pirate bounty hunter. Unfortunately, neither life is going very well. She's the least wanted pirate in the universe and her brand new scientist intern is spying on her. Things get worse when her intern is mistaken for her hostage by the Universal Police.

The Razia Series is a four-book space opera series and is available now for eBook, Audiobook. Paperback, and Hardcover.

The Madion War Trilogy

He's a prince, she's a pilot, they're at war. But when they are marooned on a deserted island hundreds of miles from either nation, they must set aside their differences and work together if they want to survive.

The Madion War Trilogy is a fantasy romance available now in eBook, Paperback, and Hardcover.

empath

Lauren Dailey is in break-up hell, but if you ask her she's doing just great. She hears a mysterious voice promising an easy escape from her problems and finds herself in a brand new world where she has the power to feel what others are feeling. Just one problem—there's a dragon in the mountains that happens to eat empaths. And it might be the source of the mysterious voice tempting her deeper into her own darkness.

Empath is a stand-alone fantasy that is available now in eBook, Paperback, and Hardcover.

About the Author

S. Usher Evans was born and raised in Pensacola, Florida. After a decade of fighting bureaucratic battles as an IT consultant in Washington, DC, she suffered a massive quarter-life-crisis. She decided fighting dragons was more fun than writing policy, so she moved back to Pensacola to write books full-time. She currently resides with her two dogs, Zoe and Mr. Biscuit, and frequently can be found plotting on the beach.

Visit S. Usher Evans online at:
http://www.susherevans.com/

Twitter: www.twitter.com/susherevans
Facebook: www.facebook.com/susherevans
Instagram: www.instagram.com/susherevans

9 781945 438189